THE HUNT IS ON

Also by Lex Sinclair:

Abducted
Diadem Books 2016.
ISBN 13: 978-1326541200

Don't Fear the Reaper Part 1
Diadem Books 2016
ISBN: 978-1-326-77008-2

Don't Fear the Reaper Part 2
Diadem Books 2016
ISBN: 978-1-326-91503-2

Don't Fear the Reaper Part 3
Diadem Books 2017
ISBN: 978-1-326-99163-0

Passion for Christ
Diadem Books 2017
ISBN: 978-0-244-35210-3

THE HUNT IS ON

by

Lex Sinclair

DB

DIADEM BOOKS

THE HUNT IS ON

Published by Diadem Books

For information, please contact:
Diadem Books
8 South Green Drive
Airth, Falkirk.
FK2 8JP
Scotland UK

www.diadembooks.com

ISBN: 978-0-244-05210-2

For Anthony & Mali Ann Thomas, with love

Fear was absolutely necessary. Without it I would have been scared to death.

—Floyd Patterson

There is a great deal of pain in life and perhaps the only pain that can be avoided is the pain that comes from trying to avoid the pain.

—Unknown

PROLOGUE

THE WOLF on the hill isn't as hungry as the wolf climbing the hill. The tall, broad-shouldered man dressed in rag clothes traipsing through the woods knew this. The hooded brown jumper hung loosely over his head concealing his visage. He moved with purpose through the woods, hearing the chirruping of birds nesting in the myriad of pines and cedars, standing like sentinels. White plumes emanated from the hooded figure and dissipated in the keen frost. Fresh snow yielded underfoot, crunching in time to the man's march.

Snowflakes sifted languidly from the grey heavens, crystalline. The knapsack drew taut around him with every stride. Puffs of snow kicked up in his wake. But none of that mattered to him. The woods were the closest he'd ever feel to a place he could call home. Amidst the curtain of flakes and the chirruping of birdsong, the man heard the distant low growling of a wolf. The noise drew him. The low, threatening growl pended something that was primitive. Something that came before man... When he emerged into the opening the man halted, nostrils enlarging with every sniff and exhalation.

The smell of death assailed his nostrils. Then he saw the wolf in the opening, paying him no heed whatsoever. The wolf faced the hill, standing on its haunches, hackles raised, saliva drooling from the gaping orifice that housed razor-sharp incisors. The ravenous hunger of the beast's rage exuded its protuberant eyes in its purity.

The wolf on top of the hill glowered down with similar malice but not identical, for it had feasted upon the fox. Crimson blood and bits of savaged flesh masked its own

1

gaping mouth. It had primal rage but not ravenous hunger. However, the mere threat to its throne induced an alarm and pending violence that belonged in the dense woods and in the woods alone.

The tall figure retraced two steps and edged around the wolf at the bottom of the hill, camouflaged in the fresh snow, using the sweet-smelling pines as cover. A fallen log provided a comfortable perch for the man. He lowered himself once he'd wiped snow off with gloved hands and watched with an insatiable alacrity. Thirst and hunger needed to be quenched soon but for the present the man looked on at the real meaning of living in the wild. His flushed cheeks tingled with anticipation as the wolf at the summit matched the growl of the wolf at the foot of the hill. The wolf at the bottom of the hill required no further invitation and began ascending. The wolf at the top of the hill began its descent. They met halfway... and pounced simultaneously.

Both wolves joined maws, intertwining, limbs flailing exhaustingly before the force of gravity toppled them over each other. Amidst the wild scratching, biting, the man stared, incredulous at the crimson spray dappling the virgin snow, blanketing the two beasts. If the fall had injured or hindered either of the beasts you couldn't tell. The savage brutality of survival was all that mattered in that moment. They met again, breaking the other's defence. The wolf at the foot of the hill howled in agony as the right side of its muzzle came free in the other wolf's mandibles.

In a flurry of limbs and heads snapping to and fro the wolf atop the hill caught hold of the hungry wolf's maw again but was thwarted by a vicious head butt. Seizing an opportunity, the hungry wolf leapt and drove down on top of the other wolf's back, biting unforgivingly into the exposed flesh, penetrating deeper until its mandibles grated against bone.

Screeching like an out-of-control banshee, the wolf that had feasted upon the fox rotated in a desperate attempt to save itself from certain death spraying blood and flesh. It found itself exposed further by lying on its back with its head at the ravenous wolf's rear legs. It whimpered in pure trepidation. Then shot up and seized the ravenous wolf's genitals in its maw and bit down. It threw its head to and fro, using the weight and taut grip to increase the hold and the unendurable agony.

The man seated atop the fallen log clapped his mitten hands over his ears and grimaced. The howl was replaced by a shriek of a dying creature realising it was moments away to never seeing, never hearing, and never feeling anything of this world ever again. A fountain of crimson liquid soaked the wolf who'd sat atop the hill, drowning it with copper-tasting spillage of its prey. It never ceased tossing its head to and fro until the creature atop it emitted another pitiful screech, whimpered and finally fell.

As violent and savage and unadulterated as the scene before him had played out the hooded figure never winced or averted his gaze for a second. He looked on with admiration for the wild beasts, both the deceased and the victor. He smiled at the blood-drenched snow. Then he rose having learnt something imperative and relevant…

It was a good hunt.

It was a good kill…

1.

DEAN FERRIS sat quiet in the back seat of the rolling BMW. His mouth was parched no matter how many times he'd licked his lips. His hands fidgeted. The driver who took surreptitious glances in the rear-view mirror thought Dean looked like a neurotic.

The black BMW rolled to a halt in front of wrought-iron gates. The engine idled for a moment. Then the gates made a mechanical whirring sound before parting, permitting the vehicle access.

Dean had been to this affluent countryside residence before. The sight of the big, drooping apple tree in the front yard obscuring the red stone façade evoked those memories. A lifetime ago it seemed Dean had been accosted by a man in a black suit at his home. The man left a message on a card reading, 'If you want to be saved and not go to prison for doing your job, accompany the messenger to my humble home.'

The multi-coloured decorative stones crunched and popped under the tyres. A hundred leaves on the towering cedars hissed in harmony. On any other day Dean would have embraced this pleasant sound.

The vehicle pulled up alongside the stone steps and the grand entrance. The driver turned the AC off, undid his seat belt and killed the engine. Dean gazed down at his clammy hands and extracted the card with the message, 'I need you for something very important. It's time to return your favour.'

Dean had no notion what that nebulous message meant, and didn't have time to deliberate. The driver had exited the vehicle and now stood by the rear door. Taking a deep breath, Dean rubbed his palms on the legs of his Levi's and emerged to the outside.

***

Tony Nivean, one of Paul Demato's remaining bodyguards, ambled slightly ahead of the anxious and wary looking Dean Ferris. He knew what was expected of this young, lithe ex-policeman. The sympathy he felt was genuine. On the other hand, perhaps it was better that Dean had no notion of what he'd be getting himself into. However, if this anxiety of being called upon had any significance to judge him then the young man would soon be acquainted with death.

He mounted the steps and approached the door beneath the four columns. The electronic keypad's red light illuminated to green once he'd punched in the six-digit entrance code.

Dean gazed over the broad shoulders of Tony into the Stygian interior. He was visibly surprised that the hallway was vacant of more guards.

Where the hell is everyone? Dean thought.

In spite of this irregularity, Dean dutifully followed Tony down the hallway.

The floorboards creaked underfoot. And when he looked down he noticed the plush tawny carpet had been replaced. Neither were there any framed pictures on the oak walls. The last time he had been here he recalled gilded photographs of Paul Demato's famous friends and family portraits.

Tony arrived at the last door on his left and knocked twice, hard. From the other side of the sturdy door came the familiar voice saying, 'Enter.'

Dean had no more time for observations or contemplation, for the mystery behind his presence would soon be unveiled. He just hoped nothing unforeseen would befall him as in the gangster films, *The Godfather* and *GoodFellas*.

2.

PAUL DEMATO rose from his leather chair behind the pinewood desk and smiled benignly at the young man following Tony into his office.

'Hey! Hey! There he is. The prodigy returns.'

Dean forced a smile in reciprocation. He was glad to see Paul again but still could not abate the unease that burrowed into his subconscious. His eyes roamed the wood-panelled office with leather upholstery sofas which met in an L-shape that spoke of Sicilian vespers and renaissance light. Unlike the walls in the dim hallway, the walls of the office still sported framed photographs of Paul and his son Leo posing with celebrities and famous athletes. Dean recognised these from the last visit but was still in awe of the photos of Tom Cruise, Mariah Carey, Sir Anthony Hopkins and Gold Medal winner, Jessica Ennis, to name a few.

Delicate amber wall sconces shone dimly. Dean returned his gaze to Paul, who had been watching him scrutiny the interior.

Paul nodded to Tony and said, 'Thank you.'

Tony closed the door behind him.

Paul turned back to Dean. 'Sit down, would ya?' he said, gesturing to the cherry-red sofa facing his polished desk. 'You look like a sudorific sufferer.'

Dean smiled meekly.

'In other words you're sweating your balls off. Stop fretting. You haven't done anything wrong. I brought you here to ask for a favour, as per card.'

Dean nodded.

'The favour you owe me and I want returned is rather complicated. Or rather the set of circumstances behind the errand I want you to do. I'll explain as best as I can though.'

On hearing the word *errand* the awesome weight upon Dean's shoulders lifted.

He exhaled. Then he began to physically relax.

'Care for some brandy?'

'Yes. But just the one.'

Paul began to pour from the decanter. When the short glass was half full, Dean leant forward and took it.

'You will return the favour you owe me, yes?'

'Yeah.' Dean didn't hesitate for two reasons. One: if it wasn't for Paul Demato's attorneys and choice of judge to take on the case of Dean killing three drug dealers whom he believed were armed when in fact they weren't. Two: If he said no there was the probability that he would not step outside again, alive.

'I know you felt bad about getting kicked off the force for that terrible incident,' Paul said. 'But how were you to know that what they were reaching for was their driving licence and a lighter. Those guys sold A-class drugs to kids and people too stupid to know side effects, effectively killing them or ruining their lives. Personally, I and many other people truly believe you did society a favour. The way the justice system carries on, people will be too afraid to stand up for their civil rights soon. But anyway we're just going over old ground here. There's nothing to be gained by it. What's done is done.'

'And I'm grateful more than I can express,' Dean said.

Paul nodded. 'I know you are. And the only reason I call upon you to do this task is because you're a man I trust more so than the two remaining guards I have left.'

'Where're the others?' Dean asked, as Paul had touched upon the topic.

'I'm legitimatising the business. I'm too old for this whatever-you-want-to-call-it. And one of the reasons is the set of circumstances that have led up to why you've been called to return the favour today.'

The exuberant façade that Paul had been wearing upon greeting Dean and inviting him into his plush office crumbled away, like a papier-mâché mask revealing the haggard features beneath.

'Are you okay?'

'Aye. I'll live. Which is more than I can say about my poor godson.'

Dean's eyebrows rose involuntarily. 'What d'you mean by that?'

'To cut a long story short without omitting too much detail, my godson, Tobias, got killed because of the family business.'

'I'm very sorry for your loss.'

'Yeah. Me too.'

Dean took a sip of his brandy, waiting patiently for Paul to repress his emotions.

'Years ago, Tobias' grandfather, Christian, gave my mother money to prevent social services putting me into care. She was a single parent and struggling like hell to work all the hours God sends, pay for a babysitter and clean the council flat. Poor soul ended up with chronic back pain from an early age to her death because of being bent over cleaning and sweeping up.'

Dean was starting to understand why Paul had got into the mafia life. How hard he had to work to get ahead in life. And even though some of his duties were immoral he could see that the world hadn't treated him right either. However, he was a man of conscience and didn't take kindly to petty criminals and drug dealers. He had also done a lot of good, albeit illegally. He had rid the streets of dealers and pimps far quicker than the police could achieve in a decade.

'If it wasn't for Christian Hill I would have ended up in a boarding school. Probably end up in one foster home after another and become a petty thug, living off the flesh of decent hard working people.'

'How did he die, if you don't mind me asking?'

'No, I don't mind,' Paul said.

***

The tall, broad shouldered man who took pleasure in seeing wolves fight to the death in the woods got into his Ford. His attire was entirely black; black jeans, black long-sleeve shirt, black trainers and black hair. His ebony eyes were expressionless as was his rugged visage.

The black vehicle camouflaged itself amidst the other cars parked alongside the suburban neighbourhood. That was good. He didn't want to be seen. He wanted to be like the chameleon. In another life distant in memory and in years the tall, dark mysterious man had a name – Anton.

Fate had mapped out Anton's life for him at the tender age of six. He had been sleeping in his bedroom when he stirred half-awake by the sounds of footfalls mounting the staircase. The stairs groaned in protest. Anton felt the pitch dark envelope him like a long lost lover and the ambience grow taut. He lay supine in his bed under the covers, squinting. The sound of his parents' bedroom door creaking open was a faint whisper to the cries of death and shrieks of horror that ensued.

Anton sat bolt-upright, eyes bulging. His ears swallowed the sounds of his mother screaming at the top of her lungs before the sound of glass shattering. The silence that came next perforated Anton's hearing.

Not wanting to yet but doing so anyway, the young boy threw the quilt off him and leapt out of bed. His bedroom door stood ajar. The darkness surrendered to dim light coming from his parents' bedroom where the hubbub occurred.

Just as Anton thought, *I had a bad dream*, his parents' door opened slowly. His heart scurried into his throat as his bony knees buckled. He gripped the doorframe. His mouth fell open at the sight of a man of six feet or more wearing a brown paper sack over his head with two eyeholes. Then he saw a severed head in each of the assailant's hands and gasped.

The figure paused at the top of the stairs. Anton blinked, knuckled sleep out of his eyes and felt his gorge rise at the two familiar heads leaking drops of blood on the carpet. He had been about to back away from the doorway unable to believe his eyes seeing the terror-stricken features of his father at the moment of death when the figure craned his paper-sack head directly at his bedroom door.

For a moment, Anton thought he would have his head chopped off too. But strangely, the figure who had brutally murdered his parents raised the hand that clutched his mother's black mane of hair and put his index finger to where the mouth would be. Anton recognised the gesticulation as don't-tell-anyone-our-little-secret. Then the figure descended the stairs. Anton stood behind the threshold feeling the warm trickle of urine run down his quivering legs in rivulets.

Now that same boy had grown into the man known by men of the mafia as Mr Death. The Cascarini Family had hired his services for this current job. Sure they had their own guys. However, no one according to gossip was as efficient and unstoppable as Mr Death.

Mr Death didn't work for any one particular organisation. He worked for himself to kill. He only took jobs specifically of an assassin. He didn't work to intimidate or threaten. He didn't kidnap one of the opposing family members in a ransom for money. And once Mr Death took a job he didn't stop until it had been completed.

The Perry family refused to pay him years ago before he got his reputation and nickname. Mr Death visited the family home and assassinated every guard on the premises. Then replaced the Christmas turkey with Oliver Perry's head and put it back in the oven. His daughter found it after her mother discovered the headless corpse that had been her husband the night before. Since then no family ever refused to pay Mr Death.

Then Cascarini wanted Leo Demato dead for making an anonymous phone call to the police about their family selling cocaine outside a nightclub. The whole family lost hundreds of thousands not to mention they had to go to court. Mr Death didn't need – nor did he want – to know the rest. It was irrelevant. What mattered to him was keeping an eye on the white detached house that had a plush green lawn out front, belonging to Leo Demato.

At some point during the day Mr Death was certain Leo would emerge. When he did he would dutifully follow him. Then he would wait and see where he went. If the environing terrain was suitable and it was deserted, Mr Death would perform his task efficiently.

Thirty-seven minutes later the front door opened and two young men emerged from the house and got into the Jeep parked on the driveway. Mr Death camouflaged the starting of his engine by the sound of the Jeep's.

The Jeep rolled backwards down the drive, onto the deserted tree-lined street and then moved forward. Mr Death waited a few moments then pulled away from the kerb and turned left, pursuing the Jeep at a safe distance. For him this was the best part. The anticipation. The hunt. Then the kill...

The Jeep made its way onto the main road, down the hill and into the town centre. Killing Leo in the centre of town where cars drove by endlessly and shoppers went to and fro was out of the question. However, the Jeep cut through town and began its ascent onto a back road. Mr Death did not notice the school, clinic, church and post office as he drove past. He saw his target and nothing more.

They were climbing hundreds of feet above the town centre now diminishing in size in the rear view mirror. And soon the traffic lessened as they followed the highway into the dense foliage. Oaks, firs and evergreens blurred by. Mr Death eased off the accelerator pedal, watching, waiting to see where the Jeep went. It was imperative to remain inconspicuous until the time was right.

This wasn't the same as the two wolves fighting to the death. However, erase the modern technology of vehicles and the same natural instincts applied. This was the case with any hunt. Whether it was two of the same kind fighting with honour and pride or a hunter pursuing its prey.

The Jeep took a left onto a muddy path rutted by a farmer's tractor. Mr Death brought the Ford to a halt. There would be no use following the 4x4 on this terrain. His car would never make it. For now he found himself stymied.

However, this obstacle presented a challenge that was unforeseen. And although the land before him worked against him performing his task, Mr Death, who like the chameleon, adapted to his environment.

He killed the engine and got out of the useless vehicle. He went to the rear and popped the boot open. In the interior laid out diligently on a tartan rug was an array of weapons. A 9-inch hunter's army knife. An AK-47 assault rifle and a .38 pistol and many more. Mr Death selected those three weapons from the boot.

Then he changed his footwear to boots. He changed the AK-47 for a different rifle with a long lens scope. Suited up, Mr Death followed the plume of dust and the sound of the Jeep's engine growing indistinct due to the fringe of the forest several hundreds of yards away. He ambled to the side of the road and mounted the sty. Then he followed the trail through the thicket at a canter. The rifle was held across his muscle-bound chest. He adjusted only to fit through the aperture of the sweet-smelling pines towards his target. He needed to be the chameleon he believed himself to be. Otherwise he would be seen by his intended target.

There were two men up ahead getting out of the Jeep. Mr Death hurried on tiptoe, moving through the thicket gracefully. Using the scope on his rifle he sighted the two men. They came into view at the rear and opened the boot. Mr Death watched and watched. He assumed they were going to extract weapons of their own. This notion excited Mr Death. It made his task all the more fun if the prey was willing to turn around and fight. Perhaps the target was aware of Mr Death's pursuit. In his fear, the target had had two options: fight or flight… and had decided on the latter.

However, the target and the other young man took out fishing rods. Mr Death still thought of them as hunters of little fish. Unlike a fish snagged on the end of a line, Mr Death intended to terminate the target in haste without being seen. He had no intention of killing the other young man. Although, he killed for pleasure as well as money, Mr Death didn't kill anyone for the sake of killing.

He moved forward, crouching under a large branch and settled between two evergreens. Through the scope he watched the two men remove their trainers for boots, just as he had done. Then the one he believed to be Leo Demato picked up a bucket by its handle and placed it by his feet. Mr Death waited for the precise moment in which intuition told him to pull the trigger…

The target put on a red and black chequered jacket. He was buttoning it up when the sound of gunfire cracked through the mountainside and reverberated.

His kneecap exploded. Shattered bone and scarlet blood flew out in one squirt.

The target crumpled, clutching the wound in agony.

Mr Death cussed inwardly. At the moment he pulled the trigger an acorn had fallen and bonked him lightly on the head which caused his rifle to lower by fractions simultaneously.

In haste he fired again and blew a hole through the boot of the wounded figure. His friend had fled, one arm flailing, the other reaching for something in his jacket pocket.

Mr Death had to move quickly. He needed to complete the job before the other young man returned with others. He sprinted through the thicket, swatting branches out of his face, in and out of towering evergreens that stood like immovable sentries. He burst into the open and rushed across the meadow brushing through the tall grass.

'Oh God! Awwwww! Oh no!'

Mr Death could hear the cries of agony now. He mounted the paddock and climbed the steep incline to the rutted path to the Jeep.

The young man who lay writhing whimpered. Then ceased when in his peripheral vision a tall, broad shouldered man armed with the weapon that had obliterated his kneecap and disabled him edged closer.

'What did I do?'

Mr Death ignored the inquiry. His breath exhaled in the crisp air.

'Soon there shall be no pain, only eternal bliss,' he said in a voice void of emotion.

'Please. Please…' the young man cried.

'There's no need to beg me. Your reward is my gift to you.'

The young man trembled from head to toe, terrified and angry at the same time. His ashen face seemed to be hanging onto his skull for dear life. He looked in the assailant's direction and had been about to cuss him when the sound of the rifle firing and a hellish thud entered his brain. After that there was nothing…

***

Paul fell silent after reciting the death of his godson.

'Your godson died in mistake for your son!' Dean said, astonished.

Paul nodded. 'My son ran to the summit to get a reception on his mobile and phoned me as it was happening, I suppose. I don't usually phone the police, as you know. But as Tobias had nothing to do with the business I thought it might have been some hunting accident.'

Dean finished his brandy in one thirsty gulp.

'But something didn't add up, so I sent one of my own to infiltrate the Cascarini Family to find out.

'I agree Leo should never have reported them to the police, no offence. But to order a hit on my own son – regardless of whether he is alive or not – was crossing the line. The Cascarini Family were resentful because I would not get involved in this drug trafficking. Because I have a lot of political connections it would've looked bad on me. And I never thought our business had anything to do with drugs. Casinos, pubs, nightclubs and so forth. But never drugs. Drugs are the downfall. The minute you get involved with drugs is the time you should get help.'

'But who is this guy "Mr Death"?' Dean wanted to know.

'As I've already said, apparently his name is Anton. No one knows what his surname is – or was – or where he was born. Although according to the Cascarini Family that hired his services, some scary-as-hell incident occurred when he was a nipper. He never spoke of it but it must have mentally scarred him ever since. His parents were killed and he was taken into care. Which is funny when you think about it, because if

Christian hadn't given my mum money I would have also been in care. It's as if our paths were destined to meet one way or another.'

'Where's Leo now?'

'Abroad. Far from here. Out of harm's way. The Cascarini's business has been liquidated thanks to the court case.'

'Where do I come into all of this?'

'Tobias' mother, Sandra, is really struggling.'

'I can imagine,' Dean said.

'I don't want nothing to do with this dirty business any more. My connections in the government approve of this. But for the time being my resources, as you have already seen, are limited. I've had to pay off some of my muscle and to protect Leo until it is safe for him to return. Meanwhile, poor Sandra Hill has moved and doesn't want anything to do with me after what happened. I would send her a cheque or money but my account has been frozen while I'm investigated, thanks to the Cascarini's.

'As a peace offering I want you to take £10,000 to her in person. It's also to help with funeral costs during her time of grief. She doesn't know who you are. I would send it in the post, but that's far too risky. God knows, Tobias would tell you if he was still alive, he worked for the Royal Mail for two months over Christmas. Packages rip open and there's a lot of theft there too. They'd have a field day if they saw ten grand in there.'

'Yeah, no worries,' Dean said. 'Seems straightforward enough.'

'Ah, wait. That's not all.' Paul hesitated for a moment. Then continued. 'Mr Death is also keeping my movements under close scrutiny, as well. Remember, for such a diligent assassin his reputation has been tainted for his error. According to my spy, the Cascarini's refused to pay him. Mr Death had been on the verge of murdering the head of the family before he'd been informed of his mistake.'

'Oh shit.'

'Yeah. Now he's seeking vengeance for not getting paid. Sandra doesn't know about my generosity. She is protected by twenty-four hour police surveillance.

'Apparently, Mr Death is aware of my intended transaction – which is why he's watching me – and is hell-bent on intercepting this transaction by killing the courier.'

Dean leant forward, proffering his glass. 'I think I'd better have another brandy.'

3.

'I DON'T SUPPOSE I'll get anything for doing this,' Dean said.

Paul sighed. 'You know I have reporters and politicians and police who are good friends and acquaintances of mine. Apart from some illegal gambling and some debts that need to be paid, I'll be all right when this is all over. If you manage to do this I'll personally see to it that you're all right for a few grand yourself.'

Dean's brow furrowed as he contemplated. 'Why doesn't Mr Death just come here and kill you or Mrs Hill?'

'Because then he won't have any money. Also, as I am under close scrutiny by the CID and Sandra is still helping the police with their inquiries it would be foolish. If he killed either me or Sandra there would be a national hunt for him and his identity would be known.'

'And then he wouldn't be much of the chameleon that he likes to think himself of,' Dean said.

'Exactly.'

'This is quite a mess.'

Paul Demato uttered laughter at that statement. 'Isn't it just.'

Dean averted his gaze from Paul, deep in thought. 'He's gonna come after me with everything he has and more. That's true, right?'

'Yeah.'

'He's got all these weapons and sublime hunting skills. So how do you expect me to be able to complete this job? I am unarmed. All I've got is a vague description of the man. But most important of all, no weapons to defend myself.'

'The weapon's part of your dilemma I can assist you with.'

Although Dean Ferris believed in his own ability to do the job that didn't prevent a tingle of uncertainty coursing through his system.

'Why me? I mean I know what you said about having to pay your muscle off. But you must have other contacts.'

Paul folded his arms behind his head, lacing his fingers together. 'You've still got a policeman's good instincts. Plus you're focused and determined. I can tell these things without you or anyone else telling me. I've been around a long time; seen a lot; dealt with a lot of eclectic people. Some of what Anton has got is in you too. A lot of my guards are ruthless and strong et cetera. But it takes a very rare man to know that he will feel the heat and yet continues to walk straight towards it knowing there's a good chance he'll get burnt.'

'And if I don't... for argument's sake?'

'If you *did* opt to refuse I would be very disappointed. Also my melancholy for having to get my hands dirty with another avoidable hit would deepen.'

Dean could see the beads of sweat glistening on Paul Demato's brow.

'Are you refusing?'

'I don't have much of a choice, do I? Could've found me something a bit less perilous though.'

A nervous smile quivered Paul's chubby face. 'I only wish I did have something better for you. But this is also a good deed. One with good moral fibre as its foundation.'

Dean frowned. 'Trouble is this time if I get caught firing a weapon – even in self-defence – I will end up doing life.'

'If it comes to that then I will come forward and say that I asked you to give money to Mrs Hill and testify about Mr Death.'

A long silence fell in the office.

'This of great importance,' Paul said, matter-of-factly. 'Everything that I have told you is the God's honest truth. I'll support you in this one hundred percent. I'll be in constant touch. Bear in mind this, Mr Death has generated a lot of heat as well.'

Dean drained the last of his brandy. Then he rose. 'The heat is on, as they say,' he said.

***

The burden of the vinyl briefcase brought home the reality of the task. Dean took Paul's clammy hand and shook on it. He thought about how the path his life had taken had brought him to this day. Had he not been so hasty in firing and seen first what that drug dealer was removing from his back pocket he would never have met Paul. There was an up-side and down-side to that. Paul Demato for no reason or purpose had come to his rescue. He'd been sitting in his bungalow with his head in his hands, relieved from duty. The home he'd worked so hard to get for so many years would have to be sold. He didn't know if he could even afford a solicitor who would get him off the hook. Even his rookie partner had spoken against him to the superintendent.

Also, if he'd gone to prison and the inmates discovered he was an ex-policeman he'd be as good as dead. He'd find razors in his toothbrush, broken glass in his porridge. Everywhere he went there would be whispers and snide remarks. He wouldn't dare fall asleep in case his cellmate ran a blade across his throat.

Instead he'd received a hefty fine for his ineptitude, which Paul had paid. And his reputation and name had been tainted ever since. He'd worked as a labourer on a building site for four months. Then as a short order cook in a café and restaurant. After that he'd got a job as a taxi driver.

When Paul contacted him he set Dean up with an old acquaintance which operated a limousine service. Dean had managed to keep up with his mortgage, albeit not as comfortably as when he'd been on the force.

So, in spite of the peril he would soon find himself in, he'd come away from that life-altering incident/mistake sunny-side up. And, as Paul pointed out, it was a good deed. He'd also get a few grand for the risk factor (if he was alive to spend it).

'You'll be taken back to your place now. Tonight I shall send Danny Sampson, an arms dealer, to your home. He'll provide you with some protection. And for God's sake don't go revealing it to anyone or firing at some stupid punk. Okay?'

'Okay.'

'He might not even risk it,' Paul said, speaking of Mr Death. 'Somehow though, I think he'll want to absolve his error and send a message to the rest of us. It's up to you to prevent that, Dean. Who knows, maybe his anger will cause him to be inefficient.'

'I'll make it my sole mission to do everything in my powers to get the money to Mrs Hill if it's the last thing I do.'

***

Tony Nivean rolled the BMW right outside Dean's bungalow.

'You want me to stick around a while, see if there's anyone loitering around   here?' Tony asked once he'd applied the handbrake.

'Are you armed?'

'You betcha,' Tony said, patting his hip where it bulged by the unseen arsenal.

'Tell you what, drive up to the end of the street, turn around and come back down again. Then get out of the car and see me to the front door.'

'Sounds like a plan of sense,' Tony said, crooking a smile to the rear-view mirror for Dean's benefit.

This is smart, Dean thought. A tad OTT but smart. Paul Demato wasn't one to exaggerate or tell untruths. If he said that this Anton assassin was efficient and precise then that was the case.

Experience and intuition informed Dean that at some point during now and the time he made his journey to Sandra Hill's house, Anton would make his move. However, as of this moment Dean was unarmed and hadn't prepared himself mentally for the task at hand. If he hadn't decided to let caution be his number one decree he would be a sitting duck until the arm's dealer arrived and supplied him with the tools for the job.

'Nice neighbourhood,' Tony said, scanning the empty suburban streets.

'Yeah, it beats city life,' Dean said. He pivoted in the back seat and craned his head out the rear window to check no one was following.

Tony spun the BMW around and headed back down the street at a snail's pace. 'Seems all clear to me.'

'It most likely is,' Dean said. 'But I can't go assuming and making rash calls.'

'Neither would I, if I were in your position.'

'Is that why you didn't take the job yourself?' Dean asked, not surprised that Tony knew about his job but was intrigued nonetheless.

Tony laughed. 'No. No. Once all the inquiries and investigations are done with, Demato will pay me what normal people call my redundancy. The whole family will move to Majorca and have nothing to do with their current affairs.'

The car came to a halt outside Dean's bungalow. The lower half of the construction was done in red brick and the top in alabaster stone. The Honda Civic sat idly on the paved drive.

'Do me a favour,' Dean said. 'Come in with me. Let me put this money someplace safe; check no one's broken in while I've been out. There's a Coke and a sandwich in it for you.'

Tony laughed again.

'What's so funny?'

'Paul was right about you.'

'Yeah. What did he say?' Dean wanted to know.

'Soft on the outside. Hard on the inside. What did he say, "Easy to underestimate".'

Tony killed the engine. They both emerged, glancing to and fro before making their way to the front door. Tony smiled inwardly at the sight of the singular garden gnome standing sentry on the front lawn.

Once the rooms had been checked and it became apparent that no one had entered or tried to during Dean's absence, Tony mounted the stool in the kitchen. Dean stashed the vinyl suitcase under his bed. When he returned he dutifully opened the fridge and handed Tony a cold can of Coke – then proceeded to make a ham sandwich, as per promise.

'Truth is, old man Demato is scared,' Tony said after his first gulp of Coke.

'Really?' Dean couldn't hide his perplexity. 'I mean he seemed anxious about everything and the fact that he's lost his godson. Not to mention Mrs Hill is no longer on speaking terms with him, and the fact his only child shoulda been the one dead. But I wouldn't have said he was scared.'

'Oh, don't get me wrong it could've been a lot worse. But Leo's grassing up the Cascarini Family has opened a can of worms. Had Leo been killed – problem solved. Not nice, but that's the business. Instead we got a pissed off Italian mafia and a pissed off deadly assassin. And all Paul wanted to do was to tie up some loose ends and retire with no money troubles, a clean record and a clear conscience.'

Dean placed the ham sandwich on a china plate and handed it to Tony.

'Thanks.'

'Yeah, no worries. I see what you mean,' he added in relation to the topic.

23

'Even if none of this had happened but the task, for whatever reason still needed doing, I don't know if I could go through with it.'

Dean sighed. The fact that Tony who was hard on the exterior as well as the interior said that made the task sound even more perilous. 'Trouble is someone – me – ends getting the shit-end of the stick.'

'You got Sandra's address?'

Dean nodded a yes. 'Tenby. West Coast of Wales. What's that, five hours?'

'Somethin' like that,' Tony said, uncertain. 'I mean we're in Sunbury. The nearest motorway to us is the M3. You get onto that almost right away. You join the M25 at the intersection, head north, past the A4 and then onto the M4. That's the motorway that will lead you directly into Wales. You'll have to either get a roadmap, SAT Nav or Google it.'

'So I go past the Queen Mary Reservoir, past Chertsey and onto the M25 that will lead me onto the M4?'

'That's right. I'm not sure from that point on though. Sorry.'

Off the top of his head Dean couldn't tell for certain. However, considering Tony sounded vague, he knew for a fact that the M4 led from London to Bristol and South Wales.

'Paul gave me a hundred for petrol and other expenses.'

Tony laughed. 'Yeah, you're gonna need that.'

'So, what do you know about this Mr Death bloke?' Dean said, changing the subject.

'Well, I imagine Paul told you about what little is known of his origins.'

'Yeah. He witnessed his parents being murdered and was taken to boarding school. From that point on no one seems to know much of him, besides he's good at his job.'

'According to our inside source during their time spent with the Cascarini's, Anton is spoken as though he were merely a shape. Not a man. Even though he is. But he's an enigma. It's one of the reasons Paul's scared.'

Dean took a Coke out of the fridge for himself and savoured the cool fizzy drink. His parched mouth greedily swallowed, moistening his mouth and throat.

'It just seems like the more I hear about him the less confident I feel.'

'Listen,' Tony said with a mouthful of food. 'Paul's under a lot of pressure. Sure Anton is a dangerous threat. I just think he told as much as he could about him to make you wary. All his money is frozen. He's being monitored like one of Britain's Most Wanted. In spite of the business he's been involved in, Demato is a clean guy. That's why he has so many political interests. Judges, politicians, lawyers and famous people don't socialise with him out of fear. Paul's a generous guy.'

'Oh, I know this,' Dean said.

'You more than anyone else, I imagine,' Tony said with approval. 'Which is why he's not used to being suspected of unlawful and ugly accusations. This is just the Cascarini's retaliating for what Leo did. Believe me, it'll pass.'

Dean leant against the worktop. 'I just want to know who's gonna be following me, that's all.'

Tony shrugged. 'Not much else I can say. The only guy that tried to kill Anton – or Mr Death – was a relative of the Cascarini's. This wasn't that long ago.'

'What happened?'

'Surprised Demato didn't tell you. I mean this is another reason the Italian family are so pissed off lately. They've been charged with and found in the possession of shit loads of cocaine, heroin, LSD and God knows what else. Then they hired Anton, who then goes and kills the wrong guy. Now they got more investigations from Demato and Tobias' parents bearing down on them. At one time it seemed – had the Cascarini's not been tied up with several lawsuits against them – there would be an all-out gangster war.

'Anyway, this relative had his house raided. The whole shooting match. He's there the day Anton arrives to collect his money. He gets in Anton's face, accusing him of being simple and creating loads of problems, blah, blah, blah. In his irate state he makes a death threat.

'Anton leaves the Cascarini family home with no money, reputation gone to the wall and some fool hurling verbal abuse at him.

'Anton must've followed this guy home. Must've remained out of sight. Then broke into the house and killed this Cascarini chump and his wife. He cut off the guy's dick and stuffed it in his mouth. When the police arrived they saw a single bullet through the woman's brow and the guy rocking to and fro in the armchair. Behind him on the bedroom wall the assailant had written in black felt, "Cocksucker".

'They had one girl. Ten years. She told the police that she saw a man wearing a brown paper sack over his head with two eyeholes. Said he stopped at the top of the stairs and put his index finger to his mouth in a, don't-tell-anyone-gesture.'

Dean didn't notice his mouth gaping until Tony stopped speaking. Finding his voice again, he said, 'Aren't you getting confused with the man wearing the paper sack over his head that Anton saw as a boy?'

Tony shook his head. 'No. Anton has been so infected – as anyone would be – of the death of his parents and the sight of their murderer, he copied him. I don't know Anton or Mr Death. Never even seen him. But I do know that he is one messed up dude who loves to kill.'

4.

TONY stayed for an hour. Dean actually enjoyed the introverted guard's company, much to his surprise. Once you sat down with the guy Dean quickly found him to be pleasant company. Tony wasn't a loquacious person; on the contrary in most cases. But when he did speak Dean found him to be prudent and cordial.

It had been so long since Dean had had company. All of a sudden the house felt empty. Dean's only serious relationship with Louise had ended when she discovered he'd killed two drug dealers. He remembered how he'd told her the first part and how she didn't even let him finish. Once she'd seen it in the local newspapers, she fled his bungalow and their relationship as though she were on fire.

Although he hadn't done time in prison – miraculously – his name would be forever tainted. Even now some his neighbours avoided him like they would the plague. This singular fact hindered his life. Of course life went on but still people stared at him.

When it had been revealed that the two drug dealers were selling gear to adolescents and had committed felonies and gone for something in their back pocket as opposed to complying, Dean tried again with his neighbours. However, to his surprise nothing had changed in the slightest. He'd made a mistake, of course. But as Paul said, if you asked people if scum like that were better off dead, most would have said yes, unequivocally.

Sighing at his melancholy deliberations, Dean consulted his wristwatch – 3:44pm.

Danny Sampson would be here in just over three hours' time, he mused. He'd finished his ham and pickle sandwiches. Then he sauntered into the cosy living room and channel surfed. He had the basic Virgin Media package, which consisted of more than one hundred channels. Sod all was on.

It was too dangerous for him to step outside yet. He doubted that Anton would know of his existence. Nevertheless, the assassin was on the prowl. Stringent methods would be taken to reinstate his position. Anton's temper would work against him though, Dean thought. A man – no matter how efficient – could not afford to allow his emotions to override his actions, especially in the dirty business Anton operated in.The one known as Mr Death had his one and only chance regarding assassinating Leo. Anton couldn't show his face in public more than once, never mind revealing his identity at an airport. That was bound to be playing on his mind. Or at least Dean hoped it was, for his sake.

A couple of minutes after five, Dean heaved himself off the sofa and got into the shower. He welcomed the inexorable downpour, feeling his muscles relax and soothe. Then just as he wrapped a towel around his midsection the phone shrilled to life. The nearest extension was right outside the bathroom. Dean hit the green TALK button.

'Yo!'

'Have you seen Tony? Is he still there?' Paul Demato asked, sounding distressed.

Dean ignored the fact that the conversation had no preamble. 'No. He left not long after three. Why? Hasn't he called you?'

'No,' Paul said. 'I phoned his mobile and got his answer do-dah. And obviously he hasn't returned otherwise I wouldn't be phoning you and asking…'

'Yeah. Okay,' Dean said, slightly vexed at Paul's rant.

'Perhaps he's just gone home to crash.'

'Was anyone following you, did you notice?'

'No. In fact we drove around, keeping an eye out. Tony came in and checked my home, as well. Made him a ham sandwich and a Coke. We chatted a while. Then he left. Incidentally, he didn't say where he was going. I assumed he was going straight back to you. But he didn't say and I didn't ask.'

'Somethin's happened,' Paul said after a long pause.

'Maybe. Maybe not. I wouldn't worry about it just yet.'

'You would if you were in my position.'

Dean considered something. Then said: 'Have you tried his home phone number? I mean I don't even know if he lives with anyone, I'm just throwing ideas outta my head.'

'No. That's good. I mean Tony lives with his mum.'

'Well, there you go. He's probably gone home for some kip and to check on his mum. He should've gone back to yours though if that's what he was supposed to do. Or maybe his mum fell ill.'

'I'll phone and see if he's there,' Paul said, placated.

'There you go. Give us a ring back when you do. It won't be long before Sampson shows. I'm gonna be heading off then, so don't leave it too late.'

'Yeah. And Dean? Sorry for being rude, it's just…'

'Apology is not necessary. Calm down,' Dean said. 'If it's true what you said, Anton will be coming after me now. So relax. Get through that shit with the police as I had to, pay off what you owe and then head off to sunny Spain. You've helped me and a lotta others out over the years. Perhaps now you should help yourself.'

After another intermission, Paul said, 'Thank you. I'll get back to you now.'

'You do that,' Dean said in a soothing voice.

But his trusty intuition attuned by his years as a policeman made the hairs on the nape of his neck bristle with trepidation.

***

Dean dried himself down and got dressed. He combed his hair and laid the Gillette razor blade on the sink by the soap dish and the Colgate toothpaste. Then he waited impatiently for the phone to ring. He knew that if he took the chance to quickly brush his teeth or shave that would be when the phone rang. Instead he watched the minutes tick by, endlessly.

'C'mon for God's sake, ring,' he muttered.

He stared at the phone as if it were some sort of peculiar hybrid deliberately frustrating him. In essence it didn't matter one iota what had befallen or where Tony was. What was paramount was that Dean had a job to do. Danny Sampson's arrival was pending. Once he'd selected what he required and got what he needed together, he'd make like a banana and split.

Sod this for a game of toy soldiers.

Dean pivoted away from the phone and proceeded to brush his teeth, vigorously. He rinsed his mouth out, checked his dentures and then sat on the toilet.

6:21pm the clock on the wall above the door read.

The phone shrilled to life. Dean was up in an instant. He snatched the cordless phone out of its cradle.

'Hello?'

'Tony hasn't returned,' Paul said, as though he'd never hung up.

'Oh shit.'

'Just spoken to his old girl. She hasn't seen him either. Probably frightened her now. She tried his mobile and left a message. He always phones her every couple of hours when he's here to make sure she's all right. She's old, frail, so on and so forth.'

'Am I still going ahead with this?'

'God yeah. But let's not hide our thoughts. Something's happened to him.'

'It doesn't look good, I admit,' Dean said. 'But we weren't followed. Or at least neither of us saw anyone trailing us.'

'Yeah, I know. And I believe you too. But...' Paul trailed off unable to finish his sentence.

'But you think he's met with foul play. Also known as Anton. Yes?'

'Yeah.'

Dean caressed his brow. 'Whatcha want me to do?'

'Nothing, I guess. I dunno.'

'Look, as soon as Sampson shows up with his toys I'll take a spin through the neighbourhood and see if I can spot the car. After that, I got to be making a move. Otherwise I'll end up facedown somewhere.'

'Okay,' Paul said, distant.

'I'll let you know if I see anything. If not, I'll be heading to Mrs Hill.'

'Be careful,' Paul said.

Dean didn't like the sound of the tremor in his voice. 'I will,' he said and terminated the conversation with a press of a button.

5.

AT APPROXIMATELY 7:00PM Danny Sampson arrived. Dean had finished his microwave roast dinner. He opened the door as Sampson ambled up the path.

'Hi.'

'You were expecting my call I presume,' Sampson said.

'Yeah. Come in.'

Sampson stepped over the threshold. He lifted the luggage carrier over the step and into the living room. Dean closed the door behind him. Then he sidled past and drew the curtains over. He pivoted and proffered a hand but Sampson ignored him and undid the clasps.

'What I've got here is some basic weaponry at the request of your employer.' Sampson said it as though there was nothing illegal about his profession. The luggage carrier unfolded. Sampson carefully removed some folded and ironed long-sleeve and short-sleeve shirts from the top and placed them on the floor. When that had been achieved, he withdrew a blanket, revealing an impressive array of arsenal and ammunition.

'Okay, what I got for you, as Paul's the one paying, is a standard AK-47 and a Colt M1911 pistol, the longest serving service pistol in the U.S. It's a nice, practical semi-automatic. It uses the energy of one shot to reload the chamber for the next. Typically recoil energy from a fired round is mechanically harnessed. After a round is fired, the pistol will cycle, ejecting the spent casing and chambering a new round from the magazine, permitting another shot immediately. There's plenty of ammunition to go with that. It's ideal for self-defence.'

Dean appreciated Sampson knew his goods. However, it became apparent that Sampson was either unaware that he used to be a police officer or thought he was obtuse.

'Next we have the AK-47, which is best described as a hybrid of previous rifle technology innovations. The trigger mechanism, double locking lugs and unlocking raceway. The accuracy has always been deemed "good enough". They are somewhat essential in combat. They are able to hit 3-5 inch groups at 100 yards. The magazine has a pronounced curve which allows it to smoothly feed ammo into the chamber.'

Sampson extracted the two weapons from their sleeves and laid them assiduously on the floor.

'That's great,' Dean said, anxious about the time being wasted. He knew how to fire guns and was more than capable of handling himself. 'But I was hoping to do this job discreetly. What have you for protection?'

'Okay,' Sampson said, nodding. He burrowed into the luggage carrier and selected two suppressors. One short. The other long. 'Okay so you know about silencers. These suppressors have a "female" threaded end, which attaches to the "male" thread cuts into the exterior of the barrel. These are the ones most used for handguns and rifles. But be mindful of harsh recoil from the AK-47 because it can cause it to over tighten, making it bloody difficult to remove.'

'Trust me if I am forced to use the AK-47 it won't be coming off. I am hoping that it doesn't even come to having to shoot anyone. But it's better to have it and not need, and need it but not have it.'

'I have some standard pepper spray and a bullet-proof vest. But if you get shot from close range and you're unable to defend yourself be warned that sometimes a bullet-proof vest merely prolongs the agony.

'There was a narcotics officer who I sold some stuff to. He got wounded by a man firing a shotgun. According to the medical examiner's report the assailant emptied twelve bullets into his abdomen. The guy was still breathing, albeit barely.'

'And the officer survived?' Dean said, unable to conceal his incredulity.

'He may or may not have. It's hard to tell. The assailant fired his last round by blowing half his head off at close range.'

***

Sampson provided Dean with the two weapons; three boxfuls of ammunition, the silencers, pepper spray, a bullet-proof vest and a laser pen. The latter Dean selected as he thought it would be a useful tool if he needed to temporarily blind his assailant in the midst of a fight at close quarters.

Sampson nodded his approval of the decision. Then he unzipped another compartment in the luggage-carrier. Dean frowned, unable to see what Sampson was extracting. And when he did see the transparent pouch filled with white powder he said, 'I think it's time you left now. I've got a long drive.'

'Not interested in this high quality cocaine?'

'No,' Dean said in a firm tone.

'How about heroin? Or some marijuana?'

'I don't do drugs and I don't deal with drug dealers. Last druggies that I came across I ended up killing.'

Sampson's face blanched. 'O-Okay. What about a sedative to calm yourself?'

Dean stared fixedly at the smartly dressed dealer. Sampson raised a hand in an I-get-what-you're-saying gesture. Then he hastily packed his belongings back into the sleeves, zipped them up before closing the luggage carrier.

I bet Demato doesn't know Sampson sells drugs, he thought.

Sampson stood up and proffered a hand. Dean only took it as he felt obligated. Nevertheless, he thought Danny Sampson was a worthless piece of crap. He was an utter loser. Yeah he had a load of impressive toys and probably a lot of contacts for anything and everything – but to sell him serious drugs as though he were selling sweets to children made Dean want to puke.

'Well, I can see I have outstayed my welcome,' Sampson said. 'So, I shall be on my way. Demato has already paid for the two weapons. I will of course be billing him for the silencers. But the laser pen and pepper spray – think of them as a gift from yours truly.'

'And what if I had bought some of your shit? Would I or Demato pay?'

'You, of course,' Sampson said. Then added: 'Did you change your mind?'

Dean raised his eyebrows.

'Thought not,' Sampson said, his throat working convulsively. 'And best of luck with your errand.'

Dean didn't bother saying an obligatory thank you. Instead he led the way to the front door. Sampson stepped over the threshold and didn't turn back. If he had he would have found a closed door where Dean had stood seconds earlier.

***

Anton watched Sampson amble down the drive after emerging from his target's bungalow residence from the comfort of his Ford. On the passenger seat was his rifle, a Remington 1100 tactical shotgun with a large metallic suppressor and his army hunting knife. On his lap was his combat knife. The blade curved and camouflaged in army hues. Anton had sharpened it while waiting patiently for Sampson to emerge. His ebony eyes looked like marbles in the dark. They narrowed with concentration and interest as he watched Sampson head towards his Jaguar with a swaggering gait.

Quietly and in fluid motion, Anton stepped out of the black Ford Fiesta. And before Sampson had even noticed his presence, the chameleon assassin was already directly behind him. In a perfect attacking position, Anton seized Sampson from behind. Sampson, bless him, did his utmost to break the fierce hold but found the sturdy, muscular arm cinched into his throat immovable. He tried to ram the top of his head into Anton's jaw. But Anton had placed his head on Sampson's left shoulder and drove his knee into his prey's back, forcing him to his knees.

Aware that he was no match for his assailant, Sampson feared for his life. His head was held precariously in a vice-like hold. His entire anatomy may as well have been paralysed for all the good it was to him now.

The cold, razor sharp knife burst through the back of his throat. Sampson choked on his own crimson blood now leaking out of his fatal wound. And just before the stars multiplied beyond infinity and a perpetual darkness blanked out every other thought, sight, sound, smell and all other senses, Sampson gasped at the pointed end of the weapon that protruded from his throat.

Anton drew the knife back in one sharp movement and watched as the mortal remains of Sampson thumped the concrete, face first. He used Sampson's suit jacket to clean the blood off his face and knife.

The assassin stepped over the ever-growing pool of coagulated blood. He got down on his haunches and stared with avid interest at the lifeless eyes seeing something he could not see. The hunter was the giver of this eternal gift, not the receiver.

Now his prey would know no pain. His prey would have no memory of his death. He was now presented with an eternal comforting of pure bliss. He would be welcomed into the arms of the everlasting by old friends and family members.

Something that Anton deeply craved: acceptance, but could never have.

Thus, the closest he could get to the feeling of love was to give it without pity or remorse. To give it wholly and completely. Then he would study the dead and try to learn and feel a trace of what they only knew. A shark was not loved by those living in the sea or by those that swam and sailed in its oceans. Nevertheless, the shark was feared and respected by those of the sea and those who merely sailed its grand oceans.

Anton was a shark. He only revealed himself to those he marked for death. It wasn't his intention to intimidate his targets. He found no pleasure in stalking them for the sake of their fear. The hunt of one mammal by another was as natural as the sunshine, as rainfall and the cold on a winter's day. The hunter's reward was a good death. The prey's an end of all suffering and to feel God's love upon their death by his hands.

He rose and ambled nonchalantly back to his Ford. He made a U-Turn in the road and brought the vehicle to a halt alongside the opposite side of the road a hundred yards or so down the road.

Anton waited with inhuman patience for his next target to emerge before the hunt began…

***

At 7:39pm Dean Ferris exited his bungalow donning a long overcoat to conceal the AK-47. His backpack contained the money and the Colt M1911 handgun and the suppressors. After rifling through his medicine cabinet he found some gauze pads, bandages and a bottle of Iodine. He also carried a wallet in his trouser pocket with his Visa Debit card and two twenty-pound notes. He'd also provided himself with a bottle of water, a can of Coke and some ham sandwiches in case he didn't get a chance to stop to eat. Once he'd locked the door, Dean pivoted and instantly froze.

There, lying face-down on the pavement drowning in a pool of crimson, was the unmoving body of Danny Sampson.

Dean cursed under his breath. Then he fumbled in his trouser pocket and fished out his mobile phone. He switched it on and waited for it to load to the main menu screen while scanning the street for the assailant. Then he selected a phone number from the memory.

The ringing cut off abruptly. 'Yeah?'

'Paul? It's me, Dean.'

'What's wrong? Did Sampson not show up?'

'Yeah, he came. Tried to sell me some additional gear. Poor fucker is swimming in a pool of his own blood thanks to our good friend, Anton. He's here. Or if not, close by.'

'Motherfucker!'

'I think it's safe to say that our friend Tony has met with similar foul play, wouldn't you?'

When Paul Demato stopped cursing creatively he answered: 'Goddamn this! Where's Sampson's body?'

'Right outside my house,' Dean said, finally realising the consequences he might face for Anton's deed. 'Someone's bound to notice sooner or later. What shall I do?'

'Can't run,' Paul said, banging his clenched fist on a table. 'If you run, it'll look suspicious.' He paused, deliberating. 'You'll have to phone the police. But before you do use your filbert. Hide your shit somewhere safe. Phone the police; tell them somethin' like you were closing the curtains and you saw someone lying down. You stepped outside, thinking they were pissed but then you saw the blood and realised it was somethin' far worse.'

Dean unlocked his front door and ambled down the hall, still listening intently to Paul's prudent instructions. 'If Anton's close by the police will frighten him off.'

'Exactly. Just turn it back around on him.' Paul was already sounding like his usual-self.

'If they turn up and scout the area, which they will do. It'll be like a goddamn circus. But they might find Tony, as well. I won't be able to go tonight; that's my original plan out the window.'

'If they do find Tony nearby, CID will identify him as one of my men and I'll be contacted. Until then don't mention my name. Got it?'

'Yeah. I wasn't going to anyway. The less I know the more convincing it'll be.'

They ended their discussion and Dean phoned the police from his landline.

Then he waited for the shit to hit the fan…

6.

THE WHIRLING red and blue beacons and blaring sirens announced the police's arrival several minutes before they came to a halt outside Dean's bungalow.

He left the front door ajar and stood by the picture window in the living room.

This couldn't have gone worse if it was planned, which it probably was, he thought. It didn't cross his mind that Anton hadn't contrived what was about to ensue. He didn't consider Anton had killed Sampson for aiding Dean in his task. Both Dean and Paul still believed that Anton would come after Dean for the money. This was only partly true. Anton wanted – needed – the money. His error had been understandable, as the Cascarini Family had not given him a full description of Leo Demato. Instead all they supplied him with was Leo's home address.

The actual kill itself had been efficient, as always. Had Leo not first revealed himself to the chameleon alongside Tobias Hill then there would have been no mistaken identity. It would have been clean cut. And Paul Demato would have still had a godson but no son of his own.

Paul always reiterated, *It takes two smart people to do a good business deal. And only one wise guy to cause an all-out mafia war*.

Dean made his way to the front door as the patrol cars screeched to the halt and killed the wailing siren. The two officers that climbed out of the first patrol car paled instantly upon seeing Danny Sampson exactly as Dean had described on the phone to the dispatcher.

Another black, unmarked car with a flashing blue beacon, minus the siren, stopped on the opposite side of the street. Two non-uniformed officers climbed out and ordered the two constables to secure the crime scene. Then they crossed the road and headed straight to Dean's front door.

Dean knew the procedure as well as the wrinkles on his cock. He beckoned the two detectives into his home. He didn't proffer a hand to them, as he knew they considered him a suspect, regardless of the circumstances and the fact that he'd informed them of the crime.

'Gentleman, would you like to join me in the living room?' Dean asked.

DI Sark nodded and then followed Dean into the living room. He lowered himself onto the sofa to the right of the armchair Dean perched himself upon.

'Do you guys want a drink?'

Sark and his new partner DI Jason refused the genial offer.

'Can you tell us what happened?' Sark said, leaning forward, studying Dean's countenance.

'No, I can't,' Dean said matter-of-factly.

'Beg your pardon,' DI Jason said, indifferent.

'I can't tell you what happened, as I did not see that unfortunate gentleman's death taking place. I mean, I assume he's dead. That amount of blood loss…'

Sark nodded to his partner, who in turn rose and stepped outside.

'You didn't phone for an ambulance?'

Dean shook his head. 'Didn't think there was any need to. I just asked for the police when I dialled 999. Sorry.'

Sark waved him off. 'My partner's gone to see if he can find a pulse. But I think your assumption is pretty accurate. Did you approach the body and check yourself?'

'No way!' Dean said. 'I was too shocked. Thought my eyes were playing tricks on me to be frank. I know that sounds ludicrous but...'

'Not at all,' Sark said. 'You did the right thing, minus calling for an ambulance.'

Dean shrugged. 'I'm sorry. My mind was kinda frazzled by the whole scenario. I mean, this is a nice, quiet, idyllic neighbourhood. There are no shouting matches. No violence or even boy racers. This a good place filled with good people. Perhaps if I had checked for a pulse or investigated I would've ruined the crime scene for your forensic guys.'

'That's true,' Sark admitted. 'But do you recognise the victim?'

'No. Having said that all I saw was some poor soul lying face-down, not moving, and a lotta blood. And I mean black blood, not like when you cut yourself shaving. But blood from deep down. I didn't hear any shouts or shots, either.'

Sark could see that Dean was telling the truth regarding the cause of death. However, he did start rambling a tad when he queried whether or not he recognised the victim. Although, this fellow was genuinely taken aback by the events that had occurred right outside his home.

'Okay,' Sark said, sounding fairly satisfied. 'We'll identify the victim soon enough. Maybe he was a neighbour or a salesman.'

'D'you reckon he was killed here?'

'What makes you ask that?' Sark said, frowning.

'I just didn't hear any cries, shouts or fighting of any sort. Having said that I have been in the shower, the kitchen – at the rear of the house – and had the T.V. on.'

It was a reasonable question Sark believed. 'I wouldn't have thought so. There wouldn't be so much blood on the pavement if that was the case.'

'Fair point,' Dean said.

Everything Dean was saying informed the detective that he was innocent of the crime itself. However, he constantly fidgeted with his hands and seemed to accept Sark's opine instantly came across as evasive. Sark believed that Dean knew something, no matter how trivial, regarding the crime or the perpetrator or the victim. Nevertheless, he couldn't put his finger on it and there was the strong possibility it was simply frayed nerves.

DI Jason popped his head around the doorframe and said, 'Our victim is dead.'

'There's a surprise,' Sark said, silently disappointed. If a victim died it made solving the crime much more troublesome and arduous, unless of course they found reliable eye witnesses.

***

Dean could scarcely believe the circus outside his once quiet suburban neighbourhood. The cacophony of onlookers resonated in the ex-policeman's head. The flashing beacons whirled incessantly causing lights to flash behind his retinas. An hour had passed quicker than a minute soaking in the shower earlier on.

He had stepped outside and felt the glowering of the onlookers boring into his back as he followed DI Sark and DI Jason outside for a closer look at the body. One of the forensic men who had donned an all-white bodysuit and gloves ducked underneath the yellow crime scene tape and approached them. He didn't bother introducing himself. Instead he said, 'Knife wound from behind through the oesophagus is the cause of death. Our victim probably didn't see it coming.'

'No gunshot wounds?' Dean blurted.

The forensic shook his head once. 'This guy wasn't shot or sedated. He didn't even see the perpetrator until it was too late.

Quick. But certainly not painless. This was no ordinary knife either. This was a big army or combat knife. There's a three-inch gash. It could only have been done with a knife with a curved and serrated blade.'

DI Jason turned to his partner. 'Checked with the neighbours and they confirmed that the red Porsche doesn't belong to any of them. Neither has anyone seen it here before for it to belong to a friend or relative of one of the locals. We checked the victim's pockets. The keys to the car are in his trouser pocket.'

Sark must have seen something behind his partner's eyes that he hadn't already told him. DI Jason had stayed outside after informing DI Sark the victim was dead and had watched as the forensics pried the luggage carrier out of his suitcase and opened it.

'There's a shit-load of coke, heroine, marijuana, speed and some guns Dirty Harry would be proud of. This guy is a dealer. Checked his wallet and found some Visa cards: turns out this guy is Danny Sampson. He is a well-known arms and drugs dealer.'

'Hence the expensive suit,' Sark said, sighing.

Dean stood motionless. Intuition told him that CID would soon make the connection with Danny Sampson and the underworld he was associated with, one of those individuals being Paul Demato. And who was Paul Demato connected with ever since the trial of two unarmed young men who were killed by a policeman?

DI Jason pulled his partner to one side. 'Just checked this Sampson's mobile phone records. Apart from his wife the last number on the memory belongs to Paul Demato.'

DI Sark looked over his shoulder and stared at Dean until they met each other's gaze. 'I think Mr Ferris knows more than he's letting on.'

'D'you think he's our guy for this?'

Sark turned back and faced his younger, less experienced partner. 'Either he is a cold blooded killer with no conscience and a great actor or no. But he definitely knows who our victim is.'

'Let's see what we can get outta him down the station,' DI Jason said.

'Need to speak to Mrs Sampson and Demato too. Something here doesn't add up. If our neighbour here is the killer why did he phone the police and not make a run for it?'

'He used to be one of us,' DI Jason said. 'Probably knew if he did it'd make a suspect.'

'But he's a suspect anyway, don't you see?' Sark said. 'He would've known that and yet called us anyway. According to forensics the body is still relatively warm. We'll get confirmation from the coroner. And had he killed him why leave him in the open, right outside his home and not get in his car and wait for it to be discovered and return none the wiser. He could've done it and then gone to a public place around the same time and had lots of eye witnesses.'

DI Sark shook his head again. His intuition and experience told him Dean Ferris was innocent of this crime. 'I don't think he's our man. Not unless we find a murder weapon on him or fingerprints or any other DNA. But he knows something.'

Dean watched as the body of Danny Sampson was finally zipped up in a body bag and placed on a stretcher and wheeled into the ambulance. His stomach performed summersaults. He buried his head in his hands.

The shit has well and truly hit the fan this time.

The whole plan of him doing a good, moral deed for Sandra Hill in her time of

grief had taken a bomb dive towards obliteration. He wasn't surprised when DI Sark ambled over to the doorstep he perched himself on and said in a calm voice, 'We need you to come down the station to answer some routine questions. You know how this works. We need to get your statement for the record.'

Dean rubbed his face, shaking his head in disbelief. 'I was supposed to be going to see my gran,' he said.

'I'm sorry about that,' DI Sark said, shrugging. 'But I don't need to tell you how important this is. We'll even get a constable to bring you straight back once we're done.'

Sighing with exertion and vexation, Dean rose. He locked his front door after turning off all the lights and then followed the two detectives to the black sedan.

'I wish my neighbours would STOP STARING!' Dean bellowed the last two words at his nosy neighbours.

DI Sark eyeballed them as if to say you-are-disgraceful. Then he closed the rear door behind Dean and got into the passenger seat. DI Jason started the engine and shook his head at the onlookers disapprovingly before turning the car around. He had to turn the steering wheel vigorously to avoid driving over the crime scene where two members of the forensics were still studying every inch of the ground for DNA.

This is gonna be a long night, Dean thought.

7.

THE MAN KNOWN as Mr Death cocked his head at the sound of sirens and approaching patrol cars. This was not how he believed his prey would have reacted at all. In fact he thought his prey would have acted hastily in trying to flee his home and drive on by without noticing he was being pursued.

Anton didn't know what to make of Dean's decision. He couldn't tell if it was indeed prudent of him or not. It didn't seem to be a wise prudent decision, as it would hinder the task of getting the money to the intended person. Whatever the case, he had to get out of there.

Instead of rushing like any other perpetrator would in blind panic, Anton started the engine, released the handbrake and nonchalantly permitted the Ford to roll down the incline onto the main road. He turned left at the junction and joined the traffic. He only briefly glanced at the two patrol cars coming in the opposite direction, beacons flashing, as they overtook the other vehicles that had dutifully pulled over.

At the roundabout, Anton took the third left turning and drove to the first set of traffic lights. In the far distance he could see the red neon Tesco sign and headed in that direction. He required car fuel and body fuel.

Anton knew Danny Sampson had died. What he didn't know was how this turn of events would affect his task. The Cascarini Family were in a world of shit thanks to Leo Demato and him. In future when he accepted a job he would insist that he be paid upfront. However, as money wasn't his main motivation (but necessary, like car and body fuel) he hadn't queried it at the time. The Cascarini Family were affluent. One only needed to be at their grandeur home or see their Rolls Royce cars and numerous sports cars and expensive Gucci suits to see that. Not for a second had Anton believed he wouldn't get paid. And although he'd killed in error, he felt assured that the Demato Family would pay.

What affected him more than anything else though, was how a trace of fear had coursed through his system when Don Cascarini started bellowing at him that he had killed the wrong guy. And that they were now being interrogated for murdering Tobias Hill. A completely innocent man who had nothing to do with their business.

The fear brought back the memories of a night of bone-chilling terror. That night was the sole reason he became a shape of the human he once might have been and nothing more. Ever since he felt no emotion. No reason. No conscience. No pity or remorse for the suffering he caused.

The fear inside him had been foreign. It made Anton vulnerable. Something he had not experienced since seeing the decapitated heads of his parents dangling by their hair from the hands of the faceless killer.

He almost missed the turning to the entrance of the Tesco car park. The tyres screeched as the swerved round the corner and followed the narrow road onto the tarmac. Anton slotted the Ford into a vacant space. It was only then that he noticed the white knuckles of his large, heavy hands clenching the leather-covered steering wheel. He relaxed them, breathed, and then erased the memory of his fear that had arisen from his mistake.

The fresh air of the crisp night filled his lungs. It felt good to inhale clean oxygen. His hands rested by his sides, loose. Emotionless once more, the chameleon headed towards the entrance of the glass enclosure.

***

48

The automatic doors made a hydraulic hiss as they slid apart, permitting Anton into the foyer. He immediately welcomed the breeze of the AC. To his immediate right was a notice board and standing in front was a middle-aged man holding a bucket for a charity titled Children in Need.

Anton ignored the man who smiled warmly at him and strode forward. He loathed public places such as Tesco. He could practically smell the acrid scent of warm blood flowing in the shoppers' anatomies. A lot of them were dead and didn't even know it. Their lives had no purpose or worth. They went about their errands as though it were of great importance. And to them – and them alone – it most likely was.

However, Anton saw them as scientists saw guinea pigs – specimens. They created a variety of problems and then complained about them. They offered asinine solutions to their predicaments (those that were capable of coming up with a solution). They bred more of their kind until they populated the country to the point of bursting. Then they complained about the very same problem they'd caused.

Anton had the reputation of a ruthless assassin. Yet he saw himself as a shape that ended suffering hastily and efficiently. At least he didn't prolong someone's suffering and then let them wait for old age to take them. These people didn't have it in them to do what he did. If he was hungry and needed something to eat he would kill for it, pure and simple. The people though would continue to complain and sit there and feel sorry for themselves.

An elderly woman carrying two bags of provisions bumped into him as she went by. She turned to face him, as though obliged. 'Excuse me.'

Anton stared with cold, black eyes.

The elderly woman shivered inwardly, not liking what she saw behind those eyes.

'Do you value your life?' Anton asked.

'Pardon?' She sounded incredulous as well as perplexed.

Anton repeated his question, looking down at her.

'Y-Yes.'

'What makes you value your life?'

The woman shifted from one foot to the other, frail and withered. 'I d-don't understand,' she said.

'Precisely my point,' Anton said, matter-of-factly.

Clearly upset by his comment, the woman said, 'What d'you mean by that?'

'You don't know what it's like to be alive; truly alive.'

The elderly woman had a good mind to give the tall, broad man towering over her a piece of her mind. But something inexplicable shimmered behind his eyes she would never be able to articulate. She knew it wasn't anything as simple as contempt. What she did know was her wrinkly old flesh crawled with goose pimples and her heart skipped a beat.

'You're bad. You have something missing deep inside you,' she whispered so only Anton could hear. 'What is it? What are *you*?'

Anton leant forward and lowered his face to the elderly lady's ear and whispered something. Whatever he had said caused her to emit a short gasp.

Then she moved with difficulty as fast as her arthritic frail form would allow her to. When her daughter phoned her an hour later the old lady couldn't swear on her life what the strange man had whispered. She didn't tell anyone about her unexpected meeting with the tall stranger who had something inside of him missing that other people had from the moment they were born to the day they died. Something that was otherworldly. But as she lay down in her bed and the darkness enveloped her Anton's whisper echoed in the valley of her heart.

In front of you, you see death.

***

Anton watched the old lady hobble outside, leaden with her shopping, struggling. Then he averted his attention away from her. He strode towards the frozen foods section next to the magazine and bookstand. Some shoppers immersed themselves in glossy magazines and the latest bestselling books.

He had read a lot of books over the years, but did so out of boredom, not enjoyment. The fridge door opened effortlessly. Anton helped himself to a bottle of sparkling water and a pack of fajitas. He also grabbed a Mars Bar. He performed this task without paying any heed to the products he had picked up, unlike the lady next to him. She pondered futilely at whether or not to purchase the cheese and onion sandwiches or the cheese and ham.

Instead of going to the checkout point where the young blonde smiled at him, wanting something to do to look busy, Anton used the self-service. He collected his loose change and carried his items in his hands. The security guard eyed him curiously as he approached the exit. Then before Anton made it over the threshold the rotund fellow blocked his path.

Halting, Anton stared at the security guard who stood three inches shorter.

'Yes? Can I be of service?'

The security guard's plump cheeks threatened to swallow his eyes into the folds of flushed flesh. He was the epitome of the chubby fat friend he had never had. 'Sir, that elderly woman you spoke to seemed very upset after she spoke to you…'

'Did she?' Anton didn't pretend to not know what the man before him was talking about. However, he was intrigued by what the guard had seen.

'Yes, she did. May I ask what you said to her?' The security guard stood with his back straight, arms out by his sides in a confident posture. His quivering jowls however told a different story.

'Yes you may,' Anton said, without a trace of humour.

The rotund gentleman took a step back, evidently not finding the sarcastic remark humorous either. He braced himself for trouble. And hated himself for trembling before this man who stared impassively at him. Most shoppers he approached either feared him or the uniform. It usually meant that they were suspected of theft or another criminal offence. The man before him could have been in a daze for all his countenance gave away.

'What did you say to her?' he said, his voice shaking.

'I told her the truth,' Anton said.

'Look…' The security guard had started sweating profusely from the brow.

'Have I broken any laws or done something?'

The guard's mouth had suddenly gone dry. His Adam's apple bobbed up and down.

'I have paid for my goods, and got a receipt to prove this is the case,' Anton continued waving the receipt in the fat man's reddening face. 'So, if you don't mind.'

'W-What did you say t-to her, sir?' the security guard bravely persisted.

The saliva of eager anticipation swam in Anton's mouth. He did well to resist the urge to put this tub of lard out of his misery and end his suffering in a body made for two right here and now. Yet if he did that and fled, the authorities wouldn't take long to track him down. They would have a hundred or so eye witnesses of his description and what vehicle he drove. The mere thought of murdering this chubby bear was obtuse. It would be as pointless as the elderly lady's life.

He had killed Danny Sampson to send a message to his prey, hoping he would panic. Killing for the sake of killing would attract unwanted attention and would ultimately be the reason for his pending arrest.

'I said "Watch where you're going". Then I said what I am about to tell you. "Get out of my way".'

The security guard, like the old woman, saw something shimmer in the ebony eyes and stepped aside, feeling the weight of his anxiety lift instantly.

As Anton passed him the security guard thought – but couldn't be certain – he heard him whisper. But he might have imagined it.

He wiped his sleeve across his damp brow before the beads of sweat ran into his squashed eyes. His whole body boiled from within. He watched the man carry his goods out of the foyer and onto the pavement. The man stopped at a zebra crossing leading onto the car park and looked over his shoulder at him.

In that harrowing moment what Anton had whispered tickled his ears as though resonating in the valley of his mind.

In front of you, you see death.

8.

DEAN might as well have been handcuffed. He walked behind DI Jason and in front of DI Sark past the information desk and down the short hall. You didn't need to be an ex-policeman to know this was merely more than making a formal statement. Still, his greatest concern was not answering a bunch of questions but how he would manage to get the stash of money to Mrs Hill in West Wales.

DI Jason opened the door to the interview room and gestured for Dean to pull up a chair. He and DI Sark sat opposite him. The plain white concrete walls flooded his consciousness with memories of when he'd been grilled for his crime against two drug dealers.

DI Jason waited for his partner to take out his notepad and jot something down. Then he said, 'Could you please tell us, without omitting anything, what you had done today leading up to discovering the victim outside your house?'

'I thought I already went through this with your partner,' Dean said.

'Yeah, you did. Now we want you to go through it again, for the record.'

Instead of telling them what had actually transpired on that day, Dean told them what happened on an average day off from work.

'D'you still keep in touch with Paul Demato?' DI Sark asked, not looking up from his notepad.

'Yeah.'

'When was the last time you spoke with him?' DI Sark went on.

'This morning,' Dean said.

Both detectives could tell Dean was telling the truth.

'Apart from his wife, the victim, Danny Sampson, last spoke with Paul Demato. Then we find him dead right outside your house,' DI Jason said, matter-of-factly.

'I can see why you brought me in here for questioning then and not just a formal statement.'

DI Jason smiled grimly. He didn't like the fact that Dean knew the procedure and wasn't showing even the slightest bit of concern. DI Sark, who had a lot more experience, ignored this unspoken duel between the two men.

'What did you and Demato talk about?'

'Usual,' Dean said.

'Could you elaborate?' DI Sark said.

Dean shrugged. 'He just asked me how I was. When I asked him the same question he said there were some changes being made regarding work and that he was hoping to move out to Spain to retire.'

Both detectives were visibly surprised by this.

'He helped you get off the hook when you killed those two young men coupla years ago, didn't he?' DI Jason said through gritted teeth.

DI Sark looked at him.

'If you want to question the judge's decision,' Dean said, remaining placid, 'then you've left it rather late to put in appeal. And as you weren't there and don't know the circumstances I suggest you keep out of it.'

'Or you'll get one of Demato's guy's to "whack" me, right?'

'Enough!' Sark snapped.

'Demato doesn't do business with drug dealers,' Dean said. 'If you say his number was on this guy's mobile, I'm not disputing that. But I don't know him. And until tonight I've never seen him.'

A knock came from the other side of the door.

DI Sark finished jotting down the sentence he was writing and called out, 'Come in.'

The door opened and a police constable held a cordless phone in his right hand. Covering the mouthpiece he looked at the detectives and said, 'Paul Demato is on the phone; said he'd like to speak with the investigator in charge.'

If DI Sark was taken aback Dean gave him credit for not showing any reaction. Instead he held his hand out and the constable handed him the phone.

'Hello?'

Sark listened intently.

'Yes, I am,' Sark said. Then he looked up at Dean. 'Yes, he is.'

Dean didn't have one clue as to what Demato was talking to DI Sark about. But he already felt relieved and vindicated.

'So, Dean here wouldn't have known?'

DI Jason continued to stare fixedly at Dean. He didn't bother to have a staring match with the detective. Instead he glimpsed him and shook his head at his juvenile behaviour.

'I will ask him right now,' DI Sark said. Then he faced Dean again.

'What is it?' Dean asked, curious.

'Paul says that he spoke with you this morning asking if you wanted to come to dinner. He sent Tony Nivean. But he hasn't heard or seen from Tony since. He was wondering if you spoke to Tony Nivean at any time today.'

Dean shook his head.

DI Sark spoke into the phone. 'No.' He paused, listening. Then he added, 'Okay. Will do. And you will give a formal statement, yes? Thanks.'

Dean watched as DI Sark terminated the conversation.

'All very interesting and complicated,' Sark said, musing aloud. 'Who is this Tony Nivean?'

'He's Paul's bodyguard,' Dean said.

'According to Demato, he sent Tony to pick you up. He waited and waited and heard nothing – although, I don't quite understand why he just didn't phone you again. Then he got in touch with this Sampson schmuck and asked him to drive by your place and around the area to see if Tony was about.'

'So what's happened to Tony?' Dean blurted.

Sark opened his hands out. 'Exactly. That's the million pound question.' He regarded the constable. 'I want a thorough search around the neighbourhood for a BMW.'

The constable nodded, repeated what Sark said for clarification into the phone and left.

'What about me?' Dean asked.

'Are you sure you don't know who that Sampson bloke is?'

Dean shook his head. 'Can I ask you something?'

'Of course,' Sark said.

'Did Demato know if Sampson was a drug dealer?'

'What d'you think?'

'I think if Demato knew this Sampson guy – God rest his soul – was into drug dealing he wouldn't be very pleased at all.'

Sark smiled benignly. 'Neither do I.'

'Am I free to go?'

DI Jason shook his head.

'Grow up,' Dean said.

DI Sark didn't even glimpse at his partner. 'If we let you go now without any more questioning, will you stay at home so we can contact you if we need any more information?'

Dean sighed. 'I have to make a trip to see a friend in west Wales a.s.a.p. They're not doing great. I promised I would drop by and see them for a day. I'll be right back though. Plus I can give you my mobile number. If you give me yours we can keep in touch like that until I get back.'

DI Sark deliberated this notion for a short while. 'Is it that important?'

'A promise is a promise,' Dean said. 'And I'll be in touch constantly. I won't be in Tenby for long. But it is very important. I know this too. But it's not as if I'm not telling you where I'm going or not giving you any information. And I have been cooperative. I could do with a short break to be honest. Even though I lost my badge and my reputation is unalterable for that mistake a couple of years ago and was found to be not guilty of purposeful murder, my neighbours still look at me like I'm Charles Manson. And all I did was react with good intentions, if a little too hasty.'

'Gimme your mobile number then,' DI Sark said. He provided Dean with his number. Then he tried Dean's mobile number to make sure it wasn't a fabricated number.

Dean had been on the verge of rising when DI Sark spoke. 'Have you ever heard of an assassin called "Mr Death"?'

'Paul mentioned a name like that by way of conversation.' Dean leant forward realising that if his posture showed he was about to get up it would appear he was hiding something. 'Apparently, there was an incident where Paul's godson got killed. I think that's what he said. I mean I don't get involved with his business or any of the details. Why?'

DI Sark wrote something down. 'His godson got murdered by mistake by "Mr Death". The Cascarini Family sent this fellow to get rid of Paul's son, Leo. Now both families are under investigation.'

'Bloody hell,' Dean blurted. 'No wonder he wanted to have dinner with me. Probably wanted to take his mind off his worries.'

'Did Paul ever mention what this guy looked like?' DI Jason asked.

Dean shook his head. 'I don't think so. I would've remembered. Is it important?'

'Make sure you don't wind up getting involved in something which doesn't concern you,' DI Sark said. 'Desperate men will sell their own grannies never mind get someone to do their dirty work.'

Dean fixed his gaze on Sark then. In all his years on the force Dean had never met a more intelligent police officer or person.

They shook hands at the reception. DI Jason offered a curt nod, which Dean thought was quite amicable considering DI Jason didn't like him one iota.

'You don't have to wait for me to phone you, you know?' DI Sark said.

'I know,' Dean said.

'If you find yourself involved in something you can't control or are forced into you got my number. We'll help you if you help us. Remember that.'

'I will,' Dean said, believing him.

***

DI Sark slotted the correct amount into the vending machine. He hit the Diet Coke button and bent down at the sound of his can sliding down into the metallic tray. He opened the can and guzzled the cold, fizzy drink.

DI Jason hadn't spoken since Dean had departed ten minutes ago. Sark could feel his stare penetrating through his back. He pivoted. 'What is it already? You still got a hard on for Dean Ferris?'

DI Jason snorted derisively. 'Seems like he was an old friend of yours. Your lips were practically glued to his arse.'

'D'you want to say that to the chief inspector, son?'

DI Jason didn't respond to that. He was seen as a rookie in comparison to DI Sark, but that didn't deter him from speaking his mind. 'What did you mean when you were going on about "desperate men would sell their grannies never mind getting someone to do their dirty work"? You think Dean is working for Demato or what?'

Swallowing the mouthful of Coke, Sark said, 'I don't know anything for certain. All I know is Demato has got a lotta heat on him since the mess up involving his godson, the Cascarini's and the investigations. Desperate men will stop at nothing to clear their name. I just don't wanna see Dean holding the shit end of the stick, that's all. Just because you don't like him, and he made a very stupid mistake a couple of years ago doesn't mean he's a criminal. He lost his job, reputation, had to do community service and pay some hefty fines over some druggies. Guys who sold drugs to teenagers and couldn't care less what the ramifications were.

'Dean Ferris was an undercover cop and solved a lot of crimes involving illegal drug deals. He also saved a lotta lives too. I'm not asking you to like the guy. I am asking that you conduct yourself professionally and you show some respect.'

DI Jason remained silent.

'You came over aggressive, hostile. All he had to say was I want a lawyer and we wouldn't have got anything worthwhile outta him. Now we know where he's headed, and we got his mobile number and Paul Demato willing to give a formal statement. It's called progress.'

Running footfalls pounded the glossy linoleum at the far end of the corridor. Both detectives looked up, alarmed. The same constable who had interrupted their informal interview with Dean Ferris stopped within five feet of them.

'What is it?' DI Jason said.

The constable regarded both of them. 'They found Tony Nivean's body…'

9.

BY THE TIME Detective Inspectors Sark and Jason arrived at the sight of the second murder one block over from where Danny Sampson had been discovered, it was pandemonium.

'Oh, I don't believe this,' DI Sark groaned.

In front of them, beyond the windscreen, neighbours had crowded around like flies attracted to shit. Worse than the public were two media vans parked up on the kerb beneath the oak trees. The BBC and ITV. The PCSO's (police constable security officers) were outnumbered and driven back by the crowds. Their feeble attempts of keeping the media and onlookers back at a safe distance would have been humorous if it wasn't so serious.

DI Jason rode the kerb onto the dewy grass and killed the engine. The night was illuminated by the whirling red and blue beacons. It reminded Sark of lights inside a nightclub. And for the amount of people emerging from their homes and crossing the street into the road it may as well have been.

Goddamn circus!

A police constable beckoned for them to come hither. Sark dug into his coat pockets and put his fingerless gloves on. He and DI Jason crossed the road to the young officer.

'Nice to see this has all been dealt with in the strictest confidence,' Sark said.

The constable had no sense of humour. Instead of laughing and bringing them up to date with the murder, his mouth fell open.

'Oh for fu…'

Sark averted his gaze from the constable momentarily. Then said: 'Who let the cat out of the bag?'

'Do you mean who let the story out?' the constable asked.

The inspector looked heavenward, pleading with God to please give this obtuse individual just a slither of intelligence. 'Yes.'

'A woman walking her two Chinese cross dogs spotted him first about two minutes after I found him. She must've told her neighbours and before you know it they're all stepping outside. Not one of them bothered to call for an ambulance – okay the victim is dead – but they did phone the media, as you can see,' he said, nodding towards the reporters standing in front of rolling cameras.

Another patrol car came screeching to a halt, siren blaring. A police officer rolled down the window and spoke through a megaphone. 'PLEASE STEP AWAY FROM THE CAR AND THE BODY. THIS IS AN OFFICIAL CRIME SCENE. YOU ARE JEOPARDISING THE POLICE AND CRIME SCENE INVESTIGATORS FROM DOING THEIR JOB. IF YOU DO NOT MOVE AWAY THIS INSTANT YOU WILL BE ARRESSTED. PLEASE STEP AWAY. NOW!'

In one fluid motion the crowd shuffled around and moved like a swarm of bees to the other side of the road. Some of them were embarrassed for gawking at the black BMW and the cadaver occupying the front seat.

As they did this DI Sark and DI Jason walked closer until they could see what the headlights of the young officer's patrol car had illuminated. In the dazzling radiance a shaven headed, sturdy built man sat unmoving in the driver's seat. His head leaned awkwardly against the door's window. The wound in his neck was lucid. Sark could tell even amidst the severed, bloody mess that it was the same perpetrator who killed Danny Sampson. Same weapon by the looks of it too.

'At least it won't take forensics long to get here,' he said.

***

A young officer dutifully dropped Dean off outside his bungalow. He was surprised to see that some of his nosy neighbours still hung around watching the forensics doing their work. They turned their attention to the patrol car. When he got out and ambled along his path towards his front door he couldn't resist facing them. He gave them a half-hearted smile. They glowered at him, already accusing him of murder, minus any facts. He considered marching over there and confronting them or glowering back at them. But they weren't worth the effort. Instead he gave them the traditional V-sign. 'Hard lines,' he said. 'You're only hoping it'd be me so you could have something to gossip about. Shows how pathetic you lot are, doesn't it? How do I know it wasn't one of you, trying to set me up?'

He didn't bother to wait for an answer. When he closed the front door behind him he exhaled explosively.

It had been one long day. His body felt leaden with exhaustion. If he left for Tenby tonight it would still appear suspicious in spite of the fact that the informal interview with the detectives had gone relatively well. Everything had gone in his favour as soon as Demato had spoken with DI Sark.

Once he drained a can of Carlsberg Dean called Paul from his mobile.

'Where are you?'

'Back home. I just wanted to phone to say thanks for calling the station. How did you know I'd be there anyway?'

'I tried your landline, tried your mobile but it was switched off. I put two and two together. It was too obvious. If you said nothing they would've known you were withholding information soon enough. What did you tell them?'

'They knew from going through Sampson's mobile you had spoken to him recently. I said I didn't dispute that but I was certain you didn't know he was a drug dealer. I told them we still keep in touch but that I wasn't part of your business. And I said you vaguely mentioned your godson dying. They know about Anton. But that's pretty much it.' Dean chose not to mention DI Sark advising him not to end up doing someone else's dirty work.

'What do they know about Anton?'

'Well, I think they only know him as "Mr Death". They didn't mention his first name. I said you might've mentioned it by way of conversation but as we didn't really discuss business and only kept in touch now and again I couldn't be certain.'

'Okay. Not bad. Perhaps you should've kept your trap shut about me mentioning Anton though.'

'But I had already told them about you telling me about your godson getting killed being murdered. I very much doubt they would've believed me then if I said no.'

'What about Tony?'

'In fairness to Inspector Sark he did tell the constable to keep an eye out for a black BMW in the area. He seemed satisfied that both of us are in blue. You phoning him like that and agreeing to give a formal statement while being under investigation looks good.'

'Well, apart from some white lies, it is true,' Paul said. 'When are you gonna make a move?'

Dean deliberated for a moment. 'It's like a CSI program have decided to film an episode right outside. And those arsehole neighbours of mine are still outside staring daggers at me. I hate all the whispering. I wish they'd just have a pair big enough to come out and say what they're really thinking… Probably tomorrow morning. I told the inspector I was going to visit a friend in Tenby and even gave him my mobile number.

The more cooperative you are with them the less they've got against you.'

'No, that's good thinking. But for God's sake make sure you keep the money out of sight and don't drive there as though you're on a jolly boys' outing. I know you're still being watched, but the bedlam up there with you is also a hindrance for Anton.'

'He hasn't stuck around. Perhaps he'll get cold feet,' Dean said, hoping more than believing what he said.

Paul chuckled. 'Trust me this guy didn't flee the crime scene 'cause he's scared. He departed of his own accord. I guarantee he'll be watching you. You may not feel his presence due to the distance or because you can't see him, but trust me, he's your shadow.'

What Paul said didn't exactly fill Dean with a surge of confidence.

A hard knock on the front door startled him out of his reverie.

'What's that?' Paul said.

'Someone's at the door. Hang on.'

Dean kept the mobile to his right ear and opened the front door. He didn't know what to make of the constable who had dropped him off at his house ten minutes ago standing before him.

'Hi,' Dean said. 'What's up?'

'They found the black BMW... and a body.'

Dean was speechless.

'Just a sec,' Dean said into the mobile. Then he faced the ashen-faced constable. 'Has the body been identified?'

'It was only just discovered,' the constable said after peeling his tongue from the roof of his mouth.

Dean nodded. He listened to Paul and said, 'Can you give a description of the victim?'

'Big guy with a shaven head dressed in a smart suit.'

65

Dean closed his eyes and cussed simultaneously with Paul who had heard as well.

'How?'

'Pardon?' the constable was just a kid, early twenties, out of his depth.

'How did he die? Shot? Stabbed?'

'Same as the first victim. His throat was slashed.'

Dean cussed again. 'Oh, will I ever get some peace?'

'The two detective inspectors have been informed. They asked if you could come and identify him.'

Dean sighed. Exhaustion had seeped into his bones. But it was nothing compared to the vexation brimming beneath the surface. 'Yeah, lemme just grab my coat.'

'Gimme a call,' Paul said. 'Or better still ask this inspector – what's his name? – to call me.'

'Will do,' Dean said.

He grabbed his coat from the hanger and followed the constable outside.

***

Dean emerged from the back seat of the patrol car. He squinted as ocean blue and scarlet light illuminated the tree-lined street. As he glanced at the onlookers standing alongside one another in a long line it appeared they were drenched in blood and not the beacons radiance. Doing his utmost to ignore those imbeciles, he crossed the road to where the detectives stood.

DI Sark offered a curt nod. 'Thanks for coming. I apologise for further inconvenience.'

The young constable glimpsed the BMW and then quickly looked away again. 'I gave him a brief description and it appears it is…' He couldn't think of the name.

'Tony,' Dean said, wincing for the uniformed officer struggling to cope.

'I appreciate that, but if you could just take a look. He'll be properly identified with his family and forensics. I just wanted to get a head start on this, that's all.'

Dean stepped up to the point where a man dressed head to toe in a white body proof suit was waiting for his colleagues to begin their investigation. A uniformed officer finished wrapping the all-too-familiar crime scene tape around the bark of the nearest tree. However, Dean didn't need to get any closer even if he wanted to. As hard as it was to believe, the man occupying the seat was the same genial bodyguard who had been inside his house not several hours ago and ate some ham sandwiches and drained a can of Coke.

DI Sark had silently approached him and now stood side by side. 'What are you thinking?'

'How different someone looks alive not a few hours ago to when they have only recently died,' Dean said in a faraway voice.

DI Sark rested a hand on his shoulder. 'But it is him, yes?'

Dean nodded. 'I was told his throat had been slashed.' He pointed to the severe neck wound that had ultimately ended Tony Nivean's life. 'His throat hasn't been slashed for crying out loud, it's been hacked. And not just hacked but hacked right down to the bone.'

'D'you think our perpetrator is this "Mr Death"?'

Dean didn't speak for a moment. He couldn't. His mouth had gone bone dry. His mind kept reverting to their conversation in the very same car and in his kitchen. How he had suddenly realised what a humble, kind and decent man Tony was once you got to know him.

'All I know is, Tony was as tough as he was kind. Whoever did this is obviously experienced. No one could do this to Tony without the street knowing. There doesn't appear to be any sign of struggle.'

DI Sark shrugged. 'We don't know that or anything else yet. Let the forensics work their magic, see what they come up with. But I agree that whoever did this is the same guy who got Sampson and is an assassin. I know as much about this "Mr Death" chap as you, by the sound of it. But it looks like he's atoning for his balls-up in killing Tobias Hill and not Leo Demato.'

'Atoning for whom though?'

'My sentiments exactly, Dean. My sentiments exactly,' DI Sark said.

10.

APPROXIMATELY half an hour later Dean strolled home. His heavy-lidded eyes threatened to close before he even got to his front door. The homicide detectives had questioned him some more. However, Dean realised that deep down they already knew he wasn't their guy. For one they already suspected Anton as their perpetrator.

His mobile vibrated in his trouser pocket, rousing him. He recognised the number immediately.

'Hello Paul.'

'Did you see the body? Is it definitely Tony?'

'Yeah, it's him.'

'How?' Paul sounded agitated.

'Same as Sampson; knife wound in the throat.'

'How could he get Tony so easily?' Paul mused aloud.

'I dunno,' Dean said, wishing he could switch off and go to sleep. 'He must have seen Tony and kept himself hidden until he attacked, perhaps from behind. I honestly don't know. I'm actually really sad. First time I ever spoke to one of your guys and realised that they weren't just the muscle. But my battery's dead. I gotta get to bed and get some sleep. Tomorrow.'

'Yeah, I apologise for calling again so late. I just needed to know for sure what the hell's going on,' Paul said. 'Do you have that inspector's number? I'm supposed to keep in touch.'

'Yeah, hang on.' Dean sifted through all the numbers on his mobile and gave it to Paul.

Paul thanked him. Then added: 'If you need to call me at any time, do not hesitate. I don't need to tell you that you're gonna have to have your wits about you. Get away as soon as possible and you ought to be fine.'

They said the obligatory goodbyes and ended the conversation.

***

At the bottom of the hill Anton could still see the flashing beacons colouring the night. He had assumed that after an hour or so at least some of the patrol cars would have made their way back to the nearest station. Instead an ambulance drove by with no siren or flashing beacon on top. Then it came to him what had most likely transpired.

He had almost forgotten about his first kill of the day. So intent was the assassin on his intended target the mere fact that he'd murdered another was somewhat inconsequential.

The fajitas and Mars bar were devoured ravenously. He didn't lick his moist lips afterwards to salivate the taste. He'd eaten because he was hungry. Now he sipped his sparkling water, without relishing the taste. He closed his eyes and relived the first kill of the day. A very satisfying kill indeed.

Anton had very nearly been spotted earlier by Tony. The shaven-headed six-foot five body guard had turned around at the top of Dean's street and came back down. Anton had been on the verge of emerging. Fortunately he'd heard the sound of the BMW's engine getting louder as it neared. He ducked down beneath his seat seconds before Tony drove past glancing his way.

He had pursued the black BMW all the way from Paul Demato's residence, but took the next turning after the body guard and whoever had stepped out of Demato's with a briefcase in his grasp.

The binoculars he'd bought were ideal for prying on from a safe distance. After approximately five minutes of sitting in his

70

car, Anton got out. He looked to and fro to see if any neighbours had seen him. Safe and unseen, he ambled down the tree-lined street and scanned the next street over.

The black BMW was parked right outside the house. The two men had gone inside. Anton succumbed to the fact that it was too risky to try to break in and enter in broad daylight and kill two men in a confined space. One would escape for sure. However, that did not prevent him from nonchalantly ambling down the street, checking again for any dog walkers or mailmen. The street was empty. He approached the BMW and to his surprise found it unlocked. He closed the back door on the right behind him as quietly as possible and lay down in the gap between the front and back seats.

It seemed like an eternity waiting. Nevertheless, the waiting heightened the anticipation. The anticipation felt like electricity coursing through his veins. His patience was inhuman. His mind didn't wander in the slightest. Anyone else would have worried or deliberated what they were doing. Their conscience would have intervened, creating fear. Anton closed his eyes and welcomed the light slumber.

Some time after (he wasn't sure how long), the front door opened. Two male voices emanated from the left of the immobile vehicle. Anton blinked his eyes open and let them adjust to the interior. He caressed his curved, army-coloured hunting knife. Then he slowly, methodically slid it from his pocket. Footfalls grew closer on the concrete. The front door closed.

Anton kept a vigilant gaze on the windows in his peripheral vision. There was a chance that Tony would walk around the car and see him lying in there. If that happened Anton would be at a huge disadvantage. He would be a sitting – or lying – target. The body guard wouldn't hesitate. He would be gunned down. It would be excruciating. Glass and metal shards would fly in all directions. Bullets would puncture his defenceless body.

Instead Tony went around the front of the car. He was delving into his trouser pocket for the car keys. An automatic *click* confirmed what Anton already knew. Then the big, beefy lump folded himself into the seat. The car rocked when the door slammed. The engine roared to life. Anton smiled to himself.

The car moved forward. Tony cussed under his breath, swinging the BMW towards the kerb to avoid collision with a DHL van heading up the road. Anton watched it pass. Then, using the din of the noisy diesel engine, he sat bolt-upright. Tony had pulled out again and was about to apply more pressure to the accelerator pedal when movement in the rear-view mirror caught his eye.

'Shit!'

He stomped the brake pedal, gripping the steering wheel fiercely. But all of this was mere reaction to the inevitable. Tony's head was wrenched back over the headrest. His throat was exposed.

Anton needed no further invitation to do what he felt was necessary.

Tony flailed and thrashed. But as strong as he was he had been caught unawares and in a precarious position. Anton had seized him and the cold, jagged blade kissed his throat in one long line.

Anton could see his protuberant eyes stretching the optical nerve and the scarlet liquid gushing out of the wound. Tony gurgled something. And it was then Anton gave his prey respect for still being so powerful as to be able to pivot in his seat and try to throw punches.

Anton rammed the heel of his hand into Tony's nose. They both heard the audible *crunch*.

The BMW had slowed considerably and managed to mount the kerb into what would appear to someone passing by as a regular parking position.

Anton finished the job by sawing into the flesh around the wound. He had to be sure this beast of a bloke wouldn't regain consciousness and start fighting again. One could never be sure. After all, Anton had been taken aback by the will to live by his prey after suffering a mortal wound.

Finished with the deed, Anton got out and opened the driver's door. He pushed Tony over where he collapsed across the passenger seat. Once he folded the weightlifter type legs away from the pedals, he lowered himself. He adjusted the position of the passenger seat until it went back all the way. Then he unceremoniously rammed Tony into a foetal position in the foot space between the passenger seat and the glove compartment. Finally he manoeuvred the car away from the bungalow where his main target resided.

When the commotion settled down, only then would he drive around the neighbourhood. He doubted his target would be charged. And he also doubted that the target with the briefcase would withdraw from his errand. But one could never be sure.

He finished his sparkling water then leant back and closed his eyes.

Dusk will soon be here, he thought.

***

Dean lay supine in bed. His mind was a conduit of thoughts. Sleep evaded him. Darkness shrouded him completely. The din outside had ebbed. However, the sound of cars passing by to and fro still came through his bedroom window inexorably. He might as well be living next door to Wembley Stadium, trying to sleep during the F.A. cup final.

But in truth the noises outside wasn't the reason why consciousness remained persistent. The day had been one long rollercoaster. His tranquillity that had slowly been restored after his court case had been obliterated. He never had any intention of not returning the favour Paul had done for him. Yet had he known of the magnitude perhaps prison…

You wouldn't have lasted five minutes inside. Even Paul knew that; thought it was an injustice to not only have your badge taken away but also be found dead in some shit hole. DI Jason didn't seem to think so though. That's the thanks I get for all the times I put my arse on the line. The good deeds are always the easiest to forget. One slight cock-up – if you could call it that – and I'm given the same treatment as a terrorist.

He threw the quilt off him and went to the bathroom. The urge to knock back all the alcohol in the house was overwhelming. But that wouldn't serve him well come sun-up. He already looked haggard.

As he stood over the washing basin studying his visage Dean ran over everything that had transpired that day in chronological order. Then he cussed inwardly. It was a pointless exercise. He wasn't a man who enforced the law any more. That wasn't to say he should turn to the dark side. Nevertheless, what would be would be. Tomorrow he had a job to do. A long drive ahead of him. He needed to focus on the task at hand.

While he stood there getting his mind into some sort of order, Dean lathered his face in shaving gel. He deleted the three-day facial hair going against the grain. His flesh blotched where the blade had scythed. It callously reminded him of Tony. Once he was finished he ran his palm over his face, softer than a baby's bum. He returned to bed and fell into a deep slumber.

Dean dreamt of a tall, broad man with a brown paper sack over his head peering out of two eyeholes…

11.

HE WOKE INSTANTLY at the shrill ringing of his alarm clock. He heaved himself up and leant against the headboard. Exhaustion was a long lost memory. Reinvigorated, Dean rolled out of bed with a spring in his step. With the proverbial battery recharged, a newfound confidence exuded his demeanour.

Nothing refreshes mind and body better than a good night's sleep.

Dean performed his waking-up routine with alacrity. He shovelled two bowls of Rice Krispies. The money and backpack and weapons were already in the car. He distinctly remembered placing them in the foot space between the passenger seat and the glove compartment.

When the two detectives had entered his home he'd been able to look them straight in the eye and answer their questions coherently. Had the money and weapons been inside the house, trepidation would have revealed itself in some shape or form.

The Honda Civic R Type required petrol as the needle was close on E the last time he'd taken it out. This could prove slightly problematic. However, if he could discreetly slip away without being seen it might not matter.

7:12 according to the digital clock on the oven.

Dean double-checked he had everything and then exited the bungalow via the back door. He closed the car door as quietly as he could. Everything was still as he'd left it, thank God. Now all he had to do was get going.

***

Anton had blinked awake as though he'd merely been closing his eyes. He consulted the radio clock – 7:15. Without further hesitation, he turned the key in the ignition and drove towards his destination.

He deliberately missed the turning for Dean's street and kept going, as before. This was preferable as it would appear inconspicuous. Yet as he turned again onto the street where he'd parked the BMW yesterday, he had to brake.

Parked at the junction were a patrol car and four cones spread out evenly across the road as a makeshift road barrier. Anton reacted hastily. He gripped the steering wheel and spun it until it locked, rolled around back the way he came and then went back down the hill.

He glimpsed his rear view to see if a uniform would emerge and watch him, but as far as he could see no one had seen him. It was too early for the rubbish collectors or the paperboy or the mailman. The uniform was probably curled up in his patrol car catching some shut eye.

Had Anton been going any faster he would have run over the cones and gone into the rear of the idling patrol car. Furthermore, if he had reacted in panic the tyres would have screeched, burnt rubber and attracted unwanted attention. As it was, this road block could be considered a minor setback, nothing more.

The Ford ascended the rise and he glimpsed the white and red-brick façade of the target's bungalow. He coasted up to the end of the street, turned around and pulled in alongside the kerb.

If the target was home he would emerge in a red Honda Civic. When he did Anton would pounce.

***

At approximately 7:42am things turned ugly.

Anton was sitting silently in his Ford, staring fixedly at the target's home with inhuman patience, when behind him to his right a woman stepped outside and stared fixedly at the black Ford Fiesta.

The rotund woman was a mere five feet two inches, and had she been a few inches taller might not have been so obese. She had been upstairs getting undressed, ready for bed when she saw the unfamiliar car head up the street and turn around. At first she thought someone had taken a wrong turn. Or their car had been facing up the street instead of down. Her night shift stacking shelves in the local Asda supermarket had dragged into the early hours of the morning, seemingly on purpose. Had she not worked this unsociable shift she would not have noticed this peculiarity.

The presence of the man in the car unnerved her for reasons she couldn't comprehend. Most likely he was a friend or relative of one of the residents and was picking them up. But had that been the case he would have got out of the vehicle and approached one of the bungalows. Perhaps he was too early. Yet if that was the case why hadn't he arrived a tad later?

Uncertain of how to proceed, the woman went back inside. She tried to forget it. Nevertheless, her conscience refused to permit her to close the door on this situation. In hindsight when the man in the car picked up one of her neighbours she'd be shaking her head inwardly, blaming her paranoia for inducing unease.

No, there's a Neighbourhood Watch scheme for a reason, she advised herself. *And that reason is to spot this type of thing from occurring. This man appears conspicuous and out of place because there's something inherently wrong and unnerving about it.*

He probably hasn't even thought about how his actions might seem to someone else. He might've woken earlier than expected, didn't want to risk falling back to sleep and forgetting to pick up his friend or colleague or whoever.

Decided on what she was going to do about this, the plump woman stepped back outside. The morning air was virginal. Her lungs appreciated the cool freshness, savouring it as though she were asthmatic. She crossed her lawn and ambled down the pavement to the idling car.

***

Anton had seen the big round arse precede the rest of the whale of the woman as she backed out of the door of her home. He knew without any forewarning why she was emerging from her home for the second time that morning. It became apparent then that she was as stupid as she was fat.

While she had been inside, leaving the front door ajar, Anton had been busying himself fitting a silencer onto the barrel of his pistol. The silencer was painted smooth black and was made out of brass map-gas burners fitted into aerosol cans. The entire mechanism had been filled with fibreglass roofing insulation.

The chamber was full with six rounds. Anton would only need one to put an end to this vermin. He wasn't too concerned that she'd spotted him and deliberated the reason of his presence. After all, with luck on his side, he would be gone from here soon enough. But now she was doing her utmost to annoy and distract him from the hunt.

He turned the key in the ignition and hit the button so the window disappeared into the door panel. He put on a pair of trendy sunglasses and watched the daft mare wobbling along the pavement. He smiled and repressed a chuckle at the sight of a cracked paving stone and thought that the woman had been the one who had caused the ground to yield beneath her weight.

'Excuse me,' came the voice of someone who thought they were in authority.

And that was as far as she got before Anton raised the pistol as she doubled over and leant towards him. The silent *pop* emanating from the weapon as it was fired sounded like someone had exhaled sharply down the barrel.

The woman's eyes rolled up in the back of her flabby head, comically. Then her body yanked her back and down. Her arse thudded the pavement followed by the back of her skull. It brought to mind a coconut falling out of its branch and splitting on the unforgiving surface.

Anton hit the button to close the window again and then drove away from the body lying sprawled out on her next door neighbours' front yard.

He showed no emotion towards the interference. However, now he had to get as far away from the body and not too close to the target's residence. Had the side street not been cordoned off this incident wouldn't have occurred. And ironically, he only had himself to reprimand.

He mounted the kerb twenty yards or so down the street and killed the engine. Then he pulled the visor down and lowered himself to a slumped position in his seat. He hoped that no one else would notice him and that his target would begin his journey. Since yesterday afternoon this quiet, idyllic neighbourhood with tree-lined streets and plush green lawns had turned into a war zone.

As he sat there in an uncomfortable position pondering, Anton realised that with his arsenal equipped with silencers he could go and finish this once and for all. There was no need to have to wait for the target to emerge. As long as he disposed of the target and got the briefcase full of money, there need not be a set plan.

But now there was a big arse bitch lying dead in the street. All it would take was one person to see her and soon the street would be crowded again. Pandemonium would ensue. Anton would be stranded, a sitting duck awaiting arrest or to be shot down by the authorities. One thing he did know was he couldn't stay here for long. He hit the button again for the window to open enough to allow some fresh air to ventilate the stuffy interior.

***

Dean rolled the car down his drive after taking the handbrake off. He hadn't started the engine on purpose. As the car rolled on the side of his home gave way to the empty street. He gently applied the handbrake, turning his head to and fro. Nothing appeared to be amiss. Satisfied that the coast was clear, he brought the engine to life. He flicked the turn signal down, indicating to go left.

By force of habit before joining any road he glimpsed both ways again and it was then his gaze fell upon the black Ford Fiesta. The tangerine sun-up shone on the horizon. The sky was a beautiful maroon canvas. The immaculately trimmed hedgerow of one of his neighbours cast a shadow across the Ford's windscreen. It was due to the shadow that Dean caught sight of the figure with sunglasses sitting bolt-upright. If it had been any later in the morning the resplendent sunshine would have reflected the windscreen and camouflaged the assassin.

Everything in Dean's peripheral got swallowed as his immediate vision zoomed in on the man known as 'Mr Death'.

He shifted the gear into first. The engine groaned in protest. Then he stomped the clutch pedal all the way down and tried again. This time the gear stick slotted into first. He rammed the accelerator pedal down so hard his calf muscle flexed involuntarily. He spun the steering wheel frantically, engine revving, blue, oily fumes coughing out of the exhaust.

The Honda's rear end swung out away from him and Dean had to grapple for control. As he righted the car and the tyres screeched on the tarmac a metallic thud came from behind him. Ignoring this and concentrating on fleeing the hunter, Dean leant forward, urging the car to go faster.

He jolted in his seat and instinctively ducked as the rear window exploded. The shower of glass fragments pebbled and pricked the back of his head and neck. For a second or two, no more, he took his gaze off the road ahead. When he looked up over the dashboard, he had to swerve the steering wheel with his entire bodyweight to avoid slamming into the rear of a transit van.

In his side mirror he saw the Ford closing the gap. Worse than that, however, was the sight of the chiselled visage of his assailant and what looked like a pistol in his right hand hanging out the window pointed directly at him.

Sure enough he had been warned beforehand but now that he was actually facing the infamous assassin which made his situation all too surreal. Not to mention perilous.

He slid down in his seat, barely able to see over the steering column. *This is what it must be like to drive a Formula 1 racing car*, he thought. The mere thought of something so ludicrous at a time when he found himself within kissing distance of death induced laughter. Tears poured down his cheeks. He shook in his seat, perplexed as to what he found so funny. And yet it hardly mattered because something his partner on the force said to him what seemed like a thousand years ago resonated in his mind. *In times when you think the worst has happened or will happen, it truly is better to laugh than to cry.*

Reminiscing that moment, Dean guffawed. And boy, it felt good to laugh out loud right then.

***

Anton watched as the rear window shattered and then disintegrated. The red Honda in front fishtailed, clipped the kerb and then righted itself. He leant out the driver's window and took aim. However, as he shot, the Ford went over a pot hole. In the oak tree birds took flight. The Honda was approaching the junction leading onto the main road. It didn't slow or stop. Fortunately, for the target's sake, there were no other road users passing by at that time. The front of the car scraped the asphalt. Orange sparks spat out.

He slowed the Ford to regain control and pursued the Honda. When the car straightened out he glimpsed his side mirror, saw that there were no vehicles behind him and fired two shots in quick succession. One hit the boot and the other shattered the brake light. Shards of red glass crumpled to the road.

Anton couldn't avoid it had he known what was going to transpire. It all happened in a blink of an eye. The Ford's front right tyre crushed the glass into the ground. Then the car tilted to the right as though there was too much weight. Anton didn't need to be told what had happened. The deflated rubber rolled along the road loose. He let the car continue to the roundabout, turned sharply in the same direction as the Honda. He pulled over in a bus stop and cut the engine, watching the red Honda grow smaller in the distance.

***

Dean screamed at the top of his lungs in jubilation. He pumped his fist into the air, shivering from the draught blowing through the rear where the window had been not five minutes ago.

'That's what they mean by poetic justice,' he said to himself, still delirious.

As sudden as the battle commenced and as unexpected and fortuitous as the punctured tyre of the trailing Ford, so did the realisation that his Honda desperately needed fuel. He cussed inwardly, knowing this would be the case prior to proceeding with the errand. Anton's misfortune had presented him with an ideal opportunity to get some distance between the Ford and hopefully lose it altogether. On the other hand what with the Tesco filling station a mile away, it gave him a clear run at filling up and getting away safe again.

Dean punched the steering wheel with a clenched fist as he came to a red light. To his immediate left was a set of CCTV cameras. They kept a close watch on superstores in case they got robbed. But nowadays even traffic lights had cameras atop of them to catch speeding motorists and other acts of crime. The urge to ignore the red light was overwhelming to say the least.

As soon as the red light changed to amber the Honda kicked forward and entered the Tesco premises. He cornered the bend like Jenson Button and rolled to a halt alongside the fuel pump. He threw himself out of the car in such a rush an onlooker would say he resembled either a scalded cat or someone who's shit themselves.

Finished filling the tank up with thirty pounds worth of petrol, Dean sprinted across the filling station into the kiosk. He withdrew three ten-pound notes and tossed them on the counter in front of the bespectacled clerk. 'I don't want a receipt and keep the change.'

The clerk who'd been perusing a Chris Carter novel, counted the money. The frantic looking customer was under by one penny. He ran it through the till and put the one penny in the RSPCA box. He gazed out the window, his bushy black eyebrows knitting themselves together as the Honda spun in a half-circle and sped out of sight. The clerk double-checked the amount owing and the amount paid and saw nothing amiss.

Had the customer owed a few quid or not paid at all then his hastiness could have been easily explained. Whoever the guy was he must have been late.

He made a note on the pad beneath the counter regarding the incident. When his supervisor came in two hours later he would inform him.

12.

THE PHONE on the bedside table destroyed all tranquillity. Mrs Sark who slept on the side of the bed next to the phone, rolled over and felt for the receiver blindly. In her half-awake, half-asleep condition, her flailing hand knocked the lampshade over. She snapped fully awake at the sound of the bulb breaking. She snatched phone out of its cradle. 'Whoever this is you owe me an antique lamp.'

She listened to the voice on the other end and elbowed her husband in the ribs.

'It's for you,' she mumbled.

Sark didn't turn around. 'Tell them to call back.'

'He wants you to call back at a more appropriate time,' Mrs Sark said.

The voice sounded urgent at the other end.

Mrs Sark elbowed her husband again. 'He say's there's been another murder in the same neighbourhood as yesterday.'

Sark growled in vexation. 'You owe us a new lamp.'

He listened to the voice of his partner.

'Do they know who the victim is?' He rubbed sleep out of his eye, hair mussed. He nodded. 'Yeah, all right. Pick me up. And make sure you've got some of those Digestive biscuits in the glove box.' He listened again, forced a smile and then gave the receiver back to his wife.

***

DI Jason brought the car to a halt right outside his partner's home. Sark opened the passenger door. As he sat down DI Jason noticed his right eye was bloodshot.

'Didn't you get any sleep?'

'Some, not a lot. Then when I did the bloody phone started ringing.'

DI Jason shook his head as he pulled away again. 'Some people have got no respect.'

Sark smiled. He fastened his seat belt. Then said: 'Where're the Digestives?' He leant forward and popped open the glove box and took out two biscuits.

* * *

When they arrived at the familiar neighbourhood Sark couldn't help thinking he spent more time here lately than at home or his desk. He'd written his report for a full-blown three hours last night before retiring. By the time he'd got home his wife had gone to bed. She'd left a note saying his food was in the fridge. He had plans to take some time off. But now it seemed that what with the latest events that would have to be postponed.

'What've we got here?' he asked his partner as they heaved themselves outside in the morning sunshine.

'Female between forty and fifty years. No eyewitnesses. Husband vaguely recalls her coming home. When he woke properly and spotted the body he immediately called for police and ambulance services. Paramedics confirmed the obvious.'

'What're you thinking?'

DI Jason didn't hesitate. 'Couple of theories. One: we have a serial killer loitering around the neighbourhood causing mayhem. Two: we got a neighbour who has had his name and reputation tainted. He gets into some dispute with one of Paul Demato's men about something-or-other and ends up killing

86

two guys. Neighbours start to assume the only murderer on the block is killing in cold blood again. He gets asked to come to the station and answer some routine questions, gets all pissed off and yells at his neighbours as he's getting into the car. He thinks he's in the clear. One of his neighbours confronts him or looks at him the wrong way. BOOM! We have a third victim.'

'Where's the husband?' DI Sark wanted to know.

'Inside. He kinda went off the rails. Paramedics sedated him.'

Sark approached the crime scene where two forensic guys were at work.

'Anything?'

One of the forensic men regarded him and shook his head. 'Not much,' he said, his voice muffled behind his mask. 'Only footprints match the husband and paramedics. The dewy grass gave us clear prints. No other footprints.'

Sark hunkered down on his haunches. A plain white sheet had been draped over the cadaver. He leant forward after putting on a pair of latex gloves and pulled the sheet back. Immediately the fatal wound became visible.

'Gunshot wound to the head?' he asked the member of the forensic team.

'And that's the only shot. No sign of a struggle. No knife wound like the other victims. Just one perfectly aimed shot right between the eyes. .38 calibre.'

DI Sark momentarily considered the possibility that this murder had been committed by another perpetrator. Yet that didn't make sense or sit right with him.

He peered closer, scrutinising the pallid features frozen for ever. The victim's capillaries had broken in her eyes. The light of her soul had gone. A red ring circled the hole in her forehead. The exit wound at the rear of her skull had dappled the dewy lawn with blood, bone and brain matter.

Sark hoped if nothing else the victim hadn't suffered.

DI Jason towered over him. His shadow blocked out the sun. He placed a hand on his partner's shoulder. 'C'mon, let's go see if the husband saw anything.'

Sark pulled the sheet back over the cadaver, covering the face masked in terror.

***

Danny Sampson was an arms' dealer and a drug dealer. He must have been aware of the risks his job had. Tony Nivean accepted those responsibilities. He was used to guys trying to get rid of him or his employer. But this woman who had donned a bright green and black uniform didn't fit. It was far more likely that she had witnessed something or interfered in something unaware of the peril she was putting herself in. She had been killed for inducing an inconvenience.

Sark rose, stretching his legs. Then he followed his partner into the home.

The interior exuded a cosy, homey ambience. Cream coloured walls, varnished wainscoting matching the exterior. A round table stood at the foot of the stairs with an old-fashioned phone and a yellow pages tome. A curved wooden beam led into the living room area. Stone walls surrounded them decorated with portraits of the Eiffel Tower, The Statue of Liberty, The Thames Bridge and Buckingham Palace. Atop the genuine fireplace a 38-inch plasma TV sat comfortably on its bracket. Piles of hardback and paperback books stood like columns in the corners of the room. Two recliner chairs faced the fireplace and TV.

Sark took it all in, marvelling at how welcoming the décor was. He imagined the married couple salivating at the smells of a Sunday roast cooking in the adjacent kitchen and the fire crackling. He imagined they had their feet up, absorbed in an intriguing yarn. God knew they had plenty to choose from.

Instead the harsh glare of the rising sun shone through the square partitions onto the grieving husband. Every line on his face appeared magnified in the glow. The tears rolling down his quivering cheeks glistened. Sark stood motionless in the doorway for a moment biting his bottom lip.

No promises, he told himself.

Bracing himself for the worst part of his job, Sark crossed the room and sat on the sofa next to the man whose entire world had been torn apart. The ambience of the interior was tainted with melancholy. Sark could feel it more so than the comforting hand of his partner upon his shoulder outside. It was as though the world knew it had lost a significant and well-loved member of the human race.

'My name is Detective Inspector Sark,' he said. 'This here is my partner DI Jason. He'll just be taking some notes.' He paused and rubbed his brow. 'I can't imagine how you're feeling right now. I won't even try. But if you can do your best to answer some questions it'll make our jobs that much easier. The sooner the better.' He paused again, swallowing with difficulty. 'I am truly sorry. I am.'

Silence filled the living room.

'It's Andrew Groves, right?' DI Jason asked.

Sark frowned at him. DI Jason shrugged.

The grieving husband used the sleeve of his pyjama top to dry his red-rimmed eyes. 'Yeah. But I prefer to be called Andrew.'

'And your wife's name is... Cathy? Is that right?' DI Sark said.

Andrew nodded. 'It was,' he said, choking on more tears.

Sark placed a hand on his shoulder. 'It still is, Andrew. She may not be here with us physically anymore, that doesn't mean she's not here though.'

Andrew faced him. 'Do you believe that? Really?'

'I choose to believe,' Sark said, honest. 'If you've done what I have and seen some of the things I have, lots of other people would too.'

'But do you *really* believe that it's true?'

Sark didn't answer.

'Are just saying it to placate me? Or are you saying it 'cause it's true?'

'I don't know if it's true or not,' Sark said, stating a fact. 'But what I do know is there is no genuine, undeniable proof that says it is or it isn't. But I choose to believe in something after all of this. And if there's not, what's the point of me, you, my partner or anything else?'

Andrew smiled. 'I hope you're right.'

'We noticed Cathy had just come off a night shift in Asda's. Is that correct?'

'Yeah. She usually works the morning shift but they've been low on staff. There was a virus going round. Cathy covered the night shift for two weeks. She didn't mind 'cause of the extra money.'

'Extra money?' Sark said.

'Night shift allowance is more than Day shift 'cause of the unsociable hours.'

'Ah, right.'

'Cathy had been planning on saving some money for a week's break in Somerset. The extra money would've come in handy she said. She gets discounts for our shopping. Neither of us smoke or drink much, unless it's an occasion. We don't live beyond our means is what I'm getting at. The mortgage has nearly been paid off. I work as self-employed welder...'

'So what time was she due home?' DI Sark asked.

'There's no set time, as such,' Andrew said. 'What with the shenanigans going on last night Cathy had to organise a lift with a colleague from work. She usually starts at ten and finishes at six. But I think she got there a little later, and therefore got home a little later.'

'Can you give an estimated time off the top of your head?' DI Jason asked. His pen hovered over the notepad.

'Well, it had to be after six this morning. Bear in mind at that time I was dead to the world.'

Sark nodded in empathy. *Yeah. So was I.*

'I heard her coming into the bedroom. I don't know what it is. My subconscious seems to kick in at that exact time, as though my brain has programmed me to be half-awake just to hear her.

'She said something like it was gonna be a nice day. She had walked home from the bottom of the hill 'cause the street might've still been cordoned off. Anyway, I think she started to get undressed but forgot to close the curtains. There was no need really. But if it made her feel better...' Andrew trailed off.

Sark nodded amicably.

'That's when she said there was a black car right outside our house. I mean I wasn't paying much heed at the time. She said there was someone sitting in the car not doing anything. I might've said "that's strange" or just thought it, I don't know.'

'Did she say what make the car was?' DI Sark asked.

'Again,' Andrew said, 'don't hold me to this. There's no way I could swear by it, but I think she said a Ford. She might've told me the type of Ford as well, but I can't remember.'

'Did she say what the person in the Ford looked like?' DI Sark asked.

'No.'

'What happened then?' DI Jason said, writing on his notepad.

'I woke up 'bout ten past seven. I rolled over and Cathy's side of the bed was empty. I stayed in bed another ten minutes,

91

expecting her to emerge from the bathroom or something. Not much time passed before I got out of bed and went downstairs to ask why she wasn't coming to bed. Usually she comes straight home, her head touches the pillow and she's out like a light.'

'And then you discovered her outside?' DI Jason said.

Andrew nodded.

DI had listened to Andrew Groves' verbal statement intently. It all made sense save one significant part.

'Didn't you hear the gunshot right outside your house?'

Andrew shook his head.

'Are you telling me you slept through the incident without hearing the sound of a gun going off?' DI Sark didn't mean to sound brusque. But he couldn't help his incredulity.

'I heard no gunshot or shouting or anything that would indicate that my wife – or anyone else for that matter – was in trouble.'

'We'll be checking with your neighbours,' Sark said.

'I asked my next door neighbour. She heard nothing, except the sound of a car engine driving away. Didn't think nothing of it.

'When I saw Cathy laying on the ground it didn't make sense. At first I thought she'd fallen. Then I saw the blood…'

'I have to ask,' Sark said. 'Did you and your wife have any dispute or arguments leading up to her death?'

'No. I loved my wife more than life itself. She is my world. My best friend. I just can't understand what compelled someone to end her life with a single gunshot wound. It wasn't as if she didn't get along with anyone, either. She had no enemies or neighbours she didn't like.'

'What about Dean Ferris?' DI Jason said. 'The guy we found yesterday with his throat cut outside Dean's house.'

'I heard what the neighbours said about him. And I vaguely recall his name being in the local papers. Apparently he shot up two drug dealers. Personally, I fail to see what the crime is.

'Cathy always used to say innocent till proven guilty. She also didn't like how the neighbours would gossip 'bout him. Her sister had been bullied. That's what people do. One person starts to speculate and then it spreads on to the next person and so on. Before you know you've got a phalanx of gossipmongers against one person. Cathy called it "safety in numbers". Cowards did that, she said. And anyway, every time I saw him he always waved and I waved back. So no, if anything my wife and I were the only ones who were tidy to him and vice versa.'

Sark levered himself out of the sofa. 'Okay. That's all for the time being, Mr Groves. We really do appreciate your cooperation. I can't tell you how sorry I am for your loss.'

Andrew rose. He and Sark shook hands. Then DI Jason leant forward and shook Mr Groves' hand. 'Thank you for your time,' DI Jason said.

'Have you got any family you can stay with?' DI Sark said.

Andrew nodded. 'I gotta start informing them before they find out off someone else. Her parents…' he trailed off and started weeping uncontrollably.

Sark hated this. He wanted to reassure the poor soul but didn't know how. Should he place a hand on his shoulder? Embrace him? Experience and years of training informed him that he needed to keep a safe distance as far as emotions went with suspects and the deceased's family and relatives.

Both detectives wanted to leave. Instead they stayed and waited patiently for Andrew to compose himself. Then they stepped outside.

'Okay,' Sark said, welcoming the warm hands of the sun of his face. 'Okay. I got it. First off I wanna check that no one in the neighbourhood owns a black Ford. I doubt it very much it was one of the neighbours.'

'What about our trigger-happy ex-policeman?'

Sark shook his head. DI Jason irritated him immensely at times. 'He owns a red Honda Civic. Also, when we go see Paul Demato, I want to see if he knows anyone who's capable of this and driving a Ford.'

DI Jason jotted this down in his notepad.

'Stay here. See if forensics have got anything new,' Sark said. 'I'm gonna see if the unpopular resident is up yet.'

13.

THE MAN known in certain circles as Mr Death had changed the tyre. He performed this task meticulously and in haste. He placed the ruined tyre in the boot and took out a Remington twelve gauge, double barrel shotgun. He propped it up on the passenger seat. Then he followed the tyre tracks of the red Honda.

He had fired his .38 pistol four times in rapid succession. Three at the Honda, two of them shattering the rear window, one that broke the taillight and one right between the eyes of an interfering cow.

Apart from the fact that he found himself out of the red Honda's distance due to the unforeseen puncture, all things considered he had done quite well. He had frightened his prey and damaged his getaway car.

The Ford Fiesta flew past a Burger King restaurant and onto the main road. Traffic was light. But soon there would be a queue of vehicles. If he got caught in that the prey would have slipped through the net and escaped.

He turned his head, slowly and smoothly. His ebony eyes behind the trendy sunglasses absorbed everything in his peripheral sight. His brain may as well have been a computer, sifting through the images, deleting them one by one. Its target remained elusive according to his radar.

After the unfortunate incident in the woods, Anton had gone back to the Cascarini's who had been informed of his error. The Don's conciliator had met with Paul Demato's conciliator. Apparently, the two families now found themselves in legal battles that the authorities had become aware of. In an attempt to prevent a full-scale gang war charges were being pressed and both the Cascarini's and the Demato businesses were being investigated. Soon, like a large company being privatised, the two families' businesses would be liquidated. They would consider themselves fortunate if they both came out of the investigations with enough money to retire comfortably.

But according to the Enzo Cascarini (the conciliator) Paul Demato had reacted with vengeance against the Cascarini's for sending him to dispose of his son. The family disowned Paul as a result. They quite rightly blamed him and his son for the death of Tobias and were now aiding the CID with their investigation. He wanted to get in touch with the Tobias family but they refused to speak. All he sought was time to explain – not to absolve himself – the circumstances and to pay for the funeral and any inconvenience. Telephone and email were his only means of communication. And as he was forbidden to leave his residence, Paul desperately required a courier to pass the money onto the Hill family.

Anton was known by such names as "The Shape", "The Chameleon! and most notably, "Mr Death" because he didn't have any family ties. Nothing bonded him to another individual. Which made him a sort of enigma in the eyes of the mafia and the authorities. He didn't become an assassin to work in the mafia. Neither did he have any personal grudges against the police forces. It was simply a chance to do something he believed he was born for and make a living out of it.

He got paid in cash and not directly into an account. He purchased with cash and not via a credit card. He bought a mobile phone from a dealer but mostly used public telephones when he seldom spoke. His arsenal came from arms' dealers. And like his prey had done business with the recently deceased Danny Sampson. But more important than that, Anton never lived beyond his means. He often slept in this stolen car. He purchased old plates and disposed of the ones belonging to the vehicle so he couldn't be easily traced.

Living off the grid had its good and bad side. He never had the luxury of his own bed. Or of his own residence. The time that he did seemed like a previous life. A time when he had not met death's acquaintance; the fateful night when an intruder had made him an orphan but spared his life. He had been spared for a reason; for a purpose. He had stared death in the face and smiled.

The boy who sucked his thumb and played with his toys and read super-hero comic books died. And something else was born…

***

A cold draught billowing through the broken rear window froze his blood. His bare knuckles protruded as he gripped the steering wheel. The hairs on his nape bristled. Then he felt something wet trickle down past his ear on his scalp. He touched the damp with his fingertips and looked at them. His fingers were wet with blood.

Dean cussed under his breath. 'Not exactly unscathed.'

In spite of the sun rising over the horizon sparkling off the rippling waters of the Queen Mary Reservoir the temperature according to the car's radio read 6'0 Celsius. Furthermore, the faster he went, doing his utmost to lengthen the gap between himself and Mr Death, the harder the wind blew, buffeting the car. This made it that much harder for him to control the vehicle.

Beneath his white Reebok hooded sweater he wore the bullet proof vest. Beneath that a long-sleeve navy shirt. However, he hadn't thought to equip himself with gloves. His hands were already frozen. The back of his head was bleeding.

He knew it wasn't serious. Nevertheless, a shard had evidently nicked him from the fusillade earlier.

Yet as time passed, the cold wind causing his eyes to water would become problematic to a greater extent. His ears already felt as though they were encased within a block of ice. His hearing would be affected. But unless he wanted to take unnecessary risks (whatever they were) he had no other option but to endure.

He was currently coasting along the M3 leaning forward in his seat, willing the car to go faster. He had thought about pulling over to pull the hood up on the sweater. But the thought of that crazy son of a bitch with his pedal to the metal gunning down on him made him reconsider.

Does he even know where I'm headed? Or how I'm gonna get there?

He silently cussed Paul and Tony to a lesser extent for telling him such morbid and sinister tales about his pursuer. In hindsight perhaps it would have been better to have done this task and not been so inquisitive about the man who'd created pandemonium for two mafia families in the moment it takes to pick someone off with a rifle.

Dean didn't think though that Paul even realised what he would be up against. Mr Death had already committed two gruesome kills in his own neighbourhood. It was as though he wanted to send him a message of what was to come. And this morning he'd been lying in wait for him to make his move. The perfect hunter.

Tenby was quite a long way to travel in these conditions.

'Damn you Paul,' Dean said through gritted teeth, shivering.

***

DI Sark strolled down the street. Last night this street was the scene of such macabre and terror that it felt surreal. Now in the early morning of a new day the street had returned to its idyllic, suburban feel-good ambience, save the yellow crime scene tape blocking off the side street.

The detective lived in the city. The sounds of birdsong and leaves whispering in a gentle breeze would be drowned out by the din of inexorable traffic going past and the city coming to life with thousands and thousands of people. For a moment he took the opportunity to close his eyes. As he walked towards the sunshine he imagined himself residing here. He envisioned himself on a deckchair in his back yard. The sweet, fresh smell of recently cut grass filling his nostrils and perfectly trimmed hedgerow surrounding him. He imagined that no one could see in as he basked in the sun's glory. There would be a cold can of Strongbow straight from the freezer next to him and a paperback novel. He imagined this Andrew Groves and he taking their dogs for a walk in the orange sunset evenings, discussing the football and exchanging books.

When he opened his eyes he had arrived at the white stone and red brick façade of Dean Ferris's bungalow. He manoeuvred himself to amble down the path when his eyes focused on the drive.

Empty.

The lovely daydream of residing here in suburbia crumpled away into dying embers. For the daydream was just that, imaginary. Reality was a hissing rattlesnake sliding its way through the undergrowth, unseen. Only when it was ready would it reveal itself. And only then would the venomous bite of reality sink in.

He tried the front door and waited, fingers crossed.

No answer.

'Oh boy,' Sark said.

***

He met DI Jason halfway up the street. The younger detective was putting his notepad in his top pocket along with his biro.

'Did you wake sleeping beauty?'

Sark shook his head. 'He's not there, and the car's gone.'

'Now tell me you can swear by his innocence.'

'In fairness, John, he did tell us for the record that he was going to see a friend in Tenby and would be back shortly. I know you're dying to nail this guy but you really got to leave your personal feelings behind.'

'Yeah. Well, we'll see, won't we?' DI Jason said. 'Incidentally, Cathy Groves was shot by someone carrying a .38 calibre.'

'Dean doesn't own a gun.'

'That we know of,' DI Jason added.

'That we know of.'

DI Jason stood relaxed, hand on hip. 'Okay. I admit the guy rubbed me up the wrong way. There's something inherent I don't like about him. Maybe 'cause he exudes so much confidence. If he did commit these crimes, he wears a face like he knows he could get away with it. But if we're to take what Andrew Groves said seriously – which I do – then Dean is one of the last people to suspect. It does seem as though someone is trying to frame him.'

'Either that or he has got himself involved in something he doesn't know the half of.'

'Or a mixture of both.'

Sark nodded, deliberating. 'Now you're starting to think like a detective again.'

14.

SANDRA HILL sat slumped in her armchair in the living room nursing a steaming hot cup of tea. Her brown, wavy curls drooped around her face. She sat in shadow watching the sun slant through the window onto the floor by her feet.

She had slept fitfully. Her anatomy had become a burden, an enormous weight upon her frail skeleton. The T.V. was on without sound. She had turned it on for comfort all to no avail. Her mind was a whirlwind. A maelstrom of thoughts assailing her consciousness. All thoughts created by a profound melancholy from which there was no escape. And the worst of it was this beat lying in bed staring at the asbestos ceiling.

By the time she lifted the cup to her lips and sipped the contents the tea was cold. Atop the T.V. was a framed photograph of her late son, Tobias. In the photo he was smiling benignly, perched on a stool in his school uniform.

On the round mahogany table with a varnished finish was a writing pad. The pad had been left open on pages filled from top to bottom and left to right with her handwriting.

Die Paul Demato. Die Paul Demato. Die Paul Demato. Die Paul Demato. Die Paul Demato. Die Paul Demato. Die Paul Demato. Die Paul Demato. Die Paul Demato...

The familiar scrawl with the same repetitive declamation went on for four pages.

Worse, she couldn't even recall doing this. Neither could she recall writing the same quotation in black permanent marker on the bathroom walls. But they were there for anyone who used the bathroom to see in her familiar scrawl.

She picked up the pad again and gripped an invisible pan. She turned the page to a fresh sheet and began scribbling and chanting, 'Die Paul Demato. Die Paul Demato. Die Paul Demato. Die Paul Demato. Die Paul Demato…'

***

Paul replaced the phone back into its cradle and sighed. Not getting an answer didn't necessarily mean something unthinkable but it didn't put his mind at ease, either.

He consulted his wrist watch and saw that it had just gone eight in the morning. He had hoped to catch Dean prior to him leaving his residence and beginning the long drive. There wasn't anything else to talk about. He merely wanted to abate the anxiety causing him to wake early.

The laptop was turned on. Paul had accessed his emails but found nothing of interest. As a result of have purchased a Kindle for Leo he received an email advertising cheap Kindle e-books to purchase directly via Amazon. He deleted this straight away and then cussed. He could have forwarded the email to his son instead.

There were no emails from anyone else.

Not that he expected to find an email from her but he had hoped Sandra would email him back. Even if the email was her calling him this, that and the other, at least it would have been acknowledgement of some kind. Instead she and her husband Matthew had given him the cold shoulder.

And it was this behaviour that brought to mind a conversation he'd once had with his son and godson, Tobias.

Leo had had some trouble concerning bullies at a popular nightclub that wasn't one of their own. A doorman had been instructed not to let him in. Leo had loudly protested. He'd been given a choice – to walk away of his own accord or be carted away in an ambulance.

Paul had dealt with the matter immediately.

'Well, you know now that that place isn't worth bothering with,' Tobias had said. 'They're just bullies. And as long as they're getting a reaction out of you or are upsetting you the longer they'll do it. Best thing to do with them is to ignore them. Make them feel as though they don't exist. They won't like it. Bullies stick with their friends. Safety in numbers. But you do what I say next time and keep doing it – they'll soon get fed up. And anyway, what's so special about that place? It's a shit-hole compared with the clubs and casinos your dad owns. Leave them to stir in their own shit.'

Both Paul and Leo had laughed at that. Quiet, shy Tobias had hit the nail on the head.

The doorman was taken into a back alley a week later and beaten to a pulp. Leo said he saw him in London a couple of months later. The doormen didn't glower or mouth off like before. And as soon as Leo had noticed him walking past he ignored him.

Tobias' parents were doing as their son had advised Leo. Paul had to admit being on the receiving end of it and how effective it was. It hurt! But worst of all it made you feel non-existent. Like he didn't matter any more. He wasn't even given the time it took a good person to notice they'd stepped in shit.

Paul nodded solemnly. Then he shut down the laptop.

***

The two detectives had gone to the nearest convenience store and purchased some Cokes and a pack of processed sandwiches. They sat in the car, feeling the worse for wear after a long night and early morning.

'Has that Andrew bloke got someone with him now?' DI Jason asked.

DI Sark nodded. He couldn't answer verbally as his mouth was full.

'That's good, at least.'

Sark swallowed some Coke and burped. 'His father-in-law came as soon as he heard. I watched them disappear indoors when we were doing our door-to-door investigations.'

'What I can't seem to get my head around is how no one – despite the ungodly hour the crime was committed – heard anything. How can not one of them hear a gun shot? I mean if we were in the woods outside an OP's nursing home and they'd all taken out their hearing aids, fair enough.'

'OP?'

DI Jason smiled. 'Sorry. Old age pensioner.'

Sark raised his eyebrows, slightly amused, slightly perplexed. 'The generation that fought for our freedom and rights have now been abbreviated. Nice.'

'Have you contacted the chief yet?'

Sark rolled his eyes at his partner. His mouth was full of bread and cheese and onion. He raised an index finger in a *wait* gesture. Once he'd chewed and swallowed he nodded. 'Yeah. He's on his way. Trouble is the media have already latched onto the story. After last night's events they'll leap on this like a bitch on heat.'

'Brilliant. Let's inform the perpetrator that we have the street covered so we can warn him beforehand. That way he can simply cease committing crimes and get away with his transgressions without punishment.'

Sark ignored his partner's facetious remark. 'The media are a pain in the arse at times. You know it. I know it, so I think the chief knows it too. But he also knows what the power of the media on your side can do to solve crimes as opposed to being kept in the dark.'

'What's his take on this murder?'

'He thinks it's of a different kind because of the victim and the choice of weapon.'

'Tony and Danny were connected to the mafia in some way. Cathy, as far as we know, wasn't. We will need to question Groves again on that subject. If he can shed some light on Cathy's hobbies and interests and anyone she might have known, besides Dean, connected with Paul Demato, then we'll know for sure.'

'Paul will shed some light on what the hell's going on. But can we trust him? He's hardly gonna want to help the same people investigating his past and illegal gambling, is he?'

'If he truly gives a toss about Dean then I think he will. I mean according to Dean all Paul wants to do is finish up business here and then move to Spain to be with his family. In comparison to the other shit-bags in his line of work he's pretty well respectable. But it's not him we also need to question.'

'Who else?'

'Cascarini is our man. Or at least I believe he is.'

'The best known dealer in South London?'

'He's known as a dealer but we still haven't proved it. His lawyers claim our evidence is all circumstantial. Some of it is. But I think we do have some substantial evidence to nail him. But will it stick? He's an intelligent, fierce businessman, and dangerous to anyone stupid enough to cross him, as Paul is beginning to find out.'

'But why Cascarini?' DI Jason asked.

'I kept thinking about what Dean told us when we questioned him. I asked him if he knew who this assassin who went by the nickname "Mr Death" was. He said Paul had mentioned it vaguely. We know that Cascarini had hired this fellow's services to get rid of Leo Demato for grassing him up.'

DI Jason nodded, concurring that this was true.

'If Cascarini hired this "Mr Death" chap he must know what he looks like,' Sark said.

'Yeah. But what does that prove in relation to this?'

'So you think it was "Mr Death's" doing?'

Sark shrugged.

'Why?' DI Jason asked, querying his partner's theory. 'It doesn't make sense. This guy messed up big time. He's more than likely doing what Leo did, fleeing the country to avoid being identified. He's got no emotional ties concerning our three victims or Dean. He's just a faceless guy who pulls the trigger.'

'But why was Paul so keen all of a sudden to get together with Dean?'

'Probably 'cause no one else wants to know him or have moved abroad to get away from this calamity,' DI Jason said. 'I mean we know he's tried contacting Mrs Hill in vain. He just wants to bend someone's ear so he can explain his actions and absolve himself of the guilt.'

'It wasn't Paul's fault though. Leo was the one who was the informant. Paul might not have known until it was too late. Bear in mind he also lost a close family member as well.'

'Was Tobias part of Paul's business?'

Sark shook his head. 'Uh huh. No. Tobias was close to Paul and Leo. He was the same age as his cousin, Leo. Pretty much grew up together. But he never got involved with the business.'

'I don't see where you're going with this "Mr Death" thing? His only involvement was the mix-up of the two young men. Nothing more.'

'But what if Cascarini hadn't just hired this guy to kill Leo? And what if Paul knew this and got in touch with Dean to help out and now this deadly killer is after Dean?'

DI Jason gave his partner a You-have-got-to-be-kidding-me look. 'Really? That's a bit far-fetched if you ask me. I sometimes wonder if you ought to write crime novels instead of trying to solve one. No offence.'

'Well, there's only one way we're gonna find out,' Sark said. Then he took another sip of his Coke.

'I seriously doubt that either of them is gonna just admit and confess everything they know. Anyway, the last thing Cascarini wants to do is be associated with the man that not only messed up big but then went and killed one of his own guys.'

Deliberating what his partner had pointed out made sense. Sark nodded.

'Yeah, I guess. Who knows? Maybe Dean knows more than he's letting on,' DI Jason said.

Sark brought to mind the first time he'd asked Dean if he recognised the dead body lying face down right outside his house. *Didn't he hesitate for just the slightest of moments?*

His reverie was broken by the din of a growling diesel engine getting louder. In the wing mirror Sark saw the familiar logo of a white van followed by two more vans and sighed. 'Here we go. The cavalry have arrived.'

DI Jason glimpsed the rear view mirror and turned away immediately. The news vans seemed to follow one another off an assembly line onto the once tranquil street.

15.

WARM AIR blew in his face from the fans counteracting the chilly breeze from the rear. It was a futile attempt to thwart the cold. But for the time being it helped. He had reached the intersection and slowed for traffic, indicating to go into the next lane.

The fan was turned up to its hottest. And only now when he had to slow and apply the brake did the cold wind causing him to shiver abate. He checked his reflection in the rear view. He wasn't at all surprised by the flushed cheeks. Road users in the other lanes who did glance at him must have thought he had a rash.

That was the least of his concern. The absence of a rear window would draw unwanted attention and eventually get him pulled over by the police. At the next turnoff he'd have to find a service station with a convenience store. He needed some gloves and a woolly hat before he froze. Furthermore, he required some masking tape and a bag he could cover the glassless window with.

There was an off ramp prior to joining the M25. But the traffic was dense and he found himself in a long queue. In the near distance the other road users were growing closer closing the gap. And unless the one called Mr Death had come across further obstruction then soon he'd have Dean in his sights. Once that happened Dean would find himself at a great disadvantage.

The traffic crawled forward. Dean flicked the turn signal down and manoeuvred the damaged Honda towards the exit. A car behind him blasted its horn, nearly slamming into his rear.

Dean realised his bad manoeuvre and raised his hand in apology. He thanked the other driver for permitting him to cut past him and up the exit ramp.

His heart pounded. The veins in his temple pulsated erratically.

'Watch the damn road you idiot. One thing at a time. Nice and cool,' he told himself.

***

Anton had depressed the pedal all the way to the floor. The needle on the speedometer leapt to almost a hundred miles an hour. The M3 was quiet. The world was still waking. The interspersed white lines at the centre of the road became one long blur. The Ford rocked and became lighter. He only slowed to cut into the centre lane and then back into the overtaking lane.

Other road users watched him fly past, both amazed and frightened at the velocity shaking their vehicles. Anton paid none of them any heed. He saw only the road ahead. He narrowed his eyes behind the sunglasses. In the far distance roads joined together. The free-flowing mobility of the motorway ended swamped with the bumper-to-bumper crawl more familiar with city centre driving.

The assassin felt his cheek twitch involuntarily. Then a thought surfaced in his consciousness as radiant as the sunrise. What he initially considered an obstacle that would guarantee his prey's escape suddenly favoured him.

As he drew closer he released the pressure from the accelerator. He slowed the vehicle by going through the gears, craning his head to see over the fringe of traffic. He focused intently. Finally his perseverance paid off.

A loud blast of a car horn could be made out up ahead. Had he not opened the passenger window upon slowing Anton

109

probably wouldn't have heard it. Instead the noise drew his attention like bees to honey. To his left the slow moving traffic had ceased to move altogether.

Keeping a firm hold on the steering wheel Anton leant over the passenger side and caught sight of the cause of the horn blast. His radar, attuned to its intended target, flashed crimson.

In reckless haste he yanked the steering wheel to the left and shot through the gap. Vehicles following in his wake screeched to a halt, nearly causing a massive pile up. The hunter ignored the din. He barely heard it and if he did it was insignificant compared to his first and foremost priority.

A Citroen fishtailed to a halt, leaving a long trail of freshly burnt rubber. Thankfully, the car was new and the tread on the tyres deep. This was the singular aspect that had prevented the driver from T-boning the black Ford Fiesta.

Anton slotted the car into the left lane. To avoid more traffic he flicked the turn signal and slotted into an emergency breakdown lane and floored the accelerator. Behind him a cacophony of horns bleated. The noise was deafening to all road users, save one.

Now that he had the prey in sight, the hunter's senses buzzed as though powered by electricity. The front bumper scraped the road at the foot of the exit ramp. A brilliant but brief firework display coughed out upon impact. His entire body shuddered but he didn't react, cry out or even flinch.

Anton slammed the brake pedal into the floor before smashing into the rear of a blue Renault. In the near distance he noticed the reason for this unexpected halt.

Traffic lights.

***

The din of numerous horns alerted Dean's attention. For a split second he welcomed the thought as it would mean he wasn't the only one who had made a driving error that almost caused a crash. Then he glanced at the wing mirror. What he saw made his heart climb into his throat. Intuition told him it wasn't a coincidence. The black Ford gleaming under the sunshine had cut across the lanes, right in front of the traffic to continue its relentless pursuit.

'Shit.'

Now what? Did he allow panic to take control and flee his vehicle on foot? Or did he remain seated in his car like a sitting duck, waiting for the man with no identity to make his move?

His heart slammed against his ribcage, doing its utmost to escape its prison. He remained focused in spite of the cold sweat.

The traffic was bumper to bumper from the foot of the exit ramp right up to the red light. This could be construed as both a good and bad aspect for Dean. On the one hand Anton couldn't get to him unless he was on foot. If he did that while carrying a weapon other road users would see him as clear as the azure sky overhead. On the other hand however Dean could no longer see him as the traffic behind him concealed the black Ford and its driver. If he did choose to attack it would be quick and sudden. Then the light changed to green.

Dean put the car into gear, removed the handbrake and floored the accelerator.

***

Anton had been unfastening his seat belt and reaching over for his shotgun when the driver of the car behind him blasted its horn. He sat bolt upright in his seat and saw that the road was clear. He glimpsed the rear view and kept an eye on the bearded man gesticulating for him to move. The hunter had a good mind to hit the brakes, emerge from the car and bring an end to the man's life with one shot. But as that would put more

111

distance between himself and the intended prey he ignored the imbecile.

There were four vehicles between him and his prey. And although he'd decided upon getting out of the car and blowing his prey's head off in retrospect that would have caused more problems. The motorway was a public place. Also, there was a CCTV camera atop the traffic lights. Had he gone with his initial plan he would have been identified.

But as it had turned out that wouldn't be the case. As he approached the junction he pulled the visor down and kept a close watch on the red Honda Civic ahead.

He smiled to himself when he noticed other road users pointing to the glassless rear window of the Honda. If the police spotted him he'd be pulled over. But if that happened, the prey might be taken into police custody. Then no one would get the money. No one would die… and Anton would be another assassin no different from any other hit man. His reputation would be forever tainted due to the mistaken identity and killing over an innocent young man.

***

It was suicidal now if he attempted to stop to conceal the damage. Anton was on his tail. His good fortune of Anton's car slowing to a stop due to a puncture had passed. Now they were on even terms again.

The cold draught swirling through the interior making his eyes water had ebbed somewhat when the adrenaline kicked in at seeing the familiar vehicle and the persistent hunter. The fan continued to blow warm air through the vents. But that would soon be drowned out when he joined the M25 and put his foot down again.

Furthermore, his hearing had diminished. Everything, even the din of bleating horns had seemed to come from far away.

His vision blurred with tears until he wiped the cuff of his sleeve over them. It felt as though this was one of those car chase simulator games kids played in the arcade. Only this was real. Dying here and now wouldn't mean Game Over. He wouldn't be able to slot another fifty pence coin into the machine to try again.

He followed the road signs until he manuovred the Honda onto the exit ramp. The traffic in front began to spread out the faster they went. Instantly the wind picked up and buffeted the Honda. Cold air blew directly into Dean's left ear. He winced at the knife-like draught. Then flicked the turn signal announcing his intention of joining the fast-moving flow of vehicles.

In his rear-view mirror he saw the black Ford close the gap. His Adam's apple went up and down involuntarily. He had to push the Honda Civic to its limit to join the motorway before a DHL artic lorry reached him. Fortunately the car was quick and efficient at accelerating from a crawl to high speed.

In his rear view the familiar Ford followed him onto the M25 without hesitation.

Dean lowered himself in his seat so the back of his head wasn't visible for a fatal gunshot. His right leg trembled with adrenaline. He focused on the road ahead now and not on who was pursuing him. Then his mobile vibrated in his pocket.

'Shit!'

***

He just made it in front of the bright yellow DHL lorry. Then cruised over the white line and fell in behind the Honda. Anton eased off the acceleration slightly to allow a safe distance between the rear of his prey and front of his car.

There was no rush to end the prey's life. The rush had only been apparent when he lost visual on the prey. Now that that was no longer a factor, rushing would go against him. As long as he made the kill prior to the prey reaching the recipient of the contents of the briefcase there was nothing to worry about.

The Honda buffeted, swaying slightly to the white line of the next lane.

The one known as Mr Death didn't need to be told that the driver of the Honda was struggling with the absence of the rear window. If the wind picked up or the Honda went faster again the harder it became to control.

He floored the accelerator and drove to within touching distance of the Honda and then eased off again.

The hunt was on…

16.

DI **SARK** and DI Jason stared in wonder at the beautiful scenic countryside residence. The hedges surrounding the residence had been trimmed inch-perfect. DI Jason slowed to a halt in front of the wrought-iron electronic entrance gate. Next to the gate fixed into the beige-brick pillar was the intercom. DI Sark pressed the button for his window to go down. Then he leant out the window and pressed the button and waited for a response. A light buzz came through the grill followed by a hoarse voice.

'Who is it?'

'Homicide detectives. I'm Detective Inspector Sark. I spoke with Paul Demato yesterday afternoon. He agreed to answer some of our questions in our investigation. Could you tell him we're here, please?'

'It's me, detective.'

Only then did Sark recognise the voice.

'Mr Demato?' Sark said, unable to conceal his surprise. 'Since when have you answered your own calls?'

'Since yesterday afternoon, detective.'

'Care to let us in.'

'Yeah. But you do need to back the car up for the gates to open.'

An audible buzz came from the intercom. DI Jason took the handbrake off and let the car roll back a few feet. The seven foot high gates whirred into life and slowly folded inwards.

DI Jason waited patiently for the gates to open fully and then put the car into gear.

An Apple tree obscured the red stone façade until they drove around the path covered with decorative stones. Innumerable Cedars sheltered the turret-roofed residence. Sunbeams slanted through the branches in magnificent, heavenly gold. A lonely robin sang a pleasant tune then took flight. The fresh smell of woods filled the detectives' nostrils. The ray of sunlight reflected off a nearby pond, sparkling in lavender hues.

The jaw-dropping residence should have belonged to a priest or a devoted Christian, not a mob boss. There were no black unmarked cars sitting idly in the driveway or anywhere for that matter around the property. No weight-lifter size men donning expensive suits standing sentinel outside.

Sark shook his head inwardly. *Been watching too many gangster films*, he told himself. This wasn't what he expected. Of course he was more than aware that Paul Demato's business was being liquidated. He'd only keep a certain amount of possessions and money if he aided the CID and the Fraud squad with their investigations. However, he didn't realise to what extent it was until now.

DI Jason rolled the car to a halt, frowning as the stones made popping sounds beneath the tyres.

'I think it's fair to say that rich people don't go broke like ordinary people,' DI Jason said, observing the property in awe.

Sark chuckled. 'Well, maybe when he moves abroad you can buy his home off him for a low, low price.'

'He's a criminal, not simple.'

'C'mon, let's see what Billy-no-mates has got to say for himself, shall we?'

They heard footfalls approaching the front door. Both detectives glanced at each other surprised that the person answering them was Paul Demato himself.

His goatee had almost grown to a full beard. His hair looked as though it hadn't been washed in days and was tousled. Shades of grey had started showing at the sides. The man before them looked nothing like the photographs or images they'd seen. Paul was wearing a pair of denim Levi's and a Chelsea football jersey.

'Gentleman,' he said automatically.

'Hello, Mr Demato,' Sark began.

'Please. Just call me Paul. You sound like two gay salesmen when you address me by my surname.'

Both detectives ignored the remark and showed their credentials.

'Well, I suppose you'd better come in,' Paul said, making an effort to be cordial.

'Since when have you been answering your own door?' Sark asked.

'Since my business got downsized and the only staff I had started dying in macabre circumstances.'

Sark and Jason crossed the threshold and followed Paul down the short hallway.

The detectives ceased walking upon entering the wood-panelled office and admired the décor. Their eyes roamed the walls and glass cabinet and pinewood desk. Paul watched their eyes enlarge as they found the framed photographs of him and Leo posing with celebrities.

'Impressed, huh?'

DI Sark turned and faced him. 'Very.'

'Yeah. Dean was impressed when I he came over for the first time.'

'When was that?' DI Jason said, not missing a beat.

'Coupla years back when you guys left him hanging for clearing the street of two scumbags. He met my attorney. He couldn't afford a good one 'cause you guys took his shield from him.'

'No need to get all defensive,' DI Jason said.

Paul shook his head. 'Not. Just stating the facts.

'Mind if we sit?' DI Sark asked, diffusing the tension of his hot headed partner.

'Yeah. D'you guys wanna drink? I got some Scotch here.'

'We're on duty,' DI Jason said. 'Just stating the facts.'

Paul smiled. 'You wanna keep the rookie on a leash, Detective. He'll frighten all your witnesses off otherwise.'

Sark quietly concurred with him. 'Bit early for a drink, isn't it?'

'Well, as I haven't slept I don't really think it makes a lotta difference, to be frank.'

Sark chastised his partner with his eyes and then lowered himself onto the leather upholstered sofa. 'Thanks for calling us last night, by the way,' Sark said. 'We appreciate your willingness and cooperation.'

'Glad I could help.'

DI Jason took out his notepad and flipped over to a clean page.

'How did you know Dean was down the station answering questions last night?' Sark began.

'I didn't,' Paul said, almost straight away. 'I was phoning to make inquiries about how long I had to wait till you could report someone missing. I got put through to you via the switchboard. I also tried Dean's number earlier in the evening and then again later. There was no answer. All I did was ask if you guys knew the whereabouts of Tony or Dean.'

'What about Sampson?'

'Sampson wasn't one of my guys. I know of him and asked a favour of him; to check if Tony was around Dean's place where I sent him. He said he would, but to be honest I didn't know if he could be trusted or not. Dean called me last night and filled me in as much as he could. Said Sampson was found with firearms and cocaine in his possession. Is that true?'

Sark nodded.

'The only reason from what I can gather why Sampson went to Dean's place had nothing to do with my concerns; it was so he could try to persuade Dean to buy drugs.'

DI Jason scribbled down the Q&A as quickly as he could. Then he looked up from his notepad. 'Would that be an incentive for Dean to murder Sampson?'

Paul Demato laughed derisively. 'Uh no. And I'm sure if Dean did – which I strongly believe he didn't – then why would he leave the corpse right outside his house for the whole world to see so he could be automatically accused?'

'I'm just asking,' DI Jason said.

'No. You want it to be Dean, for whatever reason,' Paul said, pointing his index finger at DI Jason. 'You're a detective, different division to an undercover cop. I'm not Dean's daddy so I don't feel obligated to defend him. What I will say however is that that guy put his life on the line every single day. You carry your ID around with you, ask your questions, type it all up for your chief and then put it all in a nice file. Then you go through the paperwork and look for holes or contradictions or match the evidence and DNA up. Nice job. Long hours and so on. But rarely do you have to even think about pulling out your service pistol. And even when you do it's normally when the perpetrator is alone, defenceless and unarmed, fleeing from you.

'My friend Dean had to get to know the people you put away behind bars. He had to frame them and even get his hands dirty otherwise they'd grow suspicious. Something happened to his bosses and his file went missing and according to you guys he's just another gangster, drug-dealer.

'Someone who does that knowing that everyday one minor slip-up could be the difference between him facing a loaded gun and going home is different than you and I. Don't forget that. He made one minor slip-up according to your laws. Two lives were lost for which he got punished. Okay, fine. What

119

makes guys like me disassociate from you, the police, is the fact that you blatantly ignore all the lives that were saved by one man putting his life on the line so you don't have to.'

Silence filled the office creating an unsettling ambience.

'See, where I come from guys like Dean have brass balls. If he'd done that for me and my organisation he'd be rewarded. But he didn't. He did it for the greater good, and you humiliated him and then left him to stand there by himself.'

Paul leant forward, clasping his hands together. 'And I'm the bad guy. Gimme a break.'

'Okay,' Sark said, doing his utmost to move the conversation along. 'What did you want to see Dean for that was so urgent?'

'It wasn't urgent per se.'

'Well, you contacted him and got Tony to contact him several times yesterday alone. Why?'

'I hadn't seen him for awhile. I got you guys keeping me under surveillance. My wife and son had to move to Majorca immediately for fear of the lives. I felt alone, stranded, and for what? I don't get involved with drugs or prostitution. I own some nightclubs, restaurants, hotels. In spite of what you think of me a lotta politicians, barristers and judges think quite highly of me.

'You're probably sitting there wondering why. But the reason is simple: people in the public eye who are in the hierarchy aren't embarrassed to be seen with me. I don't get one of my men to kill a policeman 'cause he looked at me the wrong way. Other families…' he trailed off.

Sark and Jason knew he was referring to the Cascarini's.

'I feel bitter and angry about what happened regarding my godson. That should've never have happened.'

'Off the record,' Sark said. He waved his hand at his partner to not write this next part down. 'Your son Leo was the one who…'

'Yeah. He shouldn't have or at least not done anything until he talked to me. He thinks guys like me are given bad names like "mob boss" 'cause of the Cascarini's operating in narcotics. Some boys' Leo's age had bought drugs before. One inadvertently overdosed. The other boy got contacted all the time by a dealer pressuring him into buying more.'

'No. I'm not saying its right or wrong what Leo did,' Sark said. 'On a personal note I believe he did do the right thing. But whichever way he chose to become an informant I can't see how that would've changed the situation.'

'Well, I guess we'll never know,' Paul said.

Sark waited for DI Jason to finish writing the last sentence. Then he continued. 'So, the guy who killed Tobias. Dean said you told him that he went by the nickname "Mr Death". Is that right?'

'Apparently so. I have never dealt, nor will I ever deal with this individual.'

'Do you suspect him of killing Sampson and Tony?' DI Jason asked.

'I don't know. Although, I wouldn't put it past him,' Paul said. He shrugged. 'D'you have any witnesses?'

Sark shook his head.

'We got nothing,' DI Jason said.

'I can tell you that if you think Dean is your suspect then you're barking up the wrong tree.'

'How so?' DI Jason asked.

'Despite what certain people think of him – he's not   a killer.'

'Who d'you think is?' Sark asked. 'You think it was this "Mr Death", right?'

Paul took a sip of Scotch and let the liquid burn his throat. 'I can't say for definite guys. If I could I'd have to prove it. What I will say is the chap that killed Tobias and one of Cascarini's men is a killer.'

'What do you know about this assassin?' Sark asked, staring attentively at Paul, studying his demeanour.

'Not a lot, Detective. If I did I can assure you I'd most likely either be dead or marked for death, which I might be anyway.'

'Because of Leo's involvement?' DI Jason said.

Paul nodded.

Sark leant forward resting his elbows on the polished desktop. His eyes roamed the mahogany-walled room again and then found their way back to Paul.

'Look, I'll level with you. We got sod all on this assassin. We know he's a loner. That he isn't tied to any family or organisation. That he doesn't do any other jobs for mob bosses besides killing someone. And we think his name is Anton. But that's it.'

Paul adjusted his wire-framed spectacles. Then he said, 'With all due respect, Detective, that's pretty much all I got which I told you guys a few days ago with what happened to Tobias.'

'Don't tell me you haven't been sitting on your arse not doing anything to find out who this guy was that murdered your godson. Don't tell me that, Paul. I may have been born, but I wasn't born yesterday.'

Paul recited the yarn that had induced Tobias' death and his son Leo's narrow escape.

'Yeah, we know all that. We read your statement,' DI Jason said, on the verge of losing his patience.

'He's not just known as "Mr Death",' Paul said. 'He's called "The Chameleon" and "The Shape". You know why?'

Both detectives shook their heads simultaneously.

'You obviously know what a chameleon is, yes?'

'A small lizard that changes its colours according to its surroundings,' Sark said, not missing a beat.

Paul nodded again. 'Exactly. In other words, gentlemen, our faceless assassin remains inconspicuous due to being able to blend into and adapt to its environment.'

'What about the nickname "The Shape"?' Sark asked, intrigued.

'He's called "The Shape" because apparently he is the size and shape of a human being but is something else…'

A long pause filled the room.

'Wait a minute,' DI Jason said. 'If all this is some fancy talk just to frighten us you're gonna be in bigger trouble than you already are.'

Paul stared fixedly at DI Jason. 'I only wish this was just some fancy talk. You're not the one who has been cut off by his sister-in-law.'

'Go on,' Sark said, not wanting to lose momentum.

'He's the size and shape of a human being. According to word-of-mouth his name is Anton. He has black hair, wears black clothes, drives a black Ford and has ebony eyes. That information I cannot vouch for as I have never seen him in person.'

'That still doesn't explain the reasoning behind the nickname "The Shape",' Sark pointed out.

'He may look like anyone else but from what I've been told he is anything but human. He has no reason. No conscience. Apparently he has no understanding of right or wrong, good or evil even in the rudimentary sense. He'd kill his own family if it was his job and not bat an eyelid. And although he does all this for money, according to Cascarini this is not what motivates him. It's not purely business. It's something else. He relishes the hunt.'

'Cascarini would have more information than what you can provide?' Sark asked.

'This Anton was hired by him. He made a huge mistake and Cascarini refused to pay him. And you know about one of Tony's men calling him a cocksucker.'

'This Anton you say is the one who the ten-year-old girl saw wearing a brown paper sack over his head?'

'That's correct. Just like the guy who entered his home when he was just a boy and decapitated his parents. Anton saw him with a brown paper sack over his head.'

Sark nodded. 'Yeah, we know 'bout that.'

17.

THE TWO CID detectives got back in the car. Their moods had darkened somewhat upon hearing the grisly, vague details of Paul Demato's account of the assassin with many nicknames but no full name or proper description. DI Jason reread through his notes that he'd scribbled down as fast as he could.

'There's still one thing that bugs me,' Sark said almost to himself.

'Go on.'

'If Paul is pretty sure that our perpetrator is the same guy who killed Tobias and Tommy Baggio then why is he now after Dean? Both Dean and Paul concur that Dean – like Tobias – has no part in the business. So why would our guy be trying to frame him?'

Neither detective spoke for what seemed like an eternity but couldn't have been any longer than a minute.

'Remember what you told Dean at the station?' DI Jason said, breaking the quiet.

'Not off the top of my head I can't,' Sark said, rubbing his temples.

'You told Dean to make sure he didn't wind up getting involved in Paul's business. And then you said something along the lines of Paul would sell their own grannies before they did their own dirty work. And that if he did get forced into doing Paul's dirty work and if he did find himself in something he couldn't control…'

'…then he shouldn't hesitate to call me,' Sark finished.

DI Jason offered his partner a weak smile. 'There ya go.'

'Paul wasn't urgent to meet up with Dean for dinner,' Sark said. 'He was urgent to get Dean to do one last job for him as he and everyone else involved in the family business are being watched like hawks. This assassin somehow knew this or had spotted Dean conversing with either Paul himself or...' He stopped, realisation kicking in.

'...or Tony Nivean,' DI Jason said, his smile broadening across his features.

Sark fished out his mobile phone and punched in Paul Demato's home phone number. Then he waited...

***

Paul answered the front door for the second time that morning to the two detectives. Only this time he cocked his head at them wearing a bemused expression. 'Gentlemen. This feels like Déjà vu. I thought I answered all of your questions. What is it now?'

DI Sark spoke before his partner even got the chance to open his mouth. 'We apologise for disturbing you again. But this is important.'

The bristled hair covering Paul's face flaked when he ran his hand through it.

'Go on,' he said, not hiding his vexation.

'You said that Tobias and Dean aren't part of your business, right?'

'That's correct. So?'

Sark ignored the impatient demeanour Paul exuded.

'So why would this "Mr Death" a.k.a., Anton, be trying to frame Dean? It doesn't make sense.'

Paul shrugged indifferently. 'I didn't say it was supposed to, did I? Whether it does or doesn't is for you to find out. That's your job, gentlemen. Not to sound impolite or anything.'

'That's what we're doing wise guy,' DI Jason cut in.

'It is my and my partner's belief that your urgency to meet up with Dean Ferris had nothing to do with getting together for dinner.'

'Oh?' Paul seemed curious how the detective had come to this conclusion.

'You were urgent to see Dean 'cause you had one last job to be done before you could pay off your debts and finally set off into the sunset.'

'A *job*?'

DI Sark nodded.

'And what was this *job*, dare I ask?'

'That's for you to tell us,' Sark said. 'If you withhold any information your intentions to fly out to Majorca might have to be put on hold.'

Something cold and dark from within Paul masked his features. His eyes threatened to bore a hole into Sark's skull.

'We also believe that this "Mr Death", or Anton, somehow found out about this – so it's most likely to do with money or drugs – and decided to pursue Dean back to his home and thereafter cause him a variety of problems.'

'My, my, my Detective, you really have yourself quite an imagination there,' Paul said, feigning humour.

'Dean said he was visiting an old friend in Tenby,' Sark went on.

Paul did a double-take. 'Well, if he's told you that and left his house then what the bloody hell are you going on about him doing some kinda *job* for me?'

It was DI Sark's turn to smile. 'You honestly expect Dean to simply just blurt everything out and get himself into hot water, more so than before?'

'What's that supposed to mean?' Paul said. He removed his glasses and rubbed the bridge of his nose where there were indentations.

'You helped him out in his time of need,' DI Sark said, hardly believing what was coming out of his mouth but knowing it was true or as close to the truth as they were going to get without a confession. 'With you guys it's always about favours. You helped Dean out before, even though he had nothing to do with you or any other connections till he lost his badge? Am I right?'

Paul chose not say anything. Instead he stared fixedly at the detective wondering how on earth he knew all of this on intuition alone.

Unfazed by the lack of response, Sark continued: 'So now Dean owed you a favour... And if I'm right Dean didn't exactly have a say in the matter. If he refused perhaps he would have a nasty accident sometime in the foreseeable future. If he did you were even.'

'You mentioned this being about money,' Paul said. 'What d'you mean by that?'

'If you wanna be evasive, fine,' Sark said. 'But it'll be your arse on the line, no one else's.'

'I'm just asking a question, Detective. You seem to be very capable of asking questions but not very good at answering them.'

'You know what I mean,' Sark said stepping back from the doorstep. 'But according to the records, doesn't Sandra Hill – Tobias' Hill's mother – live in Tenby, Wales?'

'If you're gonna waste my time, and your own, asking questions you already have information on, then I'm gonna have to say "good day" to you both.'

'Sandra Hill isn't on speaking terms with you, is she?' Sark pressed.

Paul shifted his weight from his left foot to his right. 'She's not happy about the fact her only son got killed by some ruthless assassin employed by Cascarini in mistake for Leo, no.'

Sark shook his head defiantly. 'That's not what I asked.'

'She's still in shock and not speaking to anyone for the time being. That includes me.'

'D'you feel bad about what happened?' Sark said, staring intently at Paul, looking for any indication in his demeanour that would indicate he was lying.

'Of course. Christ, that was supposed to be Leo lying on the ground, breathing his last in the middle of the woods. In case you two wankers didn't realise I'm also struggling to come to terms with all of this. On top of all that I got CID wanting to crawl up my arse. And now homicide department decide to send Beavis and Butthead to my door.'

DI Jason shook his head in disgust.

'What's the matter hotshot? Don't like the harsh truth being told to you face-to-face?'

'How 'bout you just answer the questions and wipe that smirk right off your face?' DI Jason said, doing well to control his anger.

'How 'bout you wipe my arse,' Paul said in retaliation.

'If Dean is in any trouble,' Sark said, returning to the purpose of their discussion, 'and something befalls him and we find out – and you bet your arse we will – you've held back information then look out.'

Paul raised his hand in a mock surrendering gesture. 'Wait a minute,' he said, placated after his verbal duel with DI Jason. 'Look, if he's told you he's gone to Tenby to see an old friend then that's what he's doing. He told me the same too. Okay? But when he mentioned where it was I asked if it wasn't too much trouble if he could drop by on Sandra. I was hoping she'd at least speak with Dean. Perhaps he could persuade her to at least talk to me. I want to sincerely apologise face-to-face. I want to see her face. And I want her to know how sorry I am and help with the funeral costs. And, as I just told you two cock-suckers, it should've been Leo. I love my son more than anything in the whole fuckin' world, pardon my French. But he's the one who caused all of this suffering. If there's one hang-up Leo has it is the inability to keep his mouth shut. If he wasn't my son he would've got whacked sooner.'

Sark didn't speak for a good minute. He pondered everything Paul had just said. Then he nodded. 'Okay. But that still doesn't clear up why this Anton – or whoever he is – would be following and trying to set-up Dean.'

Paul was about to interrupt but Sark waved at him dismissively.

'I can understand why Tony might've been killed. After all, due to this assassin's mistake of identity Cascarini lost one of his guys. Not to mention how the shit hit the proverbial fan when Tobias got killed in cold blood. I can even maybe allow that Cascarini wanted this "Mr Death" to kill Sampson in front of Dean's house, if he knew you and he were friends. But what I can't get my head around is why Cathy Groves, a stock replenish assistant for Asda, would be shot dead on her own front lawn in the early hours of the morning.'

'Neither can I, Detective,' Paul said, matter-of-factly.

18.

THE MOBILE PHONE rang incessantly. Dean kept alternating his attention from the road ahead to the phone. The mobile was out of reach. He supposed he could lean over and blindly grasp for it. Yet to do such a thing was perilous. He'd already had enough scares this morning to last a lifetime. Perhaps due to the fact he was no longer on the force he'd become weak. But even if this was another undercover operation, Dean didn't need to be told how risky every move he made could be.

In his rear-view the chiselled visage of his hunter drew closer. Then the Ford Fiesta backed off again, as though the driver sensed Dean might slam on the brakes and cause a vicious collision.

Dean had to admit the thought crossed his mind more than once. However, for the time being it was out of the question. There were too many other vehicles on the motorway to perform such a stunt without the chance of taking them out as well.

Soon he'd be reaching the intersection and join the M4. So far he'd managed to avoid injury, save the scrapes on the back of his head. He'd thwarted the one called 'Mr Death'. As long as he stayed focused, Dean believed that would remain the case. But sooner or later the closer he got to his destination, intuition told him Anton would make his move. No way was he merely being pursued to be intimidated or frightened.

Up until now all the deadly assassin had done was to give Dean a little taste of what was to come during their journey.

And God only knew what would happen if Anton was still tailing him when he reached Tenby, Wales.

***

DI Sark hung up, cussing under his breath.

'Still no answer then,' DI Jason said, stating the obvious.

'Gee, ya think...'

DI Jason chuckled. 'All right. I was just saying, that's all. No need to get outta your pram. Jesus!'

I knew there was something more to Dean's unexpected journey to Tenby,' Sark said, switching off his mobile.

'And you were right,' his partner said. 'But there's not really a single thing you can do about it. We could've kept Dean for at least forty-eight hours on suspicion alone. But you didn't want to do that.'

'He told us the truth.'

'Most of the truth,' DI Jason said. 'He could've told us Paul had asked him to do a favour. You suspected such a thing 'cause you asked right at the end. Why did he keep that from us? It would've put him in a better light than before and helped us with our investigation. Also, we'd have been able to protect him from any harm from this "Mr Death" character.'

'He told us as much as he could without Paul getting into hot water,' Sark said. 'You know what happens to informants: they end up in a freezer or face-down in a lake somewhere. Paul probably threatened Dean into doing this last job. Which has got to involve money in some shape or form.'

DI Jason nodded, concurring. 'But no money has been taken out of his bank according to the records. So we've got sod all. Also, we can't say that Dean or Paul have been uncooperative. On the contrary. They've been more than helpful and answered our questions as best as they could with as much detail possible.'

Sark arched his eyebrows at his partner. 'Whose side are you on?'

'I'm just saying from an outsider's point of view. Your hunches are more often than not spot on. I'm not disputing that or defending them. But you can't build a case on hunches alone.

'As far as the whole job relating to money. Just because Paul has had his bank account frozen doesn't mean he doesn't have cash around the house. Guys like Paul Demato never walk around with their pockets empty, even if they're in their pyjamas. But as you always reiterate to me – it's not what you know, it's what you can prove.

'We could get a search warrant and raid Paul's house if you pushed hard enough. But even if you found a stash of money it doesn't prove shit either way.'

'Just don't understand why he's not answering,' Sark said, heaving a sigh. 'He's probably driving at this very moment. You can't expect him to pull over straight away. And anyway, you didn't even bother to leave a message.'

DI Jason slotted the keys into the ignition. The engine growled awake.

'Say I phone him again,' Sark said.

'What, now?'

Sark nodded.

'Bound to get his answering message service. Not much point doing that if you're not gonna say whose calling. Of course he's got your number in his phone. But don't expect him to check.'

'I'll phone him again,' Sark continued. 'Only this time I leave a message…'

'You make it sound like you've really thought this over when it's quite a common thing to do.'

'… and the message I give him informs him we've just spoken to Paul. I'll say that Paul told us he's running an errand

133

for him as he's down in Tenby anyway. And the errand concerns Sandra Hill. Only, Paul and you and I, believe that this "Mr Death" is trailing him 'cause he's got money.'

DI Jason drove around the front yard. His mind buzzed as though his thoughts were roads of a Formula 1 track. 'Your telling me you're gonna phone Dean, leave a message and lie?'

'It's not a lie.'

'Yeah it is,' DI Jason said turning the car around so it faced the black wrought-iron gates. He applied the handbrake and waited for Paul to open the automatic gates permitting them to leave.

'How's it a lie?' Sark said.

'All Paul said was that he'd asked Dean if he'd time to drop by Sandra's place and speak to her; tell her how sorry he is so she'd talk to him.'

'So why's Anton – or whatever his name is – pursuing him?'

'Perhaps Cascarini will fill us in.'

'Maybe he will. Maybe he won't. Cascarini is hardly the most dependable person, is he?'

'Frankly,' DI Jason said, snapping, 'none of these guys – Dean included – are dependable or trustworthy. For all we know this could all be one big set-up. They could be sending us chasing our own tails and we wouldn't know about it till it's too late.'

'But even if my hunch is correct, Paul and Dean haven't done anything illegal,' Sark said. He shifted in his seat so his whole body faced his partner who concentrated on the road ahead.

The gates made a whirring noise as they parted open.

'Well, Paul is. He's been forbidden to do any deals while under investigation.'

'Ah, but this isn't a deal. It's one family member giving money to another family member.'

'What makes you so certain of this, anyway?' DI Jason wanted to know.

Sark's eyes rolled upwards and to the left. Something significant had suddenly dawned on him. 'Of course!'

'Oh, here we go. What now?'

'It should've been Leo, Paul said. He feels guilty, he told us that.'

'Who wouldn't?' DI Jason said, perplexed as to where his partner was going with this. 'He may be a mob boss and scum of the earth. But this is family. Family who weren't part of his business. Family who were good, honest hard-working members of the community. Tax payers. People with proper, legitimate jobs. Money earned the hard way.'

'And to try to absolve his involvement, regardless of the fact he didn't pull the trigger or order the hit, he's sent Dean to her home to give her money,' Sark finished.

DI Jason frowned. 'That doesn't make sense. Why would he trust Dean to take God knows how much cash with him halfway across the country? That's asking for trouble. Why didn't he just...' DI Jason trailed off. He finally understood what his partner had concluded.

'... send her a cheque or pay her online or straight into her account,' Sark said, satisfied that his partner had caught up with his train of thought. 'And normally, this would be how Paul, or anyone else for that matter, would conduct this type of transaction.'

DI Jason absent-mindedly flicked the turn signal and rejoined the road. 'He couldn't though.'

'And why couldn't he?' Sark said, waiting for DI Jason to say what he was thinking aloud.

'For two reasons. One: his bank account has been frozen for illegal gambling and evading tax and insurance bills. Two: even if he somehow could gain access to his bank records and account he doesn't have Sandra's details to wire her the money 'cause she's not speaking to him. And if he emails her informing her of his intentions, he'll be investigated for having withheld more money. He'll drop himself into deeper water than he's already in.'

'But if Dean can somehow get the unmarked notes to Sandra there will be nothing but circumstantial evidence – if that – to link Paul to the transaction.'

Sark nodded approvingly. 'That's right, Sherlock.'

DI Jason chanced a glance in Sark's direction. 'That might well be, but you still can't prove jack.'

'Not yet,' Sark said. 'Not yet.'

19.

THE ONE KNOWN as the chameleon focused intently on the red Honda Civic ahead. Traffic got heavier as he joined the M4 and headed westbound. The resplendent sunshine was misguiding. The temperature outside was 5 degrees Celsius. At this moment the hunter knew that the prey would be suffering from the effects of having the rear window blown to smithereens.

However, he had to admire and respect the prey's tenacity to stay out of his grasp. Fear slithered through the veins like congealed sauce and then ignited with a heart-pounding electric shock. People reacted differently to fear. Some switched off their mind and refused to accept what was happening. They'd cower away until they were boxed in. Then they would scream and pray for a quick, painless demise. Then there was the other type of individual who chose fight not flight. And although his prey was seemingly opting for the latter he was resisting.

Anton's intuition was as sharp as the draught beyond his window. No one needed to tell him that when the opportunity arose his prey wouldn't cower into a foetal ball and await death. If given the chance his prey would fight back.

The prey's fear attuned his instincts and reaction to a higher plateau. Every move was calculated. He'd seen his prey glimpsing him in the rear view mirror. The prey now used the other road users as allies. But as soon as the traffic started to thin out he'd give his prey a reminder that he wasn't going anywhere. Not by a long shot.

In his lap, Anton caressed the .38 fitted with a silencer.

20.

DI SARK ended the call and gazed out the passenger seat window at the main street going past. His partner slowed to a halt alongside the dense traffic at a set of red lights.

'What'd he say?' DI Jason asked, referring to their Chief Detective Inspector.

Sark shook his head sullenly. 'Same as you.'

The traffic lights weren't long. DI Jason removed the handbrake and put the stick into gear. The car skulked forward, bumper-to-bumper. 'Well, there's no use crying over spilt milk, is there? The chief has put an APB out for a black Ford Fiesta and anyone suspicious driving it. There really isn't a whole lot more you can do with that, pal.'

'An All Points Bulletin in this country wouldn't stop a five-year-old, never mind a ruthless killer with no conscience.'

'Don't say that, man.' DI Jason knew his partner hadn't meant his last comment. It was said out of pure vexation.

DI Sark had only been on the CID force for two years more than him. They were both young. Unusually young, considering they worked in the criminal investigation detectives, homicide unit. They were both fast climbers; hard workers. Until he'd met and worked with DI Sark, DI Jason would have sworn there was no one more determined and driven than himself. But Jonathan Sark lived, breathed, slept work.

The majority of their cases were missing persons. People who'd disappeared either on their own volition or had met with foul play. It quite often turned out that the individuals closest to their families who hadn't hinted they were going anywhere or were under no stress either at home or in work met with foul play. And the loners, or people under great stress, had taken a timeout from life to cool off.

This case was messy and complicated for all sorts of reasons. One of those reasons was the fact that an innocent member of the public had been shot dead right outside her house in the first light of day.

One thing he'd learnt about his partner was the victim's pain became his own. It was as though the dead person's spectre haunted DI Sark until they found the retribution they sought. He knew Sark suffered from insomnia. The dark shadows beneath his eyes gave his face a skeletal look in the shade.

'C'mon, buddy. It ain't over till it's over.' DI Jason tried to sound optimistic to cheer the ambience in the car if nothing else. 'Cascarini and his lawyer have agreed to answer our questions back at the Yard. He could give us something to add to this.'

Sark looked over his shoulder at his partner. 'It's not me I'm worried about.'

***

The CID headquarters was located in Twickenham, London, not far from the national rugby stadium. DI Jason sometimes went to see the odd game when he was on annual leave. It didn't seem likely that he'd be catching any of England's home fixtures in the Six Nations in a month's time though.

They entered the complex and walked silently down the hallway. The only sound came from phones ringing and soft murmurs of conversation. The sound of the detectives' footfalls on the mirror-surfaced linoleum reverberated off the alabaster walls.

The receptionist had informed them that Cascarini and his lawyer awaited their arrival in a coffee room.

Sark got the feeling that this interview wouldn't be as casual as their chat with Paul Demato. Mario Cascarini had his back up ever since he'd been found guilty of being in possession of cocaine and sending a hit man to kill Leo Demato.

It was January 12, 2006. Two years ago guys like Cascarini and Demato were nicknamed 'The Untouchables' after the gangster film based on Al Capone. The film had performed well and was acclaimed by elite critics. Robert De Niro as Al Capone had become popular.

Mario Cascarini's bald head shone beneath the fluorescent strips. Sark recalled seeing his photograph in the local paper. He'd been on page 2 along with a lengthy write-up for donating several thousand pounds to the paediatric ward for hospitals around the South London district. He'd had his beefy arms around two children bed-ridden due to cancer.

Sark had been queuing in a local One-Stop convenience store. The elderly woman in front remarked to the desk clerk what a lovely man Cascarini was, donating a good portion of his life servings and casino profits to the sick children. Sark had had to bite his lip from blurting out that the money he'd given had blood all over it. Instead he'd paid for his milk, cheese and bread. Then he took one long last look at the black and white photograph and envisioned himself seizing Tony by the nostrils and taking him down the nearest bowling alley.

The leather and aluminium chairs accommodated all four men in a half circle. Cascarini's lawyer rose and proffered his hand to the two detectives amicably.

Sark and Jason performed an obligatory handshake. Cascarini however remained seated wearing a broad grin that oozed conceit.

He's got some nerve smiling with all the court cases and fines against his name, Sark thought.

'My client and I would appreciate if you could tell us a little more as to what context these questions are regarding,' the lawyer said.

Sark noticed he was well-spoken. 'And what is your name, may I ask?'

'Kevin Thomas.'

'Okay Mr Thomas, as you are well aware your client is under investigation from the fraud squad and is also a prime suspect in an ongoing murder investigation.'

'That is correct,' Mr Thomas said. 'Is this what these questions are in relation to?'

'The money, drugs and details of what happened and in what capacity Mr Cascarini was involved in is not up for discussion. That is currently being dealt with by the court,' Sark said, speaking coherently in spite of a dry mouth. 'What we would like to ask your client involves another individual who we believe has murdered Danny Sampson and Tony Nivean as of yesterday. And a Mrs Cathy Groves earlier this morning.'

Cascarini sat up in his chair, frowning, intrigued. Once Sark had mentioned that basically this wasn't an interrogation solely against Cascarini, and that there was another suspect, the mob boss appeared interested and somewhat content.

'I heard of the two men you mentioned on the news last night,' Cascarini said, feigning concern. 'I wasn't aware that there had been another murder this morning in relation to your homicide investigation. Enlighten me. Please.'

Oh this guy truly is a piece of shit, Sark thought.

DI Jason's eyes met his partner's. They both thought the same thing simultaneously.

DI Jason explained how they'd discovered the remains of all three victims all occurring on two interconnecting streets in Dean Ferris's neighbourhood.

'Who's Dean Ferris?'

'A close friend of Demato,' Sark said.

Cascarini offered a curt shake of the head. 'Never heard of him.'

'He used to work for the drug squad,' DI Jason said. 'Got himself into hot water, lost his badge and ended up going to court.'

'Ah, I remember,' Cascarini said in an animated tone. 'Yes. Demato felt pity for the pup, didn't he?'

'In so many words,' DI Jason said. Then he rolled his eyes.

'So you suspect this Ferris chap to have killed three people around his neighbourhood?'

Sark and Jason exchanged a look.

'Didn't you employ or hire a notorious hit man to put an end to Leo Demato?' DI Jason asked.

Mr Thomas furrowed his brow. 'I thought you said we wouldn't be discussing the issues that are currently being examined in court?'

Sark shrugged. 'I'm not concerned with the ongoing court case, Mr Thomas. I am simply asking questions to help with our ongoing investigation.'

'So you don't suspect this Dean Francis...'

'...Ferris,' DI Jason corrected.

'Whatever,' Cascarini said, waving off the detective's interjection. 'But you suspect me?'

Sark shook his head. 'Please don't take us for fools, Mr Cascarini. We know full well that you were in court all day yesterday. However, we do suspect someone you've been linked to in relation to our homicide case and the court case.'

'Did you hire a hit man to kill Paul Demato's son?' DI Jason asked.

'I'm not at liberty to say,' Cascarini said after glancing at his lawyer.

'We already know you did,' Sark said, resisting the urge to bawl at this worthless scumbag. 'We just wanna know if you hired him to kill Tony Nivean, Danny Sampson and maybe Dean Ferris.'

'Wait a minute now,' Cascarini said, raising his hands in a gesture of surrender. 'So this Ferris guy is also dead?'

'Not yet,' DI Jason said.

'Did you hire a hit man whose name might be Anton to kill the aforementioned guys?' Sark said.

Cascarini shook his head. 'No.'

'But – cutting the bullshit out for a minute – you did hire him at one point, yes?' Sark said. He kept his steely eyes on Cascarini.

'I have made this gentleman's acquaintance before; that is correct.'

'Did he say anything 'bout killing Sampson and Nivean to you?'

Cascarini didn't speak for a few moments. He leant over to his lawyer and whispered something in his ear. Mr Thomas nodded his approval. Then he turned back to face the detectives once more.

'As you are aware, Paul's son has induced a hell of a lot of problems for me and his old man. This gentleman went to have words with Leo…'

'Yeah, yeah. We know about that,' DI Jason said. 'We know why you sent him to whack Leo. He ends up killing the wrong guy. Some innocent young man who has nothing to do with your shitty business winds up dying. We also know that it was the same guy who killed one of your men and his wife. Now you say to us you didn't hire Anton to kill Nivean and Sampson.'

'That is correct.'

143

'All right,' Sark said, exhaling explosively. He took out his notepad and then asked: 'What can you tell us that we might've missed on this Anton bloke?'

Cascarini leant back in his chair. The leather creaked under his weight. 'First of all his name may or may not be Anton.'

The two detectives looked at each other quizzically.

'What is his name then?' Sark asked.

'I don't know. I do know that this guy isn't part of any organisation, at least not to my knowledge anyway.'

'Does he drive a black Ford Fiesta?' Sark said, waiting for confirmation so he could put a tick next to the description of the vehicle on his notepad.

'Today he might,' Cascarini said, nonchalant. 'Tomorrow he'll be driving another vehicle.

'Paul said he's got black hair, is tall, broad shouldered with ebony eyes. Is that description accurate?' Sark asked, not liking where this was going.

'If that's what Paul was told or saw then I'm not disputing it. But what you have to remember is this guy isn't like you or me. Today he might be someone who dresses in black and drives a black car. I'm not saying that your information is inaccurate.'

'What are you saying?' DI Jason was keen to find out.

'They call him such names as "Mr Death", "The Shape" and "The Chameleon" – not because a buddy of his thought it sounded cool. He didn't give himself those nicknames either. He's been given them 'cause he'll have you chasing ghosts. By the time you locate him – if you ever do – everything that you've been told is no longer relevant.'

'Paul said this assassin kills without reason or conscience,' Sark said. 'He believes that according to you this guy is motivated not by money so much, but by the actual hunt itself. Is that true?'

Cascarini took a sip of his coffee and contorted his face at the cold liquid. 'Obviously he needs money to get him from place to place. He needs money just the same as you and I. He needs it to eat, to drink, to put fuel in whatever car he's driving and to stay in hotels and motels throughout the country and wherever the hell else he goes. But that's a necessity.

'Men work Monday to Friday for money. To pay bills and so on. But they live for the weekend. They have hobbies, interests. This drifter goes not only where the money is but where there's work. His job is his hobby. All the better if his avocation pays him. And by the looks of it he's been doing it for several years with no one being any the wiser.

'There's something primal about him that isn't in your psychology. You could have a BA and MS in criminal psychology but you'd never truly understand him. He lives to kill. It's not a duty or an obligation or even an addiction. It's some kinda compulsion. In other words gentlemen – killing is what he was born to do.'

'You spoke to him though,' Sark said. 'What can you tell us about him?'

'That's another thing,' Cascarini said holding a finger up. 'He doesn't do a whole lotta talkin'. Instead he'll sit still for hours on end and listen. Then when he does finally say something it's usually in conundrums.'

'Where's he from?' Sark asked, feeling a cold sweat surface on his brow.

'I couldn't say for certain gentlemen. But if I had to make an assumption, I'd say he was Portuguese or Spanish. Maybe even from Brazil. But as I said he is the master of disguises. So I could be judging him on one of many different, eclectic faces he wears.'

'You're not covering for him by any chance are you?' DI Jason said.

145

'No. That man killed someone very close to me. All they called him was a "cocksucker". He simply vented out his frustrations and the problems he'd caused due to his mistake in killing the wrong boy. He killed that individual in his own marital bed and took his and his wife's head. For what?'

Sark's back was aching from bending over for so long. He straightened up. He scribbled out the possible description he'd written down after speaking with Demato. And when he looked at the two sheets of paper with Paul Demato underlined on one page and Mario Cascarini underlined beneath another he realised he didn't have anything substantial.

'Anything else you can tell us about this "Mr Death" bloke?'

Cascarini put a hand under his chin and ran a finger over his parted lips.

'You're hunting this guy down, right? Using all your resources?'

Both DI Sark and DI Jason nodded in unison.

'Just remember gentlemen, if you do hunt him down there will be no arrest. Forget procedure. If you find yourself between the man known as "Mr Death" and his way out you need to ask yourself one question.'

'And what's that?' DI Jason wanted to know.

'Am I ready to die?'

Silence hit the small coffee room like a sledgehammer.

'If there's the slightest trace of doubt,' Cascarini said, more serious now than he'd ever been, 'then back down. Don't pursue. Go on sick absence. Anything. Don't listen to your bravado. Listen to your heart.

'Because believe me when I say this guy will kill you in a heartbeat. He doesn't have compassion, fear, doubt, hesitation. And if you get in his way you will die in gruesome circumstances.'

The two detectives would never say so aloud but they were deeply unnerved by Cascarini's monologue.

'What if I told you we suspect that Anton – or whatever his name is – is hunting down the aforementioned Dean Ferris. What'd you say about that?'

Cascarini stared directly into Sark's eyes. His stare didn't have a trace of menace or hate. The stare was as profound as it was blank.

'I'd say Dean Ferris is a walking dead man…'

21.

THE TWO DETECTIVES had no answer to that last ominous remark. What DI Sark had realised though was that this interview was essentially over.

Mr Thomas sensed that this was the case. 'Is that all, officers?'

DI Jason nodded.

'You said you contacted Anton, or whoever he is,' Sark said, thinking aloud.

'But how did you know about him to be able to contact him in the first instance?'

It was the first time in the interview that Sark had noticed a palpable trace of anxiety wash over Cascarini's tawny jowls.

Mr Thomas leant over this and whispered something into his client's ear.

Cascarini nodded agreement.

'If we can trace this fellow's origins that can be pivotal in tracing the man himself,' Sark said in a soft tone. He desperately wanted Cascarini to empathise his position. Then he added for good measure. 'It could make a difference and save some lives. If that happens, certain people will look at you in a different light. It'll also be on record that you assisted us in our investigation.'

Sweat beads had surfaced on the mob boss' brow. They glistened in the sunlight slanting through the gaps of the window blinds.

'Here's me expecting a good cop, bad cop routine.'

'Sorry to disappoint,' Sark said.

'Instead you make a plea to my conscience.' Cascarini said it without any sinister undertones. His tone came over as genuine. 'You've been kind, courteous and I must say professional. You can't be that old, either. But you're not a kid who's come barging in here ready to bust my balls.'

Under other circumstances Sark would have verbally thanked and appreciated the appraisal. However, Cascarini's opinion of him – whether good or bad – was insignificant. 'Will you answer that question for me? If what you said in regards to Dean Ferris being marked for death is true then we really need to act in haste.'

'What makes you think I give a damn about one of Demato's buddies?'

Sark shook his head. 'I didn't say you did or didn't. I do need to know though if you're gonna cooperate with us or not.'

Cascarini stared vacantly at the floor. 'What I tell you won't aid you in stopping this man from doing what he's already planned in his mind meticulously, Detective. I can assure you of that if nothing else.'

'Well,' Sark said, motioning to rise, 'if you're not gonna help then so be it.'

'I'll tell you, Detective. Not because of some self-righteous integrity. The CID, fraud squad, drug squad and every other authority in this damn country couldn't care less about me. But that works both ways. What I do want though is for you two to put down on your notepads and reports that I gave you all the info I had. You promise to do that?'

Sark nodded and even wrote down the question. 'You have my word,' Sark said. 'But don't expect me to go to my chief and tell him to write to the judge of your case and tell him to drop all charges against you. But you can mention it in court that you have aided the Homicide Department in this case. We'll send your lawyer a copy as your proof.'

Cascarini nodded his approval. 'Bear in mind there's not much to say about this man's past. If there was he wouldn't have all those nicknames. He wouldn't be sought after by guys like me.'

DI Jason wiped his nose with a Kleenex. Sark could see him in his peripheral vision. His partner for whatever reason nearly always had a runny nose or a blocked nose. It wasn't a winter cold or anything of that nature. He was the same all year round.

'My brother Roberto had first heard about him several years ago while on holiday in Spain,' Cascarini continued.

'Where in Spain?' Sark said, pouncing on possible key information before Cascarini could go on.

'I think it was Barcelona, or some place like that.'

Not good enough.

'Never mind. Go on,' Sark said. He needed Cascarini to get into his narrative. Then he'd be far more likely not to omit anything else from the yarn.

'There'd be some uniform policeman who'd visited a woman in her apartment. Neighbours or the owner must've heard the shouting matches at night. Anyway someone phoned the law. It was nothing special, just domestic disturbance.

'Anyway, who do they send but a young male officer to the scene. Just a kid. Hadn't been a constable for more than two months. He goes knocking on the apartment where the rows have been getting worse and worse. The couple had even argued in the early hours of the morning during the week. Neighbours heard loud crashing and glass shattering, and a woman's screams.'

'A fairly routine call,' Sark said, wanting Cascarini to pick up the pace.

'Right,' Cascarini said, gesturing that Sark had hit the nail on the head. 'So the young gun's knock on the door is answered by some Spanish senorita. Real stunner apparently.

Curvy, dark brown hair. Chestnut-brown eyes. Tits good enough to make her a highly paid glamour model. Only these weren't your plastic shite. These were the Real Deal. Legs that went on for ever and an arse that wouldn't quit.'

In spite of himself Sark laughed at the last remark. 'Yeah, we get the point.'

'So here's PC plod with his truncheon hanging on his belt and his God-given truncheon saluting her majesty.'

This time it was DI Jason's turn to laugh. He waved Cascarini to go while he wiped the snot from his nose.

'He sees the black eye that this piece of shit has given her during their latest argument. From what the guy on the fruit stall in the same building says, this policeman urges her to press charges. She does. She feels comforted by the uniform and the fact that he's in authority. She leaves the guy and rents a place further away. Somehow or another PC plod has got her forwarding address. On his day off he goes to visit her, knowing she is now a single woman.'

'Oh God,' Sark muttered, seeing where this was heading.

'Before you know it PC plod is up to his balls with this senorita, bumping uglies. Cha, cha, cha. The whole shooting match.'

Cascarini ceased talking for a moment. Then he resumed. 'Jealous ex-boyfriend finds out about PC prick slipping his ex his swollen goods. Trouble is this woman beating SOB has a lot of money and a lotta connections. He pays the guy you're after and fucked everything up for me to pay PC prick a visit at his home...'

A long pause followed.

'Yeah. And?' DI Jason said, not caring about showing his impatience.

'Presumably, PC prick is followed to his new girlfriend's apartment. Of course he doesn't have a clue about this. He's too busy thinking with the little head to give a toss about the big head that might've told him he was being followed.

'Anton – or whoever he is – is given specific instructions on the method of killing. So he waits for PC prick and Miss Ooh la la to start shagging. He picks the lock, quietly, using the sex noises to drown out the door coming apart from its hinges. He enters and roams the apartment to the bedroom where all the action is taking place like a ninja. He peeks through the gap in the door left ajar. The senorita is a seasoned pro when it comes to riding. The way she rocks to and fro like an ardent jockey she could've won the Grand National.

'Your suspect waits for her to almost reach her body-quaking orgasm before rushing into the room. He's wielding a fuckin' samurai sword. In one eye-blinking swipe decapitates PC prick. The stump where his head used to be starts pissing scarlet in geyser. Senorita is shrieking a different song. She tries to run for the door but is struck down by Anton's muscular arm.

'By the time he is finished, all he leaves for the police and forensics are two bloodied cadavers. The headless corpse of PC prick isn't the only thing he cut off. The other dismembered part protruded from the senorita's mouth. Behind the headboard on the far wall is a message written in dark red blood.

'It reads "Cock sucking whore" above the senorita's head. And above PC prick's just one word, "Dick-less".'

'What 'bout the policeman's head? Where was that?'

'Ah, good question, Detective,' Cascarini said, genuinely taken aback by Sark's alertness. 'The head was never found.'

The two detective's let that hang in the ambience, silenced to the core.

'One neighbour told detectives at the crime scene she'd seen a tall, broad-shouldered man emerge from the apartment

152

that evening and take the staircase. When she was asked for a description guess what she said?'

DI Jason immediately shook his head in an I-don't-know expression. DI Sark meanwhile contemplated it, realising that Cascarini had only queried this as Sark already had the answer. Then it came to him.

Sark gasped. 'She couldn't identify him, besides telling them that he wore a brown paper with two eyeholes.'

'Bingo!' Cascarini exclaimed.

22.

THE MAN with so many names and was considered untraceable kept a safe distance from the red Honda Civic in front. He waited for two bearded men in leather attire to overtake him riding Harley Davidson motorcycles. Then he enveloped his fingers around the .38.

For the time being both he and his prey had a stretch of the M4 to themselves.

Playtime.

He pressed the button on his right for the window to wind down. The strong wind created by the velocity he was travelling at – 80mph – whipped his black hair off his brow and cooled his granite features. The black Ford Fiesta buffeted from the unexpected draught whooshing into the vehicle.

Once he'd regained full control of the vehicle again, the man known as 'Mr Death' leant out the driver's window. He checked the road was clear of traffic behind him and then brought the weapon fitted with a silencer out from his lap. He focused his unblinking stare down the barrel that refused to remain steady in his grasp. The wind fought him. But sheer determination on his part was the deciding factor. He clicked the safety off and squeezed the trigger.

The silencer and the howling keen wind sucked the bullet into oblivion. Or at least that was what he thought until he saw the wing mirror on the Honda Civics' driver's side rip itself apart from the car and shatter onto the tarmac.

The assassin managed to tuck his head back inside the car before a fusillade of glass and plastic debris flew towards him and made a musical tune on the Ford's bodywork.

The Honda Civic swerved erratically, crossing lanes as though the white lines weren't there. It careered onto the hard shoulder. The rear tyres kicked up a rooster tail of marble and stones in its wake. Then just as the assassin with no true identity indicated to join the prey on the left-hand side of the road the Honda slipped back into the left lane. The driver of the damaged vehicle had regained his composure and continued as though nothing untoward had transpired.

What the hunter had done was effective. No, he didn't wound the man driving the Honda Civic. Nevertheless, he did manage to hit the target. What perplexed the hunter though was how resilient the driver appeared to be. He rode the unexpected storm. Then drove to the emergency breakdown lane and returned to the motorway itself when he was good and ready.

This Anton knew was a prudent move.

***

Dean exhaled and consulted the rear view mirror. The disintegration and dismembering of the wing mirror had shocked him. However, his heart hadn't climbed into his throat, pulse beating maddeningly like earlier this morning. So far he'd weathered the storm and endured.

He used reverse psychology and placed himself in his assailant's position. Sooner or later, no matter how much someone relished the hunt and thrill of killing another human being, impatience would seep into the marrow of their bone. With the impatience, frustration would be shortly accompanied by anxiety. His hunter had made a mistake before, which had induced the events thereafter. His hunter believed himself to be invincible. A true marksman. A being with no flaws.

But his mistake of killing Tobias Hill instead of Leo Demato had brought him down to earth with an unforgiving thud. Now doubt had settled into the hunter's conscious or subconscious. Either way it was there lurking in the shadows. A shape.

As a former member of the drug squad in CID, Dean was no stranger to shootouts or breaking down doors and entering the homes of men who'd kill him without a second's thought. The more he contemplated this situation the more it appeared to be not much different to any other life threatening situation he'd put himself in before. Sure this guy had a sinister background with no explanation. As Tony had said, it made 'Mr Death' come across as an enigma. But Dean knew for a fact that no human can automatically switch off all emotions like a light switch.

In comparison to him, Anton felt nothing. However that didn't mean that at some point in his life he didn't feel any emotions. It was specific emotions that had given birth to this remorseless killing machine in the first place.

'Just need to find his buttons and push them. Push 'em hard,' he said to himself for reassurance.

What did concern him was that sooner or later he would have to stop for fuel. He should have enough to get him across the Seven Bridge and into Wales. After that the hunt would escalate to perilous proportions. He didn't want to consider dying. However it was impossible not to let the thought channel through his mind. After all, last night two men had been found dead in horrific circumstances.

It was harrowing message from his assailant. A warning.

Had I lost my nerve and surrendered the money and offered to trade the briefcase in for my life he still woulda killed me, Dean thought. *Guys like this would've killed me even if I'd begged for my life. I'd have been killed for inconveniencing him. For involving myself in his affairs. Although this transaction has nothing to do with him.*

Still, Dean believed that he had a chance. He was armed and wearing a bullet proof vest. Strangely, it was the extra padding of the Kevlar vest that comforted him the most. He assumed it was due to the fact that it reminded him of the days when the fear that now swam through his veins was replaced by courage. The courage of knowing that he was sacrificing himself for a greater cause than his own life.

Was this any different?

In a lot of respects it wasn't. He was doing his utmost to aid a grieving mother. A woman whose son was shot down unmercifully when he had nothing to do with the mob business. A woman whose world had been turned upside down and shattered into a million pieces. Just like the broken wing mirror, long gone.

The money in the vinyl briefcase, dirty or not, was a gesture of sorrow and of goodwill during the harshest of times. He may not have had the shield in his possession but he did feel the pride he once felt. The pride of doing something worthwhile. The pride of doing something filled with profound integrity.

Then a melancholy thought burrowed itself deep into his consciousness. He wondered if he would ever see the sky as blue as the one overhead after today.

23.

'**OKAY**,' DI Sark said. He had listened to Mario Cascarini's detailed yarn and
had made some notes along with his partner. 'But how does any of this help us trace this 'chameleon'?'

Cascarini offered a crooked smile. 'Relax your crack, sweetheart. I'm getting there, if ya gimme a chance.'

DI Jason rolled his eyes at his partner.

'Roberto had listened to the man on the fruit stall recite this big story. Said that this fella was an incarnation of Satan or some shit. Roberto asks by way of conversation if this guy is a hit man for a mob family or establishment.

'The little fat Spaniard dude tells him he doesn't know. He doesn't ask questions that have nothing to do with him. He was merely telling the same story his friend told him. Roberto is interested in Anton – I'll call him by that name as I have no other. He asks the guy on the fruit stall who told his friend this story. Again the little fat man doesn't know but takes Roberto's number and calls his friend. He made sure Roberto wasn't a pig. Sorry a policeman.'

Sark silently reprimanded the slip of tongue with a frown.

'Anyway, cut a long story short, Roberto meets up with the little fat Spaniard's friend at a local café. Roberto makes enquiries to who this fella is and what's his story, so on and so forth.

'The guy at the café tells Roberto he is no friend of Anton's. Anton has no friends. No family by all accounts either. Kinda lives off the grid for want of a better term. But he met his acquaintance when Anton came across a fight in an alleyway involving this guy.

'He was kicking the shit outta another bloke. His gang of friends then attack the guy in the Café and proceed beating the living fuck outta him.'

DI Jason's eyebrows arched. 'Nice choice of words.'

'I mean the guy from the café found himself facing four armed blokes. They beat him to the ground and stomped his head and punched him in the abdomen. He'd just been stabbed in the thigh and was getting pissed on when a shape materialised outta the shadows.'

'He used those words?' DI Sark asked. The more yarns he heard in relation to this assassin the more the perpetrator sounded supernatural. Either that or word of mouth and parable had given him this persona.

Cascarini nodded somewhat solemnly. 'Yes, Detective. That's what Roberto said. He called me shortly after he'd had this conversation. And I thought it sounded far-fetched as well at first. That's what you were thinking, right?'

DI Sark opened his hands out in a gesture of what-do-you-expect-me-to-think?

'I'm not saying I agree or disagree with you,' Cascarini said in a placid tone. He didn't feel the need to defend himself here. 'From what I can gather it sounds as though Anton could have been in the dark alleyway the whole time, lurking in the shadows to remain out of sight. As opposed to materialising outta the wall.'

'Okay,' Sark said. 'But if we're to go on every word and type up your statement you do need to be clear about what you say and the wording, as well.'

'Anyway, Anton – or whoever – appears from behind these hoodlums. He slits the nearest guy's throat so quickly the guy in the café thought he'd imagined it. That was until the dead body thudded on the concrete and oozed dark, thick blood from the severed artery.'

DI Sark had to admit this perpetrator did sound like an incarnation of Satan.

'The guy in the café is left alone as the others stop what they're doing. But Anton is as quick as he is lithe and strong. He grabs another bloke's head from behind. In a reverse headlock manoeuvre. The guy's neck is crunched and he falls instantly to the concrete, head lolling.

'Now there are two remaining. Anton rams the heel of his hand into the first guy's nose with one hellish, fast and precise blow. The guy staggers backwards, clutching his beak. He falls over the rubbish and collapses in a heap. The last gang member standing draws a gun as this is happening. And had the safety not been on Anton might've been dead or seriously wounded. By the time he pointed the barrel of his handgun at Anton and fired Anton swiped his left arm towards the gun in the gang member's right hand. The gun is knocked outta the guy's grasp, not before tearing a hole in Anton's jacket on his upper left arm.

'The guy in the Café told Roberto Anton didn't even flinch or wince. I mean nothing. It was only a nick but still. He got shot. Even for a tough guy that's not an everyday occurrence. It is a bit of a shock.'

'Yeah,' Sark said, agreeing.

'Anton delivers a boot to the man's abdomen. This sends him sprawling backwards, but not enough to take him off his feet. The guy catches his breath from being temporarily winded then rushes Anton as he draws a .38 fitted with a silencer and pops the guy right in the forehead.

'Just like Ca...'

'Cathy Groves. This Dean what's–his-surname neighbour,' Cascarini finished for DI Jason.

'There were no survivors?' DI Sark asked, astonished at how Anton had beaten four armed and deadly men in close quarters to death with just a scratch for his troubles.

'No. He shot the guy lying in a heap holding his broken nose in the balls and head. Then he sat down on the floor amongst the dead bodies and watched this guy in the café. He told Roberto that Anton's hair was thick and full. His cheekbones were prominent, as was his chiselled jaw.

'The guy thanked Anton more times than he cared to recall. Then he said if there was anything he could do to repay him for saving his life to name it.'

Cascarini ceased talking.

'What is it?' Sark asked, puzzled.

'This bit is strange. The guy said when Anton spoke his voice sounded like his mouth was full of sand or grit. Maybe he had a speech impediment or something along those lines. Anyway, Anton asked why the men were beating him up.

'Again to cut a long story short. The guy worked for an arms' dealer. A local mob boss wanted to buy ammo and weaponry off the arms' dealer at a cheap price. As in much cheaper than he could afford to sell them for profit. So cheap, that the price of shipment would cost more than the money he'd make selling them.'

'In other words there'd be no point doing business,' Sark said, catching on.

'Exactly. The gentleman he worked for was getting on a bit in age. He wouldn't last long. He'd had a stroke the year before. It really slowed him down, blah, blah, blah.

'Anton asked what kinda profit they made if this mob boss and his muscle weren't harassing the guy in the café and the old man. He told him. I think it was between ten and twenty grand per shipment. Depending on what was sold and if it was safe to do so.'

Sark caressed his neck, tired. 'Is this why Anton is able to get guns and ammo through unconventional means?'

'As opposed to purchasing them at a local gun shop? Yes,' Cascarini said.

'Think about it. If he didn't have these connections how would he be able to equip himself and kill without anyone being able to trace his whereabouts? You may not want to hear this but Anton is no ordinary muscle, Detective. There's a perfectly good reason why he's survived on his own up until now. He's smarter than a bus load of university students and don't think I'm pulling your plonker or exaggerating either.'

Sark shook his head and grimaced. His neck was taut. His shoulders tense. He needed a proper night's rest and a long hot bath or shower to relax.

'I take it he killed this local mob boss?' DI Jason said, flexing his fingers that had gone rigid from writing for so long and in such haste.

'Oh God, yeah. And he did it with the weapons supplied to him by the old man.'

'This mob boss was having a conference meeting in one of his lavish restaurants in Barcelona. He was a big, fat bloke. Yes, even bigger than me before you say anything. Anton went with the guy from the café to this restaurant. They sat at a table on the right next to a window, overlooking the fountain outside.

'The guy from the café told Roberto this fat tub of lard even had the audacity to come over and remind him to tell the arms' dealer that he needed another supply of weaponry. That the old man was behind on his latest stock and if he was any later then his discount would increase. Then he went to the men's restroom.

'Anton watched him. Then he rose and followed.'

A wave of weariness made DI Sark lean forward in his seat.

'So Roberto asks the guy from the café to get in touch with him. If he was interested in a similar type of work or just getting paid good money to watch my back.'

'What happened to the mob boss in the restaurant?' DI Jason asked, wondering why that part of the story had been omitted.

'Anton and the guy from the café took their leave discreetly. And it was a good job they did. Ten minutes later, if that, the whole street had been cordoned off by police. No one was going anywhere without being thoroughly questioned. According to the papers the next morning, the mob boss was discovered hanging from his braces from the cubicle door. The braces had been wrapped tightly around his chubby neck. His face a purple hue. Strangled. He'd been disembowelled.'

Cascarini shrugged indifferently. 'Strangest aspect about it all for me was the fact that no one suspected someone hired by the old arms' dealer the whole time. Roberto was questioned. But he said his friend went to get some more salad and he remained at the table. This account was verified by a waiter who said that a tall, broad man with long blond hair and emerald-green eyes had asked for more salad for his starters.'

DI Sark snapped out of his weary posture. DI Jason did a double-take, eyes bulging from their sockets. 'Blond hair?' they both said simultaneously.

Cascarini's smile reached his eyes this time. The detective's shock amused him. 'You both need to pay much greater attention to the details, gentlemen,' he said. His tone was amicable in spite of the mockery. 'I told you Anton – or whoever he really is – is a master of disguise. One day he's a dark haired bloke you might bump into at your local supermarket, the next he's a grey-haired man sitting on the bus stop.'

DI Sark felt his shoulders sag from disappointment rather than exhaustion.

163

24.

THE M4 was one long stretch of road. The chameleon felt his heavy-lidded eyes threaten to close as he stared at the rear end of the Honda for hours on end. To fight the tediousness he averted his attention to the rolling pastures. There was something about the different shades of green and yellow that soothed something inside of him. It felt peculiar. Perhaps it was due to the fact that an emotion long forgotten began to swim to the surface.

The film tape in his mind's eye played a memory from a time when he'd been one of the human race. The man he called 'father' wasn't around often. He was a town constable. His mother had worked as a receptionist at a local orthodontist surgery. One day she'd been driving home from work, thinking of what she'd cook for supper when a speed racer shot out of a junction onto the main road and T-boned her.

Anton recalled his father coming home from work and finding his son all alone. The townsfolk informed his father of the accident. He and Anton had rushed to the hospital she was being treated at. When they got there a nurse told them that she was in ER. She wasn't too badly hurt, if you considered what might have been. It was the passenger side of the car that had been struck. The passenger side had folded inwards. Had anyone been occupying that seat they wouldn't have been so fortunate. However, his mother had been lacerated by shards of glass and jolted thunderously. She slipped in and out of consciousness. When she did come to at the crash site the paramedics had already arrived and were attending to her. She complained about how she felt numb all down her left-hand side.

'Feels like pins and needles. And my brain is pulsing maddeningly,' she'd told them. Then she'd passed out again.

This apparently was what concerned the doctors most. They said there was a possibility she might have been under stress prior to the accident. The hellish impact itself had then triggered a TIA (Transient Ischemic Attack). Also known outside the medical profession as a mini-stroke.

She had been heavily sedated to keep her unconscious while they removed the glass from her face. Anton and his weeping father had paid a quick visit at her bedside in ER.

She looked nothing like the beautiful woman he had married. The head brace kept her from stirring or doing any more damage to her swollen neck. They spoke of whiplash and fractured ribs. It was that and the lack of oxygen on top of the stress that had induced a blackout.

At first sight Anton had been afraid of the wounded individual lying supine on the bed. The heart monitor bleeped rhythmically. His eyes followed the green line as it curved upwards and went dead straight again the next second. Even at five he didn't need to be told that this was the place you came to when you were between life and death. This was where religious folk believed God decided who was for keeping and who was for deleting.

A middle-aged woman with grey-blonde wiry hair in the next bed rolled over, groaning. As she performed this manoeuvre Anton saw the deep red lines across her face. One very close to the black contusion that cocooned her right eye. Four red slices where her violent husband had attacked her with large bread knife. Her left eye was red-rimmed and moist. Nevertheless, it found Anton amidst the white cloaks of doctors and navy one-piece suits of the nurses rushing to and fro. Anton met her unblinking gaze, no longer afraid. Her rotund face would be forever scarred like his mother's face. The lacerations wouldn't be so discernible. Time would turn them into pink strips that resembled scratches. If she got fatter her chubby features might swallow some of those lines into cellulite. The vicious contusion bubbling over her bad eye would regain its natural hue. The swelling would deflate. But the mind would never forget the macabre of that day.

Her sausage index finger on her right hand pointed directly at him. Her lipless mouth gaped. 'You,' she croaked. Her voice came out in a husky rattlebox. 'You.'

Had she not been pointing to emphasise who she was referring to Anton might have dismissed her or thought she was speaking to someone else. But she hadn't.

'You... You are the face of death. You're here to take me. Just like you will take many others as you grow older and stronger. You're the face that will make thousands scream. You are the one whose destiny has been mapped out by Lazarus.'

By now nurses and doctors ceased what they were doing. Anton's father had whirled around, pallid face shrinking from the skull. He glowered at the obese woman.

'On this fateful night a year or so from now you will stare death in the face,' she went on. 'You will see the end of your first life. And your second, chosen, life shall be born within you. You'll be cancer for those who still have their health. You'll be the one they call "Death".'

A nurse strode across the ward and whispered something in harsh tones to the injured woman. Anton didn't need to be told that the fat lady was being reprimanded.

His mother recovered over the course of months and innumerable hospital appointments. She was forbidden to drive again (not that she craved to do so thereafter). However, as time passed, neither caring nor uncaring, towards his mother's health, her doctors had advised her that she'd need to start doing light exercises. One of those exercises included walking. His mother didn't understand the benefits of walking unless there was a destination at the end of the trip. To overcome this obstacle Anton suggested they go blackberry and strawberry picking in one of the environing orchards. To get there they had to traipse down country roads with high hedges and meandering narrow roads. This route would be perilous even on a glorious summer day. Instead they took a shortcut through the rolling pastures. The dulcet sound of unseen crickets and birdsong was the sweetest sound no human could ever beat or duplicate. It was those times that Anton (who in later life would forget his real name) cherished the most.

His doting mother had seemingly made a full recovery. She sometimes slurred her words when she spoke in haste. It had been worry that had induced her stress. Her brain had been inundated with worries without solutions. The car crash that had nearly cost her life had been the tip of the iceberg.

His mum said to him one day while crossing the golden yellow cornfield, 'God was sending me a message.'

This statement perplexed young Anton. He told his mum to explain in a way only she could so that he could understand.

'I could've died or been an invalid for the rest of my life, sweetheart,' she'd said. Her tone was a silk blanket and her touch like heavenly fingers which reached not only his skin but his heart. 'But God didn't want that to happen to me. God wanted me to stop worrying so much. He was sad that I had taken the world upon my shoulders.'

'Why Momma?' he'd asked in Portuguese parlance.

'Because that is His job, not mine. And He loves me almost as much as I love you.'

Anton remembered his whole body relaxing, surrendering to her touch. It was as if she were God's wife and had wished it with all her heart to remove all worry, all doubt from him in the second it took to run her fingers through his long brown hair.

This is what heaven must feel like, he wondered.

Her mane of hair danced around her beautiful but blemished features like an autumn Christmas tree as she spread her arms out as far as they could go and pirouetted. Then she laughed when a wave of euphoric dizziness overcame her.

Anton laughed too. He often smiled when he was his mother, and sometimes with his father.

But Anton hadn't smiled since that day, nor would he again…

25.

CASCARINI actually looked haggard from reciting the yarn of how he'd come to know of the assassin known as 'Mr Death'.

'What happens now?' the notorious mob boss wanted to know.

DI Sark rubbed his brow. 'I'll get a letter typed up that you did assist us in this homicide case and that you were cooperative. I doubt it will make much difference. The charges against you are pretty signed and sealed. But to a judge and a sympathetic jury it will show that you do have some decency.'

Cascarini forced a smile of gratitude. 'Detectives, I've got to say as far as this homicide case goes, you've got no chance.'

'Oh, really?' DI Jason said, taking offence.

Cascarini ignored DI Jason and faced DI Sark who'd been far more courteous.

'The only way you could possibly get to Anton is if your guy – Dean, was it? – calls you and gives you his location. And even then Anton has a habit of vanishing into thin air. He can make himself disappear and walk right past you in a crowd. You wouldn't even notice. He can slink back into the shadows at will. Or, as I said, he'll put a bullet through your head if you get in his way. You want my advice?'

Neither detective spoke.

As they expected Cascarini continued. 'Let it go. Put your pride aside and let it go.'

DI Sark snapped the notepad closed. He leant forward and proffered a hand to both Mario Cascarini and his lawyer Kevin Thomas. 'Gentleman we do appreciate your cooperation. I doubt it'll make much difference to the outcome of the case but it was definitely insightful.'

Sark regarded Cascarini. 'I appreciate your advice. But what you suggested is unacceptable. We cannot – and will not – let it go. But I concur that unless Dean does the right thing and comes clean then he might be marked for death.'

'He's already marked for death,' Cascarini said. 'This guy won't stop until either he or Dean is dead. The money is merely a prize for his endeavours, nothing more. Just make sure you don't get caught up in the crossfire, Detective.'

DI Sark grinned. 'I would've thought that nothing would please you more than to see one CID getting killed in cold blood.'

Cascarini gave Sark a serious look. There wasn't a trace of humour in his eyes. He shook his plump head once. 'I don't particularly like police, as you are aware. But police and judges, as proven by Paul Demato, can be bought off. Not you, though. You've got integrity. So do I, in spite of what you think.'

DI Jason snorted laughter.

'I can't say the same for your hotshot partner,' Cascarini continued, not missing a beat. 'But if you do catch up to him and you stare into his eyes don't be surprised to see no emotion or soul. That part of him died years ago... I hope you don't get the chance to stare him straight in the eyes 'cause if you do your wife will be a widow.' He paused, deliberating. 'If you love someone with all your heart, as you love your wife, you won't gamble with a life.'

DI Sark didn't bother to ask Cascarini how he knew what he felt for his wife. He didn't need to be told that his feelings could be seen lucidly in his eyes. They were the window of his soul. His wife was his life. The reason he rolled out of bed each morning and worked his arse off. He had someone worth living, fighting and loving for.

'Anton doesn't have that. That's what makes him so deadly. The only fear he has is failure. Let it go...'

***

DI Sark and DI Jason went upstairs and lowered themselves into their seats at their cluttered desk. Stationary, files, books and paperwork covered the oak tabletop. Both men had had a long day and it was only 9:43am.

'Whad'ya thinking?'

DI Sark leant back in his wooden chair, stretching and yawning.

'What did we expect?'

DI Jason remained silent.

'We knew that Cascarini didn't really have much more information. Although I will search for newspaper stories of a mob boss being disembowelled in Barcelona, Spain.' He sighed out of vexation. 'But that's not going to get us any further. The crime was unsolved. No one saw Anton go into the restroom. And even if they did...'

'...they wouldn't be able to identify him 'cause he was wearing a disguise,' DI Jason finished.

'Exactly. Cascarini is right. This is like catching a ghost.'

'Just goes to show what a piece of shit Cascarini and his brother Roberto are for hiring his services in the first place. They should've left him in the alley where they found him.'

Sark knitted his eyebrows together. 'You really ought to take your emotions outta of the equation. Or keep them to yourself. He was hired purely for business. The more muscle and men in authority on the payroll the more power. Why'd you think Demato hasn't been whacked? He's still widely respected by all the right people. Cascarini couldn't touch him if he wanted to. His son maybe. Not Demato though. If

171

Cascarini did send Anton to put a bullet in the back of his head there'd be a full scale mob war.'

'There very nearly was,' DI Jason pointed out.

'Yeah.'

'What now?'

'I'm gonna start typing up that letter I promised Cascarini and his lawyer. I've already got an approval from the chief. He's in his office waiting for you to give him all the information we got this morning. Together we'll have to type it up for the report. And I guess I'll just have to keep trying on Dean's mobile. I'll leave messages and have to hope he answers for his own sake.'

DI Jason ran a hand over his coarse stubble. 'I don't think this the end of the bloodshed,' he said, gazing up at the fan on the ceiling twirling round and round.

'There will be more blood before this hunt is over.'

'I hope you're wrong,' Sark said, solemnly. 'But I think you're right.'

26.

THE RINGING of the mobile phone jarred him from his quiet desperation. Dean checked the rear view mirror. The black Ford Fiesta was still on his tail. He knew that the longer the phone rang the patience of either Paul or the detective inspector from CID would wear thin. However, there was nothing to report. All he wanted to do was put the hunter to the back of his busy mind and concentrate on driving. The morning had hurtled forwards like an out of control Flying Scotsman. He had to do a double-take at the digital alarm clock on the dashboard. 9:53am.

He'd already ignored one call. To do so again would make matters worse and place him under suspicion if it was the detective. After all, he had given his number and promised to answer and keep in touch. To do otherwise would go against him if he did survive.

Gripping the steering wheel and making sure he made no sudden jerks, Dean leant across and blindly groped the passenger seat. His fingertips knocked the mobile further away and very nearly off the seat. Still keeping his eyes glued to the road in front, he felt around for it. He breathed a sigh of relief when he had the phone in his grasp and sat upright again. Then he hit the green answer button.

'Hello?'

***

DI Sark punched the air in jubilation.

'Dean Ferris? It's me, Detective Inspector Sark.'

The reception was filled with staccato. But he managed to hear Dean's faraway voice.

'I thought you might call at some point,' Dean said, sounding out of breath.

'I take it you're on the road as we speak. Is that right?'

'Yeah. Not really safe to speak at the mo, to be perfectly honest.'

Sark nodded. 'Okay. Are you on your way to Tenby?'

'That's right, Detective,' Dean said, exasperated. 'How can I help you?'

'Well, you can help yourself by pulling over first of all.'

'I can't I'm on the motorway.'

'Which one?'

'The M4,' Dean said.

'Just pull over onto the hard shoulder and put your hazard lights on. I won't take up too much of your time.'

A long pause.

'Dean?'

'Yeah. I'm still here.'

'Did you hear what I said?'

'Yeah. But it's out of the question. I'm not being obstructive.'

This time it was Sark's turn to fall silent.

In spite of the staccato hissing down the line, DI Sark could swear he heard the jerk of every breath of Dean's that resonated into Sark. Each passing second heightened the tension and gave him a fresh stab of dread. What he was about to say next would make or break.

And all he could think of was Cascarini's weathered, leathery face, brow furrowed when he'd said to him to 'Let it go'.

'If he's following you then, that's fine,' he said. Immediately he felt glad that he'd let the thought go and not kept it bottled up inside him.

'What're you talkin' about, Detective?' Dean's voice had become hard, defensive.

Sark wasn't the slightest bit offended. In fact to a certain degree he admired the ex-drug squad policeman for his show of defiance.

'Look, Dean we've got an APB out for a black Ford Fiesta. We've also got a vague description that the man following you has dark hair, rugged features and dark eyes. If you're not pulling over 'cause you're being obstructive then we might have to have words. But if there's another reason, we might be able to help you...'

Another long pause.

'We've spoken to Paul Demato and Mario Cascarini this morning,' DI Sark went on, hoping to gain Dean's trust. 'And I didn't want to have to tell you this but not long after you'd left this morning police arrived at another crime scene on your street.'

'Another one as well as the two yesterday?' Dean said, incredulous.

'Yes.'

'Did someone die?'

'Afraid so.'

Sark could hear Dean cussing. Then he came back on the phone. 'Who?'

'One of the only neighbours that actually thought a lot of you regardless of what your other tosspot neighbours are gossiping.'

'Just tell me.'

'Cathy Groves... We think she saw something – or someone – she wasn't supposed to have. We believe she approached this someone and questioned him. This individual didn't have an answer so he shot her in the forehead. According to the medical examiner the only consolation is she died before she hit the floor.'

175

Silence.

'Dean? You still there? Speak to me. Please.'

'Fuckin' cocksucker!'

DI Sark had to snatch the phone away from his ear. In the background he could hear something slamming three times.

'I'm sorry. But lemme tell you something, we suspect the same guy to have killed Cathy as Tony and Sampson. The same guy that's currently following you right now. C'mon, man. I can't help you if you keep me in the dark.'

'What did Paul say?'

'Let's put it this way, he didn't come out and say what I think you're doing, but he did admit that if you were heading to Tenby could you make a short visit to Sandra Hill.'

'Piece of shit!'

'Listen,' Sark barked. This drew the attention of a plain-clothed policeman who stopped what he was doing and stared at the young detective. 'Listen,' Sark said in a much softer tone. 'Just listen for a sec. You're not in trouble, as such. What we really want is this Anton or "Mr Death" guy.'

'I don't believe that dizzy mother…'

'Enough of that! Here's what I believe,' Sark said talking over him. 'It's my understanding that the Hills aren't the most affluent of folks around. They don't go to Demato with their hands outstretched for a payout. They've got too much pride for that. They don't wanna know his business. But at the same time they don't prohibit Tobias from keeping in touch with his only uncle. They're struggling financially. Demato is aware of this. He said he feels like shit and that this catastrophe was caused by Leo. His bank account is frozen like a block of ice. Sandra won't answer his emails or his calls. She's in utter shock. Probably bitter and wishes cancer upon him. So he sends a friendly face with a stash of cash to pay for a good coffin and the other funeral expenses. God knows it costs a hell of a lot. Probably why most people cry at a funeral is not cause a loved one has passed away, but cause the relatives left behind have to pay exorbitant amounts to the funeral directors.'

'How'd you know this if Paul didn't come out and say so?'

'It's my job,' Sark said in an unpretentious voice. 'Also, you still owe him for the favour he did you by helping you out with your little problem coupla years back.'

'Yeah. Well you guys soon turned your back and showed how fickle you were, didn't you?'

'Not me personally,' Sark said. 'But I understand that certain people do seem to forget what you did for them yesterday. I can relate to that.'

'I gotta go through with it,' Dean said, desperate. 'You can't stop me.'

Then the familiar sound of a dialling tone rang in his ears.

'Damn it!' Sark slammed his fist down on the tabletop. He knew then what the slamming he heard was on Dean's end.

That might've been our last chance, he thought. *It might've been Dean's last chance too.*

27.

THE MISHAR FAMILY were heading westbound on the M4 that fateful morning. They'd not long left their home in Sutton Benger. They were headed for the Weston Super-Mare shopping precinct in Bristol.

Chris kept his gaze on the road ahead while his wife Jill typed their destination into her mobile. She and her husband knew the terrain but sometimes wasted time when they got into Bristol itself taking the wrong turnings. Sometimes they went around in circles. She remembered the time they'd both gone to Cardiff, Wales. Ideally it should have taken them approximately two hours give or take. Getting to Cardiff and into the city centre had been fairly straightforward but finding the museum had been another challenge entirely. They'd ended up arguing in the confines of the Volvo over whose mistake it was when they found themselves going down the wrong road. What was good about the robotic female voice giving directions was no one would be blamed. However, the female voice was too slow to declare what lane they ought to be in.

Jenny, their sweet, angelic five-year-old daughter with her mousy blonde hair in pigtails, sat quietly in the back seat. She was occupied by the colouring book Chris had purchased at WHSmith's two days ago. She also had a couple of children's story books.

Every now again when there was a junction to get off, the robotic female voice told to them to keep going on the M4. She was already annoying Chris by not pronouncing street names in their hometown correctly. The next junction would lead to Tombarton.

Chris tilted his head left and then right, stretching the taut muscles.

'You okay, hon?' Jill asked, checking her face in the sun visor's mirror.

'Yeah, just slept awkward, that's all.'

On his left-hand side a red Honda Civic matched him for speed and then slowly moved ahead.

'Whoa!' he exclaimed.

'What's the matter?'

'That car in front hasn't got a rear window.'

Jill stopped studying her reflection for crow's feet around her eyes. She folded the sun visor up and gazed ahead. When her eyes finally found the red Honda Civic ten meters or so ahead she saw what her husband meant.

'Look,' she said, alarmed. 'You can see the jagged pieces on either side.'

'Why hasn't he covered it up?' Chris blurted.

'That's happened recently,' Jill said, shocked by the revelation.

Chris snapped a finger at the side of the car. 'His wing mirror is missing as well.'

'Ohmigod.'

'Why hasn't he pulled over? Surprised he can drive like that.'

Husband and wife didn't need to say aloud that there was something amiss.

The damaged car moved further ahead. A black Ford Fiesta followed in its wake. At first neither Jill nor Chris paid it any heed. Then the driver's side window slid into the gap and a dark-haired thick set fellow leant out. This in itself was out of the ordinary. But the sight of the gun with a silencer made Jill and Chris gasp simultaneously. They both jolted in their seats as the man in the black Ford Fiesta fired. Two silver circles dented and discoloured the bodywork of the red Honda Civic.

'Shit!'

Jill normally would have scorned her husband for cussing in the company of their young, impressionable daughter. Instead she stared ahead, her mouth an empty cavern. Her lips stretched, contorting her youthful countenance.

'Slow down,' she croaked. Her voice crept up the walls of her cavernous mouth, barely audible.

'What?'

'Slow down,' she said again. Her mouth felt as though she'd swallowed cotton balls. 'Slow down. Back off and don't get involved.'

Chris could feel his cheeks rising from the conflagration burning inside. 'Go into the glove compartment and get my little notebook and biro.'

Jill knitted her eyebrows together, anxious. 'What for?'

'Just do it!' he barked.

'Mummy,' Jenny called from the back seat.

'What, sweetie?'

'Daddy said a bad word.'

'He didn't mean to. It just slipped out,' Jill said. And as she roamed around in the glove compartment she silently chastised herself for defending Chris's slip of the tongue. She made it seem as though now all of a sudden cussing was by-the-by. A contradiction to what she'd reciprocated to her daughter on previous occasions when the topic came up.

Thankfully, Jenny didn't protest.

Notebook and biro in trembling hands, Jill said, 'Now what?'

'I want you to write down the licence plate of that guy's car.'

'Which one?'

Chris momentarily took his eyes off the road and glowered at his wife.

'Really?'

'The guy in the Ford?' Jill said, voice quaking.

'Yes. God sake, Jill.'

'Just making sure.'

She then leant forward to her passenger window and jotted down the license plate and double-checked.

Then the man in the black Ford Fiesta slid back into the car and turned. His ebony eyes fixed upon Jill's. She felt a block of ice envelope her pounding heart. Invisible fingers traced the nape of her neck all the way down to the bottom of her spine. Her thoughts froze and her nerves jangled. Pinpricks of blood vessels burst and red blotches surfaced on her quivering cheeks.

When the man raised the .38 handgun at them they both screamed.

Jill ducked. In the next second, a tinkling of broken glass filled her ears over the sound of her jackhammer heartbeat. Something too fast to comprehend severed the air and ripped into solid substance. A hollow *thunk* followed.

Jill craned her head around and her eyes protruded. Chris spat a wad of dark blood onto the dashboard. His eyes rolled languidly, losing all focus. Arterial blood had splattered the driver's window.

Jill felt the car decelerate and feared for their lives. They were sitting ducks in the middle of the M4 for traffic in their wake to slam right through them, wiping out each and every one of them as if the Volvo were made a tracing paper.

'Take the wheel,' Chris said, through fits of coughing and spitting.

Jill peered over the rim of the door and saw the black Ford Fiesta had gone. Breath escaped her in great wheezing exhalations. She took the wheel in a white-knuckled grip, seeing the knobs of her knuckles threatening to rip through the thin flesh.

'What shall I do, Chris?' she screeched.

'Hard shoulder,' Chris managed, fighting for consciousness.

Jill forgot to check the wing mirror. But even if she did she was in the wrong seat to see clearly if it was safe to do so.

An artic lorry bellowed its horn. Jill flicked the turn signal down, indicating to turn left. Chris slumped down in the driver's seat. His eyes closed over. Dark blood gushed from the wound on the left-hand side of his chest. Jill was no doctor or surgeon but she knew the bullet wound was serious.

The Volvo swerved erratically onto the hard shoulder. Tyres screeched. Jill had to struggle against the wheel to stop the car smashing into the barrier and plummeting down the bank.

'CHRIS!' she screamed. 'HIT THE FUCKIN' BRAKE!'

Chris's eyelids flickered but refused to lift open. Yet his right foot managed to stomp the brake pedal enough to bring the Volvo to a skidding halt. A plume of dust cascaded around the car.

Jill reached down and yanked the handbrake on with the last of her diminishing strength. Her top half collapsed into her husband's lap. Her chest rose and feel far too fast to be healthy.

The sound of Jenny's sobbing made her rise. Then she faced her daughter's tear-streaked face scrunched up.

'Don't ever let me hear you talk like that. You hear me?'

Jenny nodded, sobbing uncontrollably. Her lips parted. 'Yes, Mummy.'

28.

INSTINCTIVELY, Dean ducked when two bullets struck the rear of the car. Metal punctured. Then all of a sudden the gunfire ceased as abruptly as it'd begun. He didn't know what was worse, the gunfire or the absence of noise that followed.

Sitting upright again he glimpsed the rear-view mirror. His breath caught in his throat. Anton had backed off and was now pointing his weapon at a navy Volvo. Dean jolted a second after the recoil of the gun joggled the muscular arm of his assassin. A hole appeared in the Volvo's windscreen. Dean could tell the driver had been hit by the way his head snapped back and he toppled over from the waist up.

'Jesus Christ!'

He released the pressure from the accelerator to see what would transpire next. There wasn't another gunshot but the Volvo swerved out of control and eventually veered hazardously across the road onto the hard shoulder. He saw the blue engine smoke billow from the exhaust.

He didn't know whether the wounded driver was dead or alive. What perplexed him beyond reason was why Anton had fired at the man and woman in the Volvo in the first instance. Then it came to him and he couldn't help but feel a rush of hope circulate his mind.

The Volvo had been close enough for the driver and the passenger to see him being attacked. Anton had noticed this as well. He'd fired in desperation to keep the onlookers from pursuing or seeing anything else of a sinister nature. He knew it was selfish. But if the driver had survived – or even if he didn't – then they'd go to the police and report what they'd witnessed.

This would make Anton's task even more arduous. It might bring the police closer to apprehending him once and for all.

Then another thought entered his consciousness. He suddenly realised that his hunter would not stop until either he or Dean were dead. However, Dean didn't want anyone to get involved. The longer this journey became the more he wanted everyone else to stay out of the duel. This was between him and the hunter. He would kill Anton or die trying. That's what he wanted. That's what he desired.

He floored the accelerator and shot forward…

29.

DI SARK and DI Jason were sitting side by side in their swivel chairs. They had
already written a letter for Mario Cascarini's lawyer to use
during the trial that would state he had been cooperative with a
murder case. In some respects it wasn't worth the paper it was
printed on. Nevertheless, it might shave some time off
Cascarini's sentencing and innumerable fines.

Now they were using each other's notepads to type out a
statement regarding their homicide case. DI Jason was better at
typing. Sark read out what he'd written in his notepad, making
sure everything went in chronological order with the accurate
times, dates and venues.

'What'd the chief say?' DI Sark asked, putting his can of
Diet Coke down.

DI Jason shrugged. 'He's a bit surprised we got Cascarini
and Demato to say anything, to be frank. Especially Demato. I
mean he practically gave his boy up.'

'Only 'cause there's nothing illegal 'bout helping out a
family member with funeral costs.'

'Maybe. But shit, that Cascarini could talk underwater.'

They both laughed at that.

'Chief said that as interesting as it all was it wasn't much
use,' DI Jason went on. 'Although, it does give us a pretty
good idea and preparation for what'll go down if we do cross
paths with the guy with no actual name. And what he said does
make a lotta sense.'

'It's not really worth shit though if we can't stop more people from being killed,' Sark said. He ran a hand through his thick, brown hair.

'We've done what we can. And anyway, a guy who works for Tesco garage reported a flustered looking man filling his car up and darting out again. He also noticed that the car was red Honda Civic.'

Sark looked up from his lap, intrigued.

'Rear window was missing; little pieces of glass clinging to the sides.'

'What else did he say?' Sark rubbed his stubble. 'Did he see a black Ford in the vicinity?'

DI Jason shook his head. 'He only reported it because the guy had sped out of the filling station and didn't stop at the junction. Just kept on going until he was on the main road again.'

'That was Dean no doubt.'

'Yeah. But like the chief said, we can only do what we can. We've got more information in one morning than most detectives get in a few weeks of investigation. We got an APB out on our suspect. At some point between here and Tenby, Wales, something's gotta give.'

Sark read from his notepad and his partner typed down the words onto the blank page on the computer screen.

'You do need to try Dean again,' DI Jason said.

Sark noticed his partner kept his gaze on the screen when he made this comment. 'He won't talk to me. He wasn't too pleased Demato had given us as much as he did. But what worries me is he won't back off.'

DI Jason finished the last sentence. He hit the full-stop button and pivoted in his chair. 'It's not gonna make the slightest difference,' he said. 'You heard Cascarini. This Anton – or whoever – is a killing machine. The money is merely an object. Even if Dean burnt the money or surrendered, he'd still kill him.'

'I spoke with some guys who knew Dean on the Drug Squad,' Sark said, staring vacantly at the cluttered desktop. 'They said they were glad he was a cop and not a gangster or druggie. Because if it came down to it, there weren't many men on the force who'd be able to beat him in any type of fight.'

DI Jason snorted laughter. 'So you're saying we've got two men out there who are modern day Rambo's?'

DI Sark shook his head, staring despondently at the illuminated screen. The pulsing cursor matched his pulse. 'No. Rambo wasn't real. What frightens me is when these two are out of choices they'll fight to the death in the middle of broad daylight.'

'It doesn't make sense. Dean was running like a scared cat this morning.'

'I don't disbelieve the fuel attendant or the officers who reported back to us. If the guy said Dean was rushing about like a scalded cat then that's what happened. But when a cat is chased for so long and the hunter keeps on pursuing, a choice has to be made. Keep on running until you're inevitably caught and killed or...'

'Or?' DI Jason said, wondering why the pause.

'Or turn and swing a razor sharp claw in the eye of its pursuer,' Sark finished.

DI Jason didn't have anything to say. He let what his partner said burrow into his mind.

'Dean will run for as long as necessary. Then another side will surface. There's a good side and a bad side to us all. When all the good has been pushed to the limit – to the breaking point – the bad side erupts from within like a lion bursting out of its cage.'

30.

ANTON slowed the Ford and indicated to slip onto the hard shoulder. In his rear-view the Volvo had come to a skidding halt. Its hazard lights were flashing. He waited for a 4x4 to go past along with a fast sports car that resembled a Porsche. Then he pushed the Ford's hazard light button, removed the handbrake and shifted the gear into reverse.

The engine whined as he drove backwards a hundred yards. Then he hit the brake. Applied the handbrake again and saw the Volvo parked twenty meters or so behind him. Through the broken windscreen, through the webbed crack, he saw the woman he'd made eye contact with moving frantically in her seat. She shook with shock she never knew existed until right then. He watched her fumbling with her seat belt, pulling out of her seat before the belt snapped back into its holder.

He reached over and opened the glove box and took out a brown paper bag. It was folded to keep it from wrinkling or tearing. In methodical fashion, the assassin undid his own seat belt and opened the brown paper sack up. Then he slid it down over his head. It reached his neckline, completely covering his face.

***

Jill couldn't stop shaking. Her nerves were frayed beyond the point of no return. Chris's lifeless head kept falling into her lap. He weighed a tonne. His face had turned pallid. Yet his black, matted hair and brow dripped with perspiration.

Doing her utmost to control her quivering limbs, Jill willed herself to try and find her husband's pulse in his neck. She couldn't move into position due to the unexpected burden and the seat belt wrapping itself tightly around her neck. Her flesh burned where the belt dug in. The heavy metal drummer beating her heart pounded into her head.

Worse, Jenny had started wailing. Jill tried to hush her. Nevertheless, the sight of Chris's slumped form and the wound in his chest oozing blood did nothing to placate either of them. Jill didn't bother making any further attempt to quieten her traumatised little girl. The task would be fruitless. How could she possibly ask Jenny to stay calm when she couldn't?

She managed to unclip the seat belt and barely flinched when the clasp struck her cheek. Pivoting in her seat, she used both hands to lift Chris upright again. His head flopped to the right and thudded the driver's window.

'Shit! Sorry Chris,' Jill said, wincing at her clumsiness.

As she was reaching out to feel for a pulse, the sound of a car reversing nearby caught her undivided attention. For a split second she'd thought and hoped it was a motorist who'd spotted them and stopped to offer assistance.

At the sight of the black Ford Jill lost control of her bladder. Pinpricks stabbed her rosy red cheeks. Realisation seeped into her marrow and crushed her throat. A strangled wheezing escaped her. The horror didn't relent. It escalated. It hadn't crossed her mind that the man in the Ford would come back to finish what he started.

Her entire physical self went into spasmodic jerks. Hands flailed for something in her coat pocket. She whimpered and kicked her legs up and down.

Jenny could see her mother through her teary-eyed vision. Her wailing had ceased when misery and upset got replaced by panic. Her tiny, smooth hands curled and uncurled. Her chest hitched, hurting her. She sensed a change in the quality of air.

Something far beyond her limited comprehension was befalling them. Her subconscious informed her that she was merely witnessing the shrieking woman in the passenger seat that had taken over her mother. Then, as though a light switch had been flicked, the shrieking ceased.

Jenny watched dumbfounded as the mobile slipped from her mother's clammy grasp. It bounced off the seat and hit foot well. Something else was happening. Something that had stopped the frantic behaviour. Something far worse. She followed her mother's unblinking gaze out the window and knew something unthinkable was about to happen.

Jill sat catatonic. Her eyes bulged, stretching the optical nerves.

Walking towards her was a tall, broad shouldered man wearing a brown paper sack with two dark eyeholes approaching.

In front of me I see death.

***

He walked around the front of the Volvo and saw the mobile phone fall out of the woman's lifeless grasp and out of sight. He came around to the passenger side, and without any hesitation whatsoever raised the .38.

Pop! Pop! Pop...

And just like that Jill Mishar was dead.

The three bullet holes in her forehead trickled dark red liquid. Her head thumped the passenger window. A trickle of blood weaved its way down the glass Had Anton seen Jill inadvertently bump her husband's lifeless head against the driver's window he'd have thought it ironic.

He opened the passenger door and stepped aside as Jill toppled out. Then he fired another bullet into the back of Chris Mishar's skull. He couldn't afford to leave any stone unturned.

Then he saw the little girl and froze.

Her presence took a turn for the unexpected. He halted briefly, contemplating his next move.

A part of him said, *Put a bullet in the little girl's forehead. Let her join her mummy and daddy in heaven.* But another part of him that distantly resembled the boy who walked in golden cornfields with his doting mother wouldn't permit such a deed.

The little girl was wheezing like an asthmatic.

Anton removed the brown paper sack, collected the cartridges and the mobile. He retracted himself out of the Volvo and hurled the mobile into the dense foliage. Then he strode back towards the Ford. He reversed the Ford to within a few yards of the Volvo and killed the engine. He carried his arsenal and other equipment from the Ford's boot and placed it in the Volvo's boot. Once that was achieved he opened the back door and slid over to the little girl.

Even terrified beyond her wits, she was the most beautiful and innocent creature he'd ever seen. Terminating such a creature that wasn't part of the hunt and had no bearing on his task would be regrettable.

He raised an index finger to his moist lips.

Dutifully, and quite remarkably, the little girl didn't make a sound.

Hauling the cadavers would have been effortless had the location been somewhere deserted. Instead Anton had to drag Jill out of Volvo and carry her to the Ford. He placed her in the passenger seat and rested her head against the passenger window. He had to wait patiently as a line of cars shot past. Then he did the same with Chris's body.

The hauling of two adult bodies, not to mention the dead weight, didn't even make him breathe the slightest bit heavier. Calm and steady. His heart rate probably hadn't ticked north of sixty. The studious act of waiting for the right time to perform the deed had irritated him. It cost him time. Time that his prey would use to put as much distance between them.

Nevertheless, so far no one had been any the wiser.

From the passing motorists' point of view it probably looked as though one car had broken down and another motorist had pulled over. Or two cars belonging to the same family had decided to pull over unexpectedly. After that he'd carried the little girl in her child's bumper seat to the Ford and placed her gently on the back seat. Then he took one long last look at one of nature's beautiful creations.

Using the petrol can that he'd traded from the boot of the Ford to the Volvo, Anton filled the tank up. He placed his shotgun, fitted with a cylindrical silencer, and his .38, on the passenger seat and got behind the wheel and started the engine.

He didn't even glimpse in the direction of the black Ford as he rejoined the M4 and accelerated.

The image of the little girl brought back the memory of that fateful night in his own childhood. It could well have been him that had entered his family home that night when he was a boy and decapitated his parents.

That was the only reason Jenny Mishar had been spared.

One single tear escaped him and ran down his cheek, nothing more.

The moment didn't even last long enough to qualify as an emotion. Merely a trace of what he once was at that age.

31.

DEAN was nearing the River Severn. He'd cross the Severn Bridge into Wales.

Traffic would join the M4 from the M48. He eased his foot off the go pedal and flexed his fingers, seeing the dense traffic pile up.

He didn't want to assume that he was out of sight from his pursuer. Nevertheless, merely not seeing the black Ford in his rear view made a nice change. He'd spent more time in the last couple of hours consulting the rear-view mirror than he did the road in front. And for good reason.

Crossing the Severn Bridge sent a biting cold. The bones in his hands crunched. His teeth chattered. The hair on his forearms stood on end. He knew other motorists would notice the absence of the rear window. They'd point and discuss it.

If he got to a filling station he might be able to do something about it. But that didn't seem likely. He wasn't comfortable with the weapons and briefcase full of money in his possession. God only knew where the money had come from. Who'd had to die for it? And although he doubted it wasn't drug money, it didn't mean Paul had got it by unconventional means either.

The mobile shrilled to life. Dean could guess who it was without even looking at it. He didn't want to talk to anyone right now. DI Sark was too intuitive for his own good. And Paul, who was ringing him constantly, wanting to know everything that was said during his interrogation had practically given him up.

What DI Sark said about the authorities being more interested in apprehending or taking down this 'Mr Death' dude was a strong possibility. However, Dean was far too deep now to extract himself. Some of the blame would inevitably fall upon him, thanks to Paul blabbing. Worse, if he did manage to get the money to Sandra Hill and he lived to tell the tale and his pursuer vanished again, he'd be the one who'd be apprehended. And this time there would be no help from Paul or anyone else. If they put him in prison then they might as well give him the death sentence.

Here he found himself behind his ruined car stuck in limbo. There was no one to trust. This seemed to be the case not just now but during his entire life. His family had disowned him. They'd cut all ties with him as had his girlfriend when he'd lost his badge. Sure, Paul's attorney's got him off the hook. But in the end that was all so Paul could use him as another pawn. And here he was now. If he hadn't agreed to do this deed, he'd be as good as dead. If he got detained by the police between his current location and Tenby or even thereafter he'd be as good as dead. And finally, if Anton caught up to him, he'd be as good as dead.

He recalled times when his colleagues had applauded him after a tough undercover case. They looked at him with genuine awe at his bravery. He'd smelt death and survived. He'd even touched death with pale fingertips and survived.

But now putting his life on the line to take down numerous crack-heads and keeping A-Class drugs off the streets was all for nothing. His insides roiled with rage. His biceps flexed. Veins surfaced on taut skin. One lousy mistake had driven the proverbial stake through his pounding heart.

He knew people who suffered greatly often talked about the world being against them. This is what they must have meant. To be endlessly trying to do good and being despised for his troubles. Not once during the myriad of emotions did he ever consider taking the money for himself. If nothing else, didn't that make him a decent man?

A sign welcomed him to Wales. He smiled wanly. He was halfway there. Furthermore, he was familiar with Wales. His ex-girlfriend had hailed from Wales. They often drove to and fro so she could visit her parents. They lived in Neath. A nice, quiet little town.

Another more harrowing thought came to him, shattering the tranquillity. If Anton was still trailing him then Dean would end the chase. He suddenly realised what had been bothering him from the moment he'd grudgingly accepted the task. The source of his fear wasn't from putting himself in a perilous situation. No, not at all. It hadn't made sense even when he'd almost jumped out of his skin upon leaving his home. And when his rear window had been shot to bits it hadn't been fear he'd felt. It was adrenaline.

As his memory had highlighted his consciousness, risking his life had never bothered him. He'd never even thought of himself as a tough guy. Or dare he think it, a hero. So it wasn't fear of dying or being mortally wounded. Although he didn't relish the idea either. It was being chased. The hunt itself.

Since yesterday afternoon he'd been hunted and toyed with. He'd been chased like a scalded cat, running hell-bent away from the fire. And he supposed, in hindsight, he had acted like a scared cat.

But now the time for running was drawing to a close. Now the time came to turn and fight back. Yet Dean needed to extract any bravado. Just because he knew the only way to confront true evil was to face it head on did not mean to behave recklessly.

To execute this plan he needed to use intelligence, not muscle. He had the arsenal to protect and hurt his hunter. What he needed now was familiar terrain. A foreign place to his hunter. Then he'd have an advantage.

His heart bit slower, steadier.

Dean nodded inwardly, approving of the idea.

The incessant thrumming of tyres on tarmac soothed him.

32.

SANDRA HILL had lived in Tenby, Wales, for the last twenty-three years. She and her husband Darren Hill had moved to a council house opposite Marsh Road. The quiet, scenic cul-de-sac of Newell Hill had given them an ideal and humble setting to raise their only child. The exterior of their home was painted a sky-blue; not all that unusual than the other homes in Tenby. The town was an old-fashioned cobble-stoned seaside attraction. The beach, stores and pubs were a ten-minute walk away.

Tobias' cadaver was currently stored in the morgue. His body would be released by Saturday, in three days' time, ready for the funeral. His untimely death had occurred almost two weeks ago now. Yet time had blinked past

Sandra in a daze, as though this was all in her imagination. Of course that wasn't the case. Nevertheless, she'd never even considered still being alive and fairly young to be present at her son's funeral.

There were times when her brother, Paul, would call her up and query what she wanted for Christmas of her Birthday. She knew he meant well. But on occasion she could hear the undertone of conceitedness in his voice. They both knew that they lived worlds apart.

Paul Demato was well-known amongst the underworld. He was the man with judges, barristers, solicitors, doctors, specialists and even the police on the payroll. Of course no one would admit to being his acquaintance. But whenever Paul needed a favour he could buy anyone from any profession to come to his aid.

Contemplating it now made Sandra's tummy rumble. Her gorge rose. Bile burned her throat. He'd truly believed he was untouchable. That he'd actually achieved something of great importance and worthwhile. When all he'd done was attain enough men who knew what buttons to push to force others to succumb to his desires. And here she was living an honest, humble existence. Yet there was something tremendously earnest in struggling like everyone else. Sandra had never ordered the death of another human being to get further ahead in life. She'd never needed to threaten someone in authority to do something corrupt or to turn a blind eye. As children they hadn't had much, save each other. The only thing that kept them from becoming strangers was Tobias. He loved his Uncle Paul and his cousin, Leo.

Sandra knew Tobias didn't ask questions regarding his uncle's business. He didn't care. He was one of the rare people who treated others as he found them. He never listened or believed rumours, merely because someone told him. Tobias always said, 'Innocent till proven guilty.'

She recalled the day he'd come from comprehensive school with his final exam results. All A's and B's. He was beaming from ear to ear. Then he phoned Leo and asked him how he'd done, seen as they were both the same age. It turned out Leo hadn't done quite as well, but was nonetheless satisfied overall. When he'd come off the phone Tobias sat down on the sofa next to her. And in one sentence her joy was instantly replaced by a deliberating dread snaking up her spine.

'I told Leo my marks,' Tobias began as though faraway. 'He said that was great news. Uncle Paul was there too. He wanted to know. He always said I had a good head on my shoulders. I mentioned that I was interested in doing something like being an accountant or working with computers. Organising files for businesses and so on...'

Sandra knew it was coming. An overwhelming urge to interrupt tickled her parted lips. Instead she willed herself to let her son finish what he was going to say.

'Uncle Paul said that could easily be arranged,' Tobias had continued, evidently taken aback by the proposal. 'I wasn't quite sure what he meant, and he said that he'd pay for me to go to either Cambridge or Oxford University to become a qualified accountant or a financial advisor. If I was interested and I passed then there'd be a job waiting for me in the family business.'

At that precise moment Sandra Hill's heart turned to stone. Everything what she'd hoped for her only child had come true. Yet in doing so had opened a can of worms. Her rich and successful brother, who could buy anything or anyone at any given time, was now lining her baby up to work for him in the mob business.

Tobias had previously enquired why Uncle Paul and his mother never got together for Christmas, birthdays or any other special occasions. And at first when he first started enquiring at the age of eight, Sandra told him it was because of the distance. Nevertheless, as he got older and inevitably wiser it became apparent there was much more than distance keeping the siblings apart.

Tobias would spend the weekend, no more, over at Leo's house. When he returned words would spill out of his mouth too fast. She even had to remind him to slow down and breathe.

'Mum! Mum! Leo said Uncle Paul bought a villa in Spain. And in the summer they're going to Barbados. He asked if I can go. Can I? Please?'

This was the worst type of pain. A part of her desperately wanted Tobias to see a part of the world he'd never see again. But two weeks living the life of luxury and being under the influence of her brother would misguide her son. Two weeks of taking these pleasures for granted would distort the boy's mind.

Before long he'd want to know how Uncle Paul and Leo could do these wonderful things, go to these amazing places when they couldn't.

The only holiday they ever had was in the spring. Their neighbours – the Bale's – would let them use their caravan located at Kiln Holiday Park roughly half a mile down the road.

Watching his face crumble, tears brimming, wrenched her heart. In some respects her refusal was cruel or at least unfair. He didn't hate her or storm out of the room and slam a door. Perhaps if he'd reacted like that it might have made it easier to cope with. Instead he stared at her, crestfallen, unable to fathom her refusal. Not only that, she wouldn't even entertain a discussion behind her decision.

'What's the family business?' Tobias had asked.

When she thought about it, Sandra realised then that at some point during her son's life she'd have to tell him who her brother was and what he did. She didn't have a choice in the matter. As much as her brother seemed to be a different person than the boy she'd grown up with, for her son's sake he had a right to know.

This was in June. Tenby was a seaside town that came to life during the spring and summer. Tourists from all over came to get away from their busy, city lives and relax.

Tobias often said, 'When I'm feeling my worst a nice long walk on the beach listening to nothing except the crashing of waves and the squawk of gulls always makes me feel better.'

Sandra never forgot when he made that comment two years ago.

'Come with me to the beach,' she'd said. 'I'll tell you everything you need to know.'

And that's what they'd done. They'd strolled across the beach, leaving two trails of footprints in their wake. And Sandra had told him everything.

At the end Tobias had seemed full of melancholy and incredulity. 'How'd he end up being a mob boss, Mum?'

Sandra had shaken her head. 'I'm not sure of all the intricate details, sweetheart. What I do know is that your brother and I struggled and had a tough upbringing. Neither of us did well in school, through no fault of our own. God knows we tried but we just had too many other worries on our minds.'

Tobias had lowered himself and pulled his knees up to his chest. 'This is why you never let me go on holiday with them or spend any longer than the weekend, isn't it?' His tone wasn't the slightest accusatory. He just asked it by way of conversation.

Sandra had lowered herself next to him. The resplendent sun speckled iridescent hues across the rippling waves. From their vantage point it looked as though the ocean had swallowed the rainbow.

'I always felt really bad about that,' she'd said. 'I felt like I was holding you back, and being selfish. But I wasn't.' She paused, bracing herself to carry on. 'Uncle Paul isn't the only mob boss in the country. But he is a very powerful and influential man. Money is power. If you have money or men working beneath you doing what you say, when you say it, that's power. But there are others like him. It's hard to explain…' she trailed off.

A wave crashed in the distance, waterfall effect.

'You only need to look at someone the wrong way or say something that offends someone else and before you know it you're lying face-down in the earth in the middle of nowhere.

'I was always afraid that if you were seen in Uncle Paul's presence they might mistake you as another son or Leo.'

Tobias' eyebrows came together. 'I don't understand. What's Leo got to do with this?'

'Nothing,' Sandra had said. 'But sometimes to hurt a protected man, like my brother, they might hurt someone close to him instead.'

'Why?'

'To make him listen. To make him take them serious. To hurt him. Men like that believe in vengeance. An eye for an eye. But men like that have too much dominance and not enough sense to realise that nothing lasts forever. Men like that don't realise that an eye for an eye and the world goes blind. They don't take into account that all the shortcuts they've taken will catch up with them. I like to believe in an old adage that goes something like, "what goes around comes around". In Hinduism the devotees believe in Karma.'

'What's that?'

'That a person's actions affecting his or fate will come back to haunt them in his or her next reincarnation.'

'That's why we never see each other on special occasions, isn't it?'

Sandra nodded solemnly. 'But that's not the only reason,' she added in haste. 'Uncle Paul may well seem like a nice, caring uncle. And, to a certain extent, he is. He is a kind, caring uncle who loves you very much. But there's always some hidden agenda. My brother never does anyone a favour without contriving something well in advance, even years. If he helps you now you'd be for ever indebted to him. There'd be no refusing him if you disagreed on something. There's his way and there's a hole in the ground.'

Tobias arched his left eyebrow at his mum. 'I somehow doubt Uncle Paul would kill me,' he said.

'No. But he'd order someone to do it for him. And if he didn't go that far he'd make your life a misery. He'd pay journalists and tutors to conjure up a story about how you cheated in your exams. You'd be followed day and night. No one would employ you. The minute you stepped out of line.

Even if it was going three miles over the limit on a deserted road you'd get a fine. Or something of a similar nature.'

Gulls circled overhead. Tobias and Sandra rose from the sand and started walking. If you stayed in one place long enough in plain sight of seagulls they both knew not to be surprised if one of them shat on you.

'There's a perfectly apt reason why I don't stay in touch with Uncle Paul,' Sandra went on. 'A part of me loves him. But I think the part of me only really loves the sweet, sad boy who comforted me on those cold winter nights when there was only one quilt and a draught coming through the attic.'

Tobias didn't utter a word for five minutes. Then he'd said: 'Okay, Mum. I know you'd never lie to me. It's just I really wanted to go to uni so I could get a good job and do well for myself.'

Sandra had slung an arm over his shoulder and rested her brow against the side of his head. 'You will,' she said loud enough so he could hear over the breaking of waves. 'You will.'

Tobias' trust in her never faltered, not once.

And yet now an empty cavern in her chest that had once housed her heart suffocated her. In spite of her advice. In spite of Tobias' unwavering trust, her son was dead.

Once in a blue moon he spent a weekend with his cousin. And that was the reason – the exact same reason Sandra had urged him to take the righteous path – he was being buried long before a boy his age should have been. That was the reason Sandra had lost her only child and hadn't slept properly in the last couple of weeks and would never sleep peacefully ever again.

33.

DI **JASON** was reading through the statement he and DI Sark had put together, checking for any typos or grammatical errors. His partner had gone outside for some fresh air. DI Jason also knew his partner needed to be alone to mull everything over. In a lot of ways he admired him. However, sometimes a case was a lost cause. Sometimes you had to move on. Otherwise you'd end up going crazy, going over and over the same details until none of it made an iota of sense.

But Sark was too conscientious. He cared. You weren't supposed to have any emotional ties towards a case as it could affect one's actions. Nevertheless, when an innocent person died and they went to investigate he'd always catch a glimpse of Sark staring into the vacant eyes of the victim. DI Jason used to wonder why. But as they spent more time together and worked cases in close proximity, he believed Sark was searching for something. Or perhaps the absence of the victim's soul fascinated and appalled him simultaneously.

He saved the document to the computer's hard drive and on the key drive for back-up. Then he used the cursor to bring the little arrow of the print symbol and clicked.

The laser printer whirred to life and coughed out a hard copy onto the tray. He left it there for the ink to dry and leant back in his chair. Jason stifled a yawn, picked up the written statement and carried it over to his chief's glass-enclosed office. Through the pane he could see his superior on the phone. He returned the paperwork to his desk and waited.

Two minutes later Sark returned. He nodded a greeting to his partner and sat down on his side of the desk and took the phone out of its cradle.

'Who're you calling?'

'The wife,' Sark said.

DI Jason understood that on occasion when a case wasn't going particularly well some detectives did something or spoke to someone which had nothing to do with work. It helped them cope with the responsibility and the stress. Fresh air and talking to his wife was Sark's way of coping.

DI Jason was fortunate that he was able to extract himself mentally from a case. A lot of officers who'd had to fire their gun or witness a death were usually given a leave of absence. However, instead of doing nothing the force would send them to a counsellor to discuss their feelings.

Both Jason and Sark had yet to open fire. Nevertheless, the chief did ask them on a regular basis if there was anything disturbing them and if they were sleeping and eating well.

If a policeman, no matter what rank, wasn't taking care of themselves or functioning properly, they were a risk to themselves and to others. Lack of sleep or nourishment could affect their decisions and cost someone their lives or ruin an entire case by not adhering to the correct procedure.

DI Jason only pondered this because of what Cascarini had said about the man they were after. Not many men on the force thought about dying. Sure they put their lives on the line all the time, but the minute you started really worrying about such things and letting fear control you it was time to retire or go back to being a PCSO in your district.

If you love someone with all your heart, as much as you love your wife, you won't gamble with a life, Cascarini had said. *Anton doesn't have that. That's what makes him so deadly. The only fear he has is failure. Let it go...*

DI Jason recited this in his mind as he watched his partner talking on the phone.

Then he thought of his duty. To serve and to protect. Maybe it was the fact that he and Sark had love and compassion made them feel for the victims and their grieving families.

When he'd stepped out of the Groves' family home and into the sunshine his anger outweighed his fear. His determination overwhelmed his own wellbeing. Going into that cosy home and listening to Andrew tell them about what kind of person his wife had been was what drove him to fight for justice and to prevent anyone else suffering the same fate.

A hand clamped down on his shoulder jolted him from his reverie. He gazed up and saw his chief detective inspector towering over him. His face was a mask of serious concern.

'What is it, Chief?'

'They found the black Ford Fiesta...'

34.

DEAN was at a Texaco filling station on the outskirts of Cardiff city centre. His wrecked car wouldn't make it much longer on the quarter tank. Also, due to the constant gust of wind howling through the rear window his hearing was muffled.

When he stepped out of the car he groaned. The muscles in his calves and thighs screamed in protest, numb with lactic acid. It was only when attempting to stand next to the petrol pump, stretching, that he realised how much tension he had. He almost fell out of the car. For a split second he thought the bottom half of him was still in the Honda. Then an asinine thought suggested he might be paralysed.

Nevertheless, as he stretched his legs taut, feeling returned slowly. He caught a glimpse of his reflection in the passenger window and realised he'd be perfect for a zombie extra in one of George A. Romero's living dead films.

He shook out his feet and leant back, relishing the pull in his hamstrings and back. This was why many drivers took a couple of breaks during long distance driving. It wasn't merely to fill up the tank. Sometimes they needed to get out of being in the same position, unmoving for long hours.

A thick blanket of exhaustion crushed his shoulders into a hunched posture. His whole head felt like it housed a fire and pins and needles afflicted his hands as he squeezed the nozzle. When the tank was full again, Dean returned the nozzle to its holder. Then he fastened the cap back on. He made sure to stretch his legs as he ambled across the filling station to the kiosk.

The fan blowing hot air directly above the doorway caressed his exposed head and shoulders. Dean got his bearings and crossed to the refrigerator and shelves that stocked soft drinks and juice. He grabbed a Pepsi Max and picked up a Yorkie chocolate bar on his way to the counter.

'Hey, love,' the obese and bespectacled woman attendant said.

Dean didn't know what she was going to blurt out, but her anxiety surfaced through the layers of skin.

'You got blood all the way down the side of your neck. You been in some kinda accident or what?'

Dean stood like a dithering wreck, unsure what the safest response would be.

'Yeah...' he trailed off. The nothingness that ensued was unsettling. 'Yeah. Uh, some tosspot bumped into the back of me.'

'You got whiplash, love?'

'Little bit,' Dean said, nodding. Then he stopped nodding.

The obese but cordial attendant shifted her ample butt and faced the window. The rolls of flab that had swallowed her neck quivered. 'Christ on a bike! You ain't got no back window!'

Dean sighed inwardly. 'Yeah. It shattered on impact,' he said, cringing at his lie.

'You sure as shit must've been hit real hard then, mister.'

'Just a bit.'

'You called the police?' the attendant asked, pushing her black lens specs up on her broad squishy nose.

'Yes. They told me to drive to the nearest station. So here I am.' He forced a smile.

'But you can't go drivin' off without no back window. How 'bout I give you one of our black rubbish bags so you can cover it up? Least till you get a new window... or car.'

Dean appreciated the offer, and was in two minds to accept. However, he didn't want anyone else getting involved. He'd end up stranded. And if he did bump into a patrol officer how would he explain the guns and twenty grand?

'No, it's okay. I'm almost there now.' With that said he took out three ten-pound notes and laid them on the counter.

'Still can't let you leave here with your car like that.'

'What?' Dean said, flushing a beetroot hue.

'Against the law. If you caused an accident or got hurt and I knew 'bout it I'd get into trouble. Plus, it'd be on my conscience.'

I don't believe this shit. I'm gonna get outdone by some busybody's conscience.

'Don't make me call the police on you,' the attendant said. She looked solemn at Dean, pleading with him not to force her to do this.

'I don't have any tape,' he said, matter-of-factly.

'We do. Just stick the big black plastic bag over the window,' she said, smiling warmly at him. 'And go to our toilet and get yourself cleaned up. You might need some medical attention.'

'It's just a scratch,' Dean said, trying to diffuse the situation.

'That may well be the case. Still, you're on CCTV and it's my duty to see that you are all right to drive away from here safely.'

Dean exhaled slowly, both from fatigue and exhaustion. 'Don't exactly have much of a choice in the matter when you put it like that, do I?'

'Uh, huh.'

'Where's your toilet?'

'Men's room behind the magazine stand on your right.'

Dean was about to walk towards the magazine and newspaper stand when the attendant said, 'Aren't you forgetting something?'

Pivoting, Dean rolled his eyes as the attendant proffered his change.

'Thanks,' he muttered.

'I'll go get the tape and a black rubbish bag,' she said, pleased that he'd listened to her advice.

Suppose it doesn't make any difference if he catches up with you now. You know you two are gonna have to cross paths at some time. Just don't want it to happen when my back is turned and when I least expect it.

***

A brown Volvo slowed as it took the turning off the three-lane roundabout and crawled past the McDonald's and KFC restaurants. Then the driver stopped abruptly as the Texaco filling station came into view.

A man driving a Fiat Doblo stood on the brakes, screeching to a halt. He narrowly avoided going into the back of the stationary Volvo. He blasted his horn, and poked his head out the window. 'You fuckin wanker!' he bellowed, veins surfacing on his neck like blue cables.

Anton made to grab his Remington shotgun. Then he refocused as he spotted the cameras overhead atop a towering pole. He ignored the man behind him, shaking his clenched fist and spun the Volvo into the filling station. He parked the car next to the cage of propane tanks. Then he reloaded his .38 and tucked it into his black jacket. Seated behind the steering wheel he could see the familiar number plate and the obliterated rear window.

It was his target all right.

The question now was, what was he going to do?

***

The men's room consisted of two washbasins, two urinals and one cubicle. Although small, unlike a lot of public toilets, Dean had to admit it was very clean. A few inches above head height a frosted glass window stood ajar. Dean welcomed the fresh breeze. He finished his business and washed his hands. Then he hoisted himself up using the urinals and poked his head out.

Beyond the window was a gravel car park. A wire fence held upright by timber posts separated the gravel area from the overgrown meadow stretching up and out over the hillock. As Dean gazed out at the scenic yet ordinary vista he couldn't help but feel a pang of envy. Maybe if he hadn't been so ambitious and such a do-gooder he might be working at a Texaco garage giving someone their change. Sure it was tedious, even thinking about it. Yet what had once seemed tedious to him now appeared serene.

People who worked at kiosks rarely faced true horror. They clocked in at the start of their shift and clocked out at the end. In between they would assist members of the public from all walks of life. Probably read a book or magazine or listen to the radio or watch a portable TV when it was quiet. But most important of all they didn't get into trouble. They didn't face adversity or become beleaguered with stress.

An azure-blue Vauxhall Corsa was the only vehicle sitting deserted on the gravel. It had to be the obese attendant's vehicle.

Suspension's probably shagged though, Dean thought. Then he immediately chastised himself for thinking such a callous thought.

He jumped down again and lifted his hands up to the shiny metal nozzle of the hand dryer and felt the hot air gushing out. The din of the dryer and the closed door of door leading to the men's room and the one leading to the shop floor made it nigh on impossible for anyone to hear anything inside the store.

Dean retracted his hands and was approaching the door when he recoiled at the sound of something heavy crashing. It sounded like items and the shelves themselves had collapsed. The ex drug-squad police officer instinctively went to grab hold of the lever to haul the door open... then halted.

His old ally, intuition, prevented him from acting in haste.

The absence of sound that ensued bored into his consciousness. If the lady had fallen he'd have heard a cry upon impact or a groan thereafter. But that was not the case. What came after were slow, methodical footfalls, *click, clacking* over the linoleum and the crunching of crisp packets yielding to the enormous weight.

Shit!

That maniacal, inexorable hunter had found him.

It was almost as if fate or God was guiding this deranged killer. Yet what perplexed Dean was the fact that the backpack filled with money and peanut-butter sandwiches was still in the wrecked Honda. Had Anton checked the car? And if so, was he still now going to kill him?

There was only one way to find out...

However, a thought came to Dean as he whirled around. How would Anton know where he kept the money? For all the assassin knew he had the money on him. And in hindsight perhaps that's what he should have done.

It was a good job he'd found the frosted glass window ajar when he had. If it hadn't been there and there were no windows, he'd have been a sitting duck.

***

Anton aimed the Remington at the monitor showing himself from four different angles and fired. The recoil jolted his shoulder. The screen disintegrated. Debris cascaded to the linoleum. What was left of the monitor clung to the wall bracket and the lead, dropping bits and pieces, spitting sparks.

Wasting no time the big mother of a man lifted the flap and crossed the counter. He found the DVD player recording the CCTV footage. He opened the CD tray, took the disk out and snapped it once, twice and three times. The shards glittered under the lights. Then he shot the DVD player for good measure, flinching from the fragments of plastic flying back at him.

The obese, bespectacled woman lay in a heap on the floor behind the counter. Her body had slammed back into the cigarette and cigar shelves. Marlboro and Pall Mall packets covered her lower half. Her head and slammed the counter as she bounced involuntarily off the wall. Her spectacles had smashed and tiny bits of glass protruded from her vacant eyes. A trickle of blood ran across the bridge of her broken nose and down over the ridges of her four chins.

Satisfied that he'd taken care of not being identified, the chameleon scanned the kiosk. A dark recess behind the magazine and newspaper stand caught his undivided attention. He headed in that direction, discharging the cases of spent bullets and recharging.

A sign above the heavy blue door read 'Toilets'. And there was a depiction of a figure with his legs apart on one door and another figure with legs closed on the other. There was no question that this was where his prey had escaped to. The question was which toilet had he gone into. If he knew he was coming which he most likely did then maybe he wanted to trick him by going into the female toilets.

Without further deliberation, Anton pushed open the female toilet and entered the pink walled restroom. The ladies' room consisted of three washbasins and three cubicles. As he crossed the tiled flooring, Anton caught a glimpse of his reflection in the mirrors above the basins. Both he and the shotgun filled the room. One by one he studiously pushed open the cubicle doors. Then he strode out of the room.

When he entered the men's room bewilderment struck him like a fierce slap on a brisk winter day. Both cubicles were empty and there was no one at the urinal. He went to the washbasins. One was bone dry... the other dappled with droplets of blood. The frosted glass window was closed over but wasn't shut.

Gripping his chosen weapon, the hunter turned and threw the big, heavy door open and marched out.

The big man's eyes widened with rage as the red Honda Civic screeched out of the filling station. He raised his shotgun and fired. The ding of metal being punctured and ripped apart reached him simultaneously. Then the prey flew out of sight.

***

Dean instinctively kept his head down. He fought strenuously against the steering wheel. He rejoined the road without looking or indicating where he was going or what lane he intended to join.

A blast of a horn reached his ears but not his frantic mind. He kept his eyes on the road, seeking a lane that would lead him back onto the M4 west. Adrenaline surged through him. He could actually feel his brain throbbing against his forehead. Dean wouldn't have been surprised if it exploded or shut down.

Once he was back on the M4 and heading west he eased into the left lane. A quivering hand caressed his brow. All he could see in his mind's eye was the cordial, bespectacled, obese woman who lived an ordinary, tedious, calm life. She'd never seen or had any obligation to him or anyone else. Yet she'd expressed her concern for his wellbeing the moment he entered the kiosk. Her genuine kind-heartedness had touched him. No doubt that nice, kind-hearted woman was now gone from the world and never to return; never to express her concern and show compassion to anyone else.

Hot tears pricked the corners of his eyes. His emotions simmered beneath the surface. Soon the whistle of the kettle would signal that the water was – like his fresh tears – indeed hot.

Whatever happens from here on in you make sure that the money reaches Mrs Hill. Nothing else matters. The misery ends today.

Dean stared absent-mindedly at the motorway.

35.

DI SARK and DI Jason had arrived at the crime scene on the outskirts of Bristol on the M4 via police helicopter. After running from the helicopter across the high grass and up the bank they now stood alongside the vehicle described on the local news.

What no one had expected was the two dead bodies and the screaming infant harnessed in the back seat.

'Jesus Christ!' Sark exclaimed.

DI Jason got down on his haunches and leant closer to the vehicle. He was mindful not to touch anything. Crime scene forensics were busy going over the abandoned car.

Behind them two patrol cars with their neon red and blue bubbles splashed the motorway with whirling lights. The emergency breakdown lane and the left lane had been closed. Traffic cones had been placed from where the detectives were standing five hundred feet ahead. All vehicles were dutifully slowing.

What DI Sark loathed more than anything though were the onlookers gawking out of their windows, trying to get a glimpse of the tragedy. It made him physically sick. Some people had no decency at all. And yet wherever a crime had been committed in the country that he'd investigated it was always the same.

DI Jason rose and then approached his partner. 'Cascarini may well talk for Britain but he sure as hell is right 'bout our perp,' he said so only Sark could hear him.

Sark's neck was sore from the joggling around in the helicopter. 'So, what we got here is for some reason or another our badass killer has murdered these two travellers, swapped cars and spared the little girl.'

DI Jason nodded in agreement.

'I'm surprised he didn't off her as well.'

'Why didn't he?' DI Jason asked.

'Apparently, he's not so evil that he'd put a bullet through an infant's head. But he did make her an orphan.' He paused, deliberating. 'As soon as we get the bodies identified we ought to be able to identify the girl and contact her next of kin.'

'Meanwhile we got an ex-cop fleeing, hell-bent on reaching Tenby with a shit-load of cash and our ruthless assassin leaving a trail of death in his wake.'

'A penny for your thoughts?'

DI Jason pulled out a pack of Opal Fruits and offered one to his partner. Sark took one and tore the wrapping off. Together they chewed the succulent sweets.

Then DI Jason spoke. 'We can follow these two right across the country. No matter how many Anton kills, no amount of evidence is gonna bring us any closer to him. We've got an APB out on him and a brief description. Now, we got a deadly assassin driving an unknown vehicle, at least till we identify our victims. What we do know is their destination…'

'So…' Sark prompted.

'So, let's go to Tenby. We know where Sandra Hill lives. Let's go there. If Dean arrives, great. In doing so he'll lead Anton to us, as well. If not, our killing machine will either have to change his appearance or go into hiding. Whatever the case we've done all we can and covered ourselves in the process.'

After musing what his partner said, Sark spoke. 'Even if I phoned Dean now, which I'll do anyway, he won't give up. To do so now is suicidal. You heard what Cascarini said. What I can't quite fathom is why Anton would kill two innocent people in broad daylight on the M4 where he could easily have been spotted. Seems like one helluva risk just to swap cars.'

216

'I'll ask forensics to see if they can find a fault with the Ford to explain if that has anything to do with it,' DI Jason said. 'But to be honest, I think this guy isn't just a killer. I agree with Cascarini. There's a reason why he's so elusive. He can change vehicles to throw us off, change appearance. But someone must know him for him to have obtained a driving licence and weapons. He must live somewhere. How else does anyone get in contact with him?'

Sark frowned. 'He came from Portugal and was discovered in Spain by Cascarini's brother.'

'No. I mean since he came over here with Cascarini,' DI Jason said.

'But even if we knew all that, like you said it's not gonna make a blind bit of difference. What we gotta do is get these two identified, get the girl to her nearest relative and get to Tenby. We also need to trace the licence plate.'

'If he is still alive and Dean does lead us straight to him,' DI Jason went on, without missing a beat, 'are you willing to sacrifice everything to bring him down? Because Cascarini may be an arsehole but he's right. Anton won't surrender. The only way anyone can stop him is by doing what he did to these unfortunate people – by putting a bullet through his skull.'

Sark placed his hands on his hips and inhaled the fresh countryside fragrance from the foliage and the rolling pastures. When he spoke he didn't speak to anyone in particular. 'I used to think that fearing death made me weak. Now I am older I see that fearing death is what keeps me alive.'

DI Jason didn't know what to make of that vague comment and remained silent.

36.

THE WIND continued to howl through the rear window.
However, as midday drew ever closer the sun and the hot
air from the fan warmed Dean. Or perhaps he'd just got used to
the numbing cold. Furthermore, his adrenaline had reddened
his face and brought his veins to the surface.

The Kevlar bullet-proof vest made him look twenty pounds
heavier. He glimpsed the weapons on the passenger side, still
surprised to see them there.

Anton must have spotted his car alongside one of the petrol
pumps. Once it became apparent he wasn't there, the big guy
had gone straight to the kiosk. Had he paid more heed he'd
have obtained the briefcase full of money and disarmed him.
Instead his M1911, AK-47 both fitted with suppressors jutted
out from beneath the passenger seat. His bandages, pack of
gauze pads and iodine were in his backpack with his peanut-
butter sandwiches.

He was driving through Margam on his way to Port Talbot.
A harrowing yet pertinent thought arrived at the front of his
consciousness, unable for him to ignore.

As he wasn't too familiar with the road layout the further
west he went, Dean knew that at some point he'd have to stop
again and consult the Google map on his mobile. He knew the
town of Neath was approaching. His plan of taking a detour
onto familiar terrain was vital for his survival and to achieving
his goal. Yet what concerned him was due to sweating
profusely and being driving constantly he was growing weary.
He wasn't used to so much travelling in one go without
intervals.

He supposed the break at the Texaco garage on the outskirts of Cardiff could be classed as an interval. However, if five minutes constituted a break and then having your heart treble its beat as he fled by the skin of his teeth, it wasn't considered a break after all.

To outsmart the maniacal hunter he had to recharge his batteries. His stomach rumbled and he had to peel his lips apart they were so parched. Swallowing became arduous.

Pressing his foot harder on the accelerator didn't achieve much. All that happened was the Volvo increased its speed to match his Honda. Furthermore, he needed time to organise and set up a plan that would work. He may have been willing to die, but that didn't mean behaving recklessly. After all, he still had possession of Sandra Hill's money and a task to complete. And he'd be damned if some maniac was going to prevent him from doing this one final deed before he made peace with God.

You're not going all religious on me now, are you? he asked himself, grinning.

He was now passing the town of Port Talbot.   Port Talbot, Dean knew, was home to one of the greatest actors of all time – Anthony Hopkins. He snorted laughter at thinking what would Mr Hopkins' character in The Silence of the Lambs, Hannibal Lector, would've done if he was in his position.

His arms were leaden with numbness from being locked in the same posture for so long. The fact that he gripped the steering wheel until the leather creaked didn't help matters either. Five minutes wasn't enough. 'Not by far,' he muttered to himself. His hair was windswept and his eyes felt dry. This was difficult to fathom as he wasn't driving a car with the sunroof down. Yet the warm air blasting out of the vent and the cold draught swirling through the rear window had afflicted his exposed skin more than he first realised. His knuckles crackled as he flexed them, trying to release the rigidity. He consulted the rear-view mirror and sighed as the Volvo still occupied the space behind. He had to take his hat off to the assassin. Anton lived up to his reputation. Not once throughout the journey had he let up on him. If he did fall behind and Dean let the thought cross his mind that he might be free, sooner or later there he was again firing the odd shot into his ruined Volvo, deliberately reminding Dean he was there. In some respects, his adversary's determination spurred his own determination to never give in.

But one idea did cross Dean's busy mind. *Surely Anton must be feeling weary, as well. I mean he's only human, just like anyone else. At least in the physical sense. He couldn't have slept all that well if he was keeping watch on my home all night long.*

'You got some stamina. I'll admit that,' he said aloud.

The town of Port Talbot lay beneath the motorway. Dean barely caught a glance. *On a beautiful, cloudless day the United Kingdom was one spectacular vista of splendour,* he remarked. The mountains dwarfed the M4 and the town below like coliseums. Dean knew if he stayed on the M4 he'd soon pass the Baglan Energy Park, go across the bridge and on towards Llandarcy business park.

He recalled going to the Llandarcy sport's centre with his girlfriend. His girlfriend's parents were members. They used their membership cards to play on the Tennis Courts and use the saunas afterwards. He remembered it vividly as it was one of his fondest memories.

A pang of pain and regret stung him. Perhaps if their relationship had worked out and he'd not lost his badge and had his once unblemished name and reputation destroyed and ridiculed across the tabloids he'd still be in a relationship and have something worth fighting and living for.

Evidently that was not to be his fate. For whatever reason – it couldn't have purely been one misguided error – doing this last honourable deed at whatever cost to himself was what he was meant for.

Dean supposed he could have refused and got whacked and disposed of, like the proverbial rubbish he considered himself to be. In hindsight, he realised that was one of the reasons he never liked his neighbours, save the Groves' family. Their lack of forgiveness reflected his own culpability. The fact that every day he was reminded of the one colossal error and wouldn't let him in live in peace never mind consider exonerating him had burrowed into his consciousness. It was one of – if not the sole reason – why he took prescribed sleeping pills. And why he took anti-depressants first thing in the morning and last thing at night.

Unexpectedly, the dam broke and his shoulders shuddered. Sobs afflicted him, blurring his vision. He realised one of the single most imperative acumens a person needed to understand before heading out to face the world, regardless of race, religion, sex or education, was this: Be kind to yourself and others.

Cathy and Andrew Groves had been kind to him, and so had Paul Demato when everyone else, family and close friends turned their backs on him. They didn't even have the decency to listen to his side of the story. But most of all, Detective Inspector Sark had been kind. He'd been the only policeman in all the years since he'd pulled the trigger and killed two drug dealers that had treated him like a human being.

'I'm sorry, God,' he sobbed. 'I'm so sorry.'

37.

THE HOLIDAY INN EXPRESS was located at the first left turning at junction 43 on the M4. When Dean had gone to the men's room in Cardiff Texaco service station he'd consulted the road map on the internet via his mobile. And although he was fairly familiar with the town of Neath he needed to double-check. Getting his bearings might be one of the differences and give him an advantage.

He could see the edifice growing larger as he approached. If he wasn't being pursued the way he was ordinarily he would have flicked the turn signal indicating where he intended to go. Instead he continued forward and swung the steering wheel down in one rapid force. From there he climbed the two-lane road to the roundabout.

Behind him he could hear the Volvo swerving at the last minute so as not to lose him. Dean's heart was jacked. His hands steady. The roundabout was busy. He crouched down in his seat in case Anton decided to take a shot at him. Then when the road was clearer, he got onto the roundabout and took a sharp left.

The tyres of the wrecked Volvo struggled for traction. Dean released his right foot from the accelerator pedal and turned the wheel. There was no time to check his mirrors to see if the Volvo was behind him, still. The road took a sharp left and if he went too fast he'd collide with the parked cars.

There were two adjacent car parks. One for The Harvester restaurant and one for the Holiday Inn Express. If he followed the road around he'd come to the Llandarcy Sports Centre.

Tyres screeched as he entered the Holiday Inn Express car park and reversed into a space on the far end. He applied the handbrake and killed the engine. Sliding further down in his seat, he watched the car park and waited for the Volvo. Twenty seconds passed. Then Dean wasted no more time. He stuffed his Colt M1911 pistol into his backpack along with the other items and his sandwiches and Yorkie bar. Once this was achieved he lifted the vinyl briefcase up and took out the slip of paper with the code to open it. 157-295.

The clasps snapped back, and when he lifted the top up there was so much money in front of him it couldn't have been real. But what was most astounding was the fact that the notes were all in fives and tens. Dean understood why. If he managed to get the money to Sandra Hill and there were fifty-pound notes or one-hundred pound notes it'd be conspicuous. However, if she was found with a bundle of five-pound notes or ten-pound notes, she could always say she'd got money from her bank account.

Due to the fact that the briefcase was filled to the brim, it seemed as though there was more than twenty grand occupying the space. But that didn't matter to Dean. He upended the briefcase and shovelled the elasticised bundles into his backpack.

Ramming the car keys into his jacket pocket, Dean scanned the car park. From his limited vantage point he could see no Volvo loitering around close by. Instead of waiting for an invitation that would never come, Dean burst out of the Honda, locked it and half-walked, half-ran to the beige and brown façade.

He knew he couldn't hurry into the entrance. He had to be cool and natural. Yet in his peripheral vision he caught sight of the brown Volvo parked alongside the entrance.

'Fuck!' he hissed.

Anton stared daggers at him.

If Dean didn't make it inside the building with the money, not only would he die but he'd also fail his mission and Anton would get Sandra Hill's money.

Taking a big, deep breath, Dean pivoted and jogged to the entrance. He never saw the hunter pull out his .38. However, the sound of a violent cough and the involuntary jolt forward, knocked him off balance. He struggled to exhale and catch his breath. Consciously however, he remained on his buckling legs. The next hard jolt felt as though some had jabbed him with a metallic walking stick on his rear shoulder.

Dean collapsed into the glass door and dropped to one knee just as a third bullet whizzed past his head and shattered the glass. He rolled into the entrance further over the shards, cutting his hands. Then he rose to full height, spitting a wad of congealed blood into a tissue. He folded the stained tissue up and moved forward, doing his utmost to appear inconspicuous.

Fortunately there was a bathroom on his left and instead of approaching the broad reception desk Dean elbowed his way into the toilet. One man stood at the urinal, focusing intently on not missing the drain to notice him. He locked the cubicle behind him, put the toilet seat down and groaned in discomfort. Arching his head back caused a muscle spasm. He slapped a hand over his gaping mouth just as he was about to gasp.

On the other side of the door, the man now washed his hands. Next came the blow dryer and then the heavy timber door on pneumatic hinges swinging closed again.

Blood trickled down his arm where he'd been shot in his triceps muscle. The other wound was very close to his neck and spinal cord. A few inches over and blood trickling down his shuddering frame would have been the least of his concerns. Nevertheless, he'd made it thus far.

Opening his backpack he took out a kitchen knife and the roll of bandages. He also ripped open the pack of gauze pads. Removing his jacket proved to be both arduous and painful.

But once he was naked above the waistline he applied pressure to the wound at the rear of his arm to stop the bleeding. He wiped the wound clean and then fingered the bullet embedded in his arm.

Making sure no one else was in the toilets with him, Dean then gripped the blade of the kitchen knife precariously and tried to pry the bullet out. His fingers were too large to get into the wound itself properly. However, the tip of the blade scraped the bullet until it got leverage and pulled the bullet back out through the hole it'd made.

By the time he'd completed this task Dean was ashen-faced and numb with pain. He leant back against the cistern and controlled his breathing rate. Then he pressed the gauze pad absorbing the blood hard against the wound. He did that until it lost its effect, then wrapped a bandage tight around his injured arm.

Once he put his clothes back on, Dean flushed the blood-drenched gauze pad down the toilet, placed his items back into the heavy backpack and carried it in his left hand.

At the washbasin he washed his face with hot water and combed his hair so it at least looked presentable. If asked why he appeared so pale, he'd say something along the lines 'long drive without rest and I didn't eat a proper breakfast'.

What puzzled him more than anything else as he emerged from the toilets and crossed the capacious lobby to the reception area was how Anton had not managed to fatally kill him with one shot?

Then another far more harrowing thought came to him. *He could've killed you, but first he wants me to suffer and feel pain for causing him so much trouble.*

The reception area was brightly lit, lavish and modern in appearance. A smartly dressed employee approached from the left. She was no more than five feet five inches and had her hair tied back in a bun. Her face, especially her cheeks, shone a bronze hue. Dean assumed it was the effect of make-up. When she smiled Dean noticed she had perfect white teeth, as though they'd never been used.

She could sell a lotta toothpaste.

'Hi,' she said in an overly sweet voice.

'Hi.' Dean tried to sound chirpy. Instead his throat caught and he barely coughed the word out.

'Welcome to the Holiday Inn Express,' the receptionist said. She might as well have been practicing her greeting pitch aloud.

'Thanks,' Dean said. He wished she'd stop grinning like a fool. 'Do you have any rooms available?'

'Yes,' she practically squeaked. 'We have family rooms. Rooms with double-beds and single rooms.'

'A single room will do.'

'The breakfast for a night stay comes free when you book a room.'

'I won't be staying that long,' Dean said. 'How much is it?'

She told him the price. Then added: 'Do you have any luggage you'd like a member of staff to carry for you to your room, sir?'

'No. This is all I got,' he said, lifting the heavy backpack.

She handed him his change and then opened the glass cabinet and took out a key attached to a ring with tags on it. 'Your room number is 56. It is on the first floor. When you reach the floor turn left and your room is towards the end of the building. There is a TV on the wall. The remote control will be on the bedside table. You'll have an en suite bathroom, a writing desk and a clean white single bed. They're quite cosy. If you'd like to contact the reception area just dial 1 and we'll be with you right away. Is there anything else, sir?'

Dean envied the carefree aura emanating from this young lady. 'No, I don't think so. Thank you.'

'Are you sure you don't want a concierge to escort you?'

Dean smiled. 'I'll find it no problem.' He was just about to head through the interconnecting double-doors into the hallway that led to the carpeted stairwell when he regarded the polite lady. 'Oh. There is something you could do for me.'

'Yes sir. What may that be?'

'If a tall, well-built guy with dark hair comes here and asks for someone of my description, don't tell him where I am. He's a pest.'

The receptionist's smile became a distant memory in moments. Now her brow furrowed and her eyes grew larger under the light from the wall sconces. 'If he comes here is it in my and everyone else's best interest to call the police?'

'No, don't do that,' Dean said, shaking his head. 'Just tell him I came here and then left again. Can you do that?'

The young receptionist couldn't hide her concern even if she wanted to. The unblemished features that she wore upon first making his acquaintance were now a map of lines. 'I will.'

Dean felt bad in the pit of his stomach. 'Really it's nothing to worry about. Just some reckless driver I had the displeasure of meeting on my journey here from London, that's all.'

'There're a lot of them about, sir,' the cordial lady said in a timid voice.

'Tell me about it.' Dean left the receptionist standing motionless behind the counter with the trace of a smile touching her glossy lips.

38.

DEAN FOUND THE ROOM effortlessly. He unlocked the door, pushed it open and had to snort a laugh. In fairness to the receptionist whom he'd inadvertently unnerved her brief description of the room was just as he'd envisioned ascending the stairs.

White and navy-blue curtains had been opened revealing a splendid vista through the double-glazing windows. The TV was mounted on the white wall, the bed looking as though it'd never been used. Not a speck or crumb anywhere to be found.

Once he locked the door behind him, Dean dropped the heavy backpack onto the mattress and entered the en-suite bathroom. The room itself had a fresh grapefruit aroma. It smelled good. He stood by the window and gazed out.

Room 56 was on the other side of the building from the hotel's car park. Still, caution and vigilance were required at all times. *Never let your guard down*, he told himself.

The M4 looked like a child's Matchbox model set. Vehicles of all shapes and sizes and colours whizzed past, never ending.

The time was 12:16 according to the digital clock on his mobile. A few more moments passed before Dean moved away from the window and lowered himself onto the mattress. He opened up his backpack and ended up having to upend all the contents so he could get to his softening peanut butter sandwiches and Yorkie chocolate bar.

First things first, he thought. Then he slipped his sore feet out of his Addidas trainers. He emitted a groan of pleasure and slid back onto the mattress. Placing the two pillows on top of each other he propped up his head and stretched out languidly.

As he relaxed on top of the comfy mattress, savouring the taste of his sandwiches and Yorkie while washing it down with natural mineral water, his mind wandered. The TV was on but he'd only been channel surfing, comforted slightly by the background din of a *Friends* episode on cable.

Initially he didn't know what to think regarding his minor breakdown in the car. At first he worried it might be the first time he'd shown himself any weakness. But contemplating it now with some food being digested and replacing some of his bodily fluids he'd sweated out all morning he had a clearer perspective. It had been a good reaction; to cry; to let his inner emotions out. He felt better for it. Now he knew for certain that his decision to go through with this aware that he was living on borrowed time wasn't based on a rash decision or a surge of adrenaline or any other emotion induced while enduring phenomenal stress.

Dean reached down over the side of the mattress, blindly groping for his bottled water. His fingers missed it and touched what felt like a cardboard box under the bed. He thought he dropped something. However, he couldn't fathom which of his belongings he'd dropped that had fallen under the bed that was definitely a cardboard box of some kind.

Averting his attention from the TV screen, Dean bent over and pulled out what he'd inadvertently discovered. He winced at the sudden spasm at the top of his back on his rear deltoid. The bullet was still lodged in there, deep. Dean was no surgeon but what he performed on his arm in the cubicle had been fairly easy. The wound over his shoulder was hard to reach at the best of times. It didn't immobilise him. That was part of the problem. Because he could still move, albeit with much discomfort, Dean had put it to the back of his mind. He ignored it while he lifted the cardboard box up into sight and laughed heartily.

***

Having finished eating his lunch and drained his bottled water, Dean killed the TV using the remote control. Then he started writing a text to Paul.

Paul, it's me Dean. I am currently at the Holiday Inn Express in Llandarcy, Neath. I still have Sandra's money in my possession, but I'm not sure for how long. I've been shot... twice. I'm okay but I'm not sure if I'm gonna make it all the way to Tenby. Could you please give me Sandra Hill's full postal address, please? I know I got the address but I need the exact postcode to do this. I won't be able to stay here too long. Just taking a timeout to recuperate then me and Anton are gonna get better acquainted. If you don't give me Sandra's postcode then don't hold your breath on her getting the money. It's up to you.

He read the message back to himself before sending it to Paul Demato's mobile. Then he rose and ambled over to the en-suite blue and white tiled bathroom and drew himself a hot shower.

He was drying his hair when his mobile started vibrating. Dean knew it was either Paul or the cordial detective. Whoever it was he didn't feel like talking right now. The last thing he needed on top of everything else that had transpired since yesterday was for one of the two to distract him with their opinions and advice.

The mobile had gone quiet by the time he'd finished drying himself and got dressed. He ambled over to the phone on the bedside cabinet and checked who had called. Not surprisingly it was Paul's number. He'd also left a text message.

Dean opened it up and read the text.

Dean, I want to apologise for telling the detectives too much info. But if I'd kept too many details back and they'd found out the real story they'd have me for withholding key

230

evidence. Plus, they already sussed it out. I'm a bit anxious about you, pal. I'm sorry you've been wounded. I really am. Perhaps in hindsight I could've sent Tony with you. But I needed protection for myself. The other mobs know I'm at a fragile state right now and are itching to get a chance to pop me. As for your request for my sister's postcode, I'm begging you not to send it in the post. Unless you tell me what your intentions are I must refuse that request. But whatever you do don't let that God-awful man get his hands on it. That's all I ask. And if you do survive this, I'll pay you extra and pay your medical expenses too.

Dean appreciated the offer of extra money. However, he didn't think he'd be alive to see the sunrise let alone be able to enjoy the materialistic luxuries that money could buy. In the next text message he sent he didn't mention any of this. But he did tell Paul his plan. Then he waited for a response.

His mobile buzzed intermittently for several seconds. Dean picked it up and opened the new text message.

That's a fuckin' ingenious plan! I knew you were more than meets the eye. That's why you'd have excelled in this business. You keep your head down and your mouth shut and your eyes and ears open all the time. Tony or any of my or anyone else's guys wouldn't have thought of that. Not even Anton.

Phone reception and ask if they have any stamps. This is the only problem with this plan. If they don't have any stamps, how're you gonna get to a post office to buy one without getting shot again? Sometimes they do though. And offer them a few quid for one letter. That way they'll be able to see how important it is. Best of luck, pal. I just wanna thank you again for doing this. I know I didn't exactly give you an alternative, but I do appreciate what you're going through. Only you could handle it. I mean that.

Here's the full address...

Sandra Hill
15 Newell Hill
Tenby
Wales
SA70 8RT

One first class stamp should be enough. Just keep the letter brief. Just tell her that you've left something of grave importance at the hotel you're at (make sure to give her the full address of the hotel and directions). Just tell her it belongs to her and if someone else sees it will take it immediately. God help us if one of the maids finds it. Also tell her it's not just hers but belongs to her son, Tobias. Tell her that Tobias would've wanted her to keep it.

Let me know how you get on. And I'll speak to you soon. Oh, and next time, answer your damn phone and don't begrudge me.

Dean laughed hard at the last sentence. Shaking his head derisively, he said, 'That's easy to say when you're sitting at home twiddling your thumbs, Paul.'

***

Dean called reception from his room, remembering to dial 1. The pleasant if slightly cheesy receptionist answered in her chirpy tone. Dean went ahead and enquired if the hotel had any first class stamps, a piece of paper and an envelope. He added he'd pay extra money for the stamp as an incentive.

'We definitely have some writing paper and some small white envelopes,' she said. 'But I'm not sure if we have any stamps. I'm just checking the drawers.'

232

He braced himself for her to add that they didn't have any stamps. And if they didn't, the envelope and piece of paper were as useful for this task as a chocolate teapot.

'Can I ring you back in a couple of minutes, sir?' she said.

Only if you stop calling me sir!

'Yes,' he said. 'That'd be perfectly all right. I'll be right here.'

Putting the phone back in its cradle he thought, *You sounded just as cheesy as her.*

***

He snatched the phone out of its cradle before the second ring.

'Hello, sir,' the receptionist said.

Dean withheld a sign of vexation. 'Yes,' he said in a clipped tone.

'I asked my manager for some first class stamps. He checked his desk drawers and couldn't find any…'

He punched the mattress.

'… but luckily for you,' she went on, 'a man sitting in the lobby overheard me talking to my manager and has two first class stamps that he's willing to sell you for two pound. Is that all right?'

'I'll give him five pound, tell him,' Dean said with alacrity.

'Just a moment.' Then Dean could hear her telling someone close by how much he'd offered.

He heard a gentleman's voice saying, 'Okay, great!'

'Your offer has been accepted,' the receptionist said unaware that Dean had overheard the conversation.

'Excellent. Could you please bring me a clean sheet of paper, one single white envelope – I'll pay you for the items, as well – a biro and some Sellotape as well as the stamps, please? I will then pay you five pound for the kind gentleman and five pound for the items I've just asked for. How does that sound?'

'There's no need to pay me or the hotel for the piece of paper and envelope or the Sellotape, sir. But I will send one of the concierges up to collect the gentleman's money and bring you what you requested.'

Apart from being called 'sir' yet again everything was going to plan.

***

Dean tidied up the room, putting his rubbish in the bin and his belongings back inside his backpack out of sight. He removed a five-pound note from the money Paul had given him for travel expenses and waited for the anticipated knock.

The concierge rapped hard three times. Dean opened the door ajar and poked his head around. The young man before him standing in the corridor couldn't be any older than twenty-five. His black hair had been slicked back. His face was as smooth a baby's bum. And like the receptionist his teeth shone enamel.

'Sorry,' Dean said. 'I'd invite you in but I've just come out of the shower.'

Initially he did intend to permit the concierge into the room. Yet he felt safer lying to his face. 'Here's the five-pound I promised that gentleman.'

'Thank you, sir,' he said, smiling amicably.

Oh for God's sake not another one. When the fuck was I knighted?!

'One more thing,' Dean added. 'I'm unable to reach a post office at any time soon. But this letter is of grave importance. May I leave it with someone in reception knowing they'll send it or can you guarantee that you'll post it?'

The concierge's smile dissolved into concentration as he listened intently. Then he spoke with certainty. 'That is perfectly fine, sir. We have two postmen arrive here daily –

one to deliver post and one in the afternoon who collects post. Other customers have done the same before if they were away on business.'

Dean didn't particularly need to hear the history of the post with regards to the Holiday Inn Express Hotel. Nevertheless, he nodded comprehension. 'That's good to know. And thank you again for your kind service.'

'No problem, sir. Will there be anything else?'

On the verge of saying no, Dean held his tongue. Then: 'Actually, there is something. I know it's only midday, but I was wondering if I could order a drink and some strawberries, if you have them to order.'

'Of course, sir,' the concierge said. 'I shall send a waiter up with a bottle of white wine and a bowl of strawberries a.s.a.p.'

Dean thanked him again and closed the door. He rolled his eyes at being called sir as if he'd adopted the name. Although he should be grateful the young man didn't salute him.

Now that he had a biro, a clean piece of paper and a white envelope and two stamps Dean needed to consider what he was going to write. He'd read what Paul told him to write from the latest text message. However, another side of his consciousness insisted that he write to Sandra Hill in his own words.

If Paul Demato wasn't under investigation and having to pay innumerable tax and other bills for his discrepancies he could afford a lot more money. Yet it wasn't the money per se. The money was a symbol. Furthermore, Paul was only giving the last stash of his money away to buy forgiveness. Now that his empire was falling all around him, he desperately sought the love of his family. But for Dean this task was his salvation.

Unless something unforeseen befell Anton in the very near future then Dean was as good as dead already. This letter would be his final statement of his life. Although it wasn't about him, at the same time it was all about him. After all, he was the one taking all the risks. He was the one who'd barely escaped the clutches of death today and witnessed the gruesome deaths of innocent human beings who just happened to be in the wrong place at the wrong time.

The only reason he'd accepted the task was that he feared being popped right there in Paul's plush office or when he least expected it. If he didn't have any compassion he'd have taken the money for himself and fled the country or gone into hiding and watched the end of the much feared mob boss Paul Demato immigrate to Spain, defeated and made a fool of.

This letter wasn't just for Sandra Hill. The letter was for everyone who'd suffered, including himself. With that in mind, Dean sat at the writing desk and wrote his letter.

39.

THE TWO CID homicide detectives had driven to the Texaco filling station on the outskirts of Cardiff City Centre when they were informed of a gruesome murder from their chief superintendent.

They'd shot past the traffic using the wailing siren and flashing blue and red beacons to their current destination. The inexorable zigzagging in and out of traffic at speeds of up to one hundred plus miles an hour made them buzz with intensity. During the hellish ride DI Sark could barely hear himself over the hammer of his own pulse, the windstorm of his breath. In Hollywood action movies where the cops chase the bad guys through the streets it looked awesome. Reality however was far crueler to his senses. One error or misguided judgment call from one of the other road users and they'd be the ones lying next to their victims whose crimes they were trying to solve. His flushed face boiled from within. What made it worse was when they entered the crime scene and could smell the spilt blood. Patrol cars circulated the Texaco garage. Only citizens passing in their cars, slowing for traffic, took an interest.

'I think I've aged ten years today alone,' DI Sark muttered to his partner.

'I know the feeling,' DI Jason said leading the way into the kiosk. 'But on the plus side, CCTV footage should've captured all of it and we can identify our guy for ourselves and see what vehicle he's driving.'

'It won't be soon enough though. God knows what Scotland Yard are making of all of this.'

'C'mon, man,' the younger detective said. 'We don't know that. Dean might make it to Tenby and by then we'll know what our perp looks like to make an arrest.'

'Yeah, you're right,' DI Sark said, patting his partner on the shoulder. 'Just tired, that's all.'

They made their way down the aisle towards the counter where the murder took place. On the other side of the counter, amidst the cigar and cigarette packets and broken glass and other debris, was their victim.

'This guy makes Ted Bundy look like a saint,' DI Jason said, horrified by the state of the dead woman.

DI Sark removed his sweaty hands from his coat pocket and rested them on his slender hips. 'Forensics will be here shortly,' he said, matter-of-factly. 'But from what I can tell she's been shot and struck directly in her face.'

DI Jason noted the attendant had been shot by a big gun in the chest. Crimson blood dripped down the wall in rivulets. 'If he shot her first she'd have been knocked back and fallen down. That's a fatal wound. There'd be no need to strike her in the face afterwards. Unless she was still breathing.'

DI Sark nodded, appreciating the valid point made. 'She was either still breathing or she hit her head on the way down. Look how her specs are all smashed.'

DI Jason grimaced at the shards of broken lens protruding from the obese lady's eyes and plump cheeks. He shook his head in revulsion. 'Just to let you know; looks like our guy figured he was on camera.'

Sark followed DI Jason's gaze to the obliterated monitor. The last remnants were dangling from the bracket in the top corner. 'Well, Cascarini said he's no fool. Guess he wasn't lying 'bout that either, huh?'

'Wish he was.'

40.

ANTON sat in the Volvo wondering how he ought to proceed. He had no idea how long his prey intended on staying in the hotel. For all he knew Dean had planned to stay the night. Normally, it wouldn't have mattered how long it took, as long as it got done. But patience was a virtue that seemed to be slipping from his sweaty grasp as hours went by.

This prey was far more resilient and resourceful than anyone he'd ever faced. That included Mario Cascarini and the old man back in Spain. He kept fidgeting, unable to stay motionless for longer than five minutes. To kill the time, Anton turned the car radio on. He didn't know one radio station to the other in London. He wasn't a resident of London any more than he was a resident of Barcelona.

One of the main reasons he was untraceable was that he'd immigrated without anyone, save Cascarini's men, knowing he'd arrived at the old man in Spain. He didn't have a passport. This fact had appeared troublesome at first. Then Cascarini had the ingenious notion of placing Anton into a caravan that his brother purchased. From Barcelona he'd travelled all the way to the north of France. Prior to going onboard a cruise liner to Portsmouth, Cascarini's brother told Anton to hide in the compartment beneath the couch in the family caravan. Once the caravan, attached to a Vauxhall, rolled off the cruise liner and onto British soil, Anton was able to come out of hiding and ride in the car to London.

In this day and age it was unfathomable to even consider someone able to live off the grid. Yet Anton had done precisely that, and until present had managed to keep a low profile.

'Scotland Yard are investigating horrific murders along the M4 and the death of a Texaco garage assistant. The bodies of Chris and Jill Mishar were discovered in the assailant's Ford Fiesta on the emergency breakdown lane on the outskirts of Bristol earlier this morning. Police believe the assailant to be a hired hit man and is armed and very dangerous. The assailant is believed to be chasing an ex-police officer for a large amount of money...'

Anton snapped the radio off. Harsh breaths escaped him. That awful feeling that resembled bone-dread fear threatened to crowd his consciousness and affect his one-track mind-set.

A bead of sweat slid down his brow and into his right eye before he had a chance to wipe it away. It stung momentarily then obscured the vision in his right eye. After blinking several times he finally got his full vision back.

Anxiety crept up upon him like a secret lover. If he'd been acquainted with the emotion and not switched himself off for his adult life he might have been able to cope with it a lot easier. In the boys' boarding school back in his native country, his mind was constantly in a catatonic state. He was numb, void of any human emotions. The nurses believed him to be a deaf mute at first. But after thorough examination by doctors and specialists the physical records showed the experts that there was nothing wrong with the boy. However, mentally he was like a computer on standby.

The fellow orphans accepted his silence and uncooperativeness as a sign of weakness. But that all changed in the summer of 1979.

The boarding school was an early nineteenth-century edifice of brown stone. The building was large enough to be a prison. The main building housed a dining room and living room. The four turrets housed the boys' dormitory. On the west wing a long exterior portico led directly to the library. The east wing had an adjacent exterior portico consisting of transparent panels leading directly to the assembly hall and where P.E. classes took place. Another short portico at the end of both assembly hall and the library interconnected to two cabins – one used as a nursing station, the other a study hall.

The environing woods and football field were where most of the boys preferred to spend their leisure during the day. Not Anton. You didn't need to be observant to notice the palpable difference between the other orphans and the mysterious young boy. The boy who'd become arguably the most deadly hit man and most elusive killer in modern times opted to spend his days in the library. Although he had a speech impediment, Anton read in his head voraciously. He devoured books considered far too old for him to fathom. And as the library was used by the teachers and headmaster and other staff there were adult books available to him.

A psychologist would say after studying his life from past to present, it was the life-shattering experience of seeing the decapitated heads of his loving parents and his ensuing isolation that induced this radical difference. Of course, every orphaned child had been traumatised at some point in their short lives. But like a lot of children, they'd adapted in time, as they knew no different. This was life. This had been the hand they'd been dealt. They dealt with it – but not Anton.

Instead he immersed himself in books of serial killers, such as Jack The Ripper, Ed Gein and others. Had one of the teachers taken a closer look at the boy's avid interest in further detail, they'd have seen that Anton had discovered some unparalleled connection with these killers. Unbeknown to the headmaster and the teachers, they assumed that his consumption of book after book could only be a good thing. A pivotal element in the boy asserting himself to a better life than the one he'd been given. The prudent headmaster quietly admired and was even in awe of this unique child. He believed that the boy had learnt that life itself can – and often is   – a mean and nasty place that will beat you to your knees if you allowed it. And instead of crumbling to ground with an earth-shattering impact like a fragile wraith, he'd consciously decided to grit his teeth and fight for every inch with raw determination.

If they'd only known!

Anton had recently had his ninth birthday – not that birthdays meant anything to him anymore. He wouldn't have known unless his teacher had wished him happy birthday and given him a card and a present. The boy nodded his appreciation but refused to speak. He opened the card first and read the birthday wishes. Then he tore the wrapping paper off the solid object and revealed a first edition paperback copy of *The Shining* by a bestselling author by the name of Stephen King. He flipped the book over and read the blurb, salivating in the sinister plotline suggested.

This had been the third year he'd been at the boarding school. He remembered that, regardless of his catatonic state throughout that time. He remembered it because he'd been silently counting down the days of his years as a child and then an adolescent. After that, providing he stayed out of trouble, he'd be free. Then the world would pay for what it had allowed to befall his parents. What some maniacal killer had done that fateful night. The enormous silhouette moving down the hall, materialising into a mountain of a man. The towering figure whose features were concealed in a brown grocery bag with two eyeholes, gesturing for him to stay silent, as he pissed himself. And in all that time no one had ever wished him happy birthday or Christmas or Easter. But now all of a sudden, his teacher who evidently knew he loved to read substantial books had given him a present, just like his parents used to.

Hot tears welled up in his eyes. He pivoted before the teacher could reach out and embrace him and ran down the hall to his dorm.

Later that night when the other boys were pillow fighting Anton lay atop his mattress and inhaled the sweet aroma of the crisp brand new paperback. This wasn't a library book. This was his – to keep. And yet he was hesitant to open it in case he creased the spine or ruffled the pages. Nevertheless, with fingers that buzzed with electricity he opened the book and began reading and was taken aback by the first line, stifling a laugh.

Officious little prick! he thought in both shock and amusement.

Although Anton was a slow reader, he devoured thirty pages in one go before lights out. That night his dreams were filled with endless possibilities.

The next morning was a Saturday. After going through his morning ritual, Anton followed the other boys to the dinning room. He sat in his usual place in the top corner, wolfing down his cereal and gulping his orange juice. He still had to wait for the other boys to finish their breakfast before he could be excused.

Friday evenings were spent doing homework. This Anton thought was actually a good idea. The sooner the homework got done the sooner he could enjoy the rest of the weekend without having the thought burrowing in the back of his mind.

The resplendent sunshine exuded a sanguine glow on the day. Anton may not have enjoyed playing football or any other sports but he knew not to waste a beautiful day like the one that day. He followed the boys outside, inhaling the sweet fragrance of the pines. The boarding school property was surrounded by a barbed wire fence. There was a sty at the far end that joined a well-worn path obscured by overarching branches and foliage.

The on-campus weekend teacher and supervisor, Mr Greer, opened the barn and took out two miniature goalposts. He placed one at the end nearest the library and one down the far end close to the sty. The boys spread out, eager for the ball and waited for a game to start. They didn't bother asking Anton if he wanted to play. They already knew it was pointless, as did Mr Greer.

Instead Anton ambled around the makeshift football pitch to the shaded area beneath the fronds. He sat down with his legs spread out and noticed two boys were missing, Roberto and Wagner. Perhaps the reason he noticed this was due to the fact that Roberto, an eleven-year old, tawny-skinned boy with a shaven head always gave him the thousand yard stare. They'd never spoken to each other in the three years since Anton had been a resident. Yet Roberto had despised him the moment he'd laid eyes on him.

Roberto and Wagner were football mad. Not only did they never fail to miss a game but they were the first in the queue. They always chased after the ball, and if they couldn't reach one of the smaller, faster boys, they'd dive in feet first, sweeping the other boys' legs from behind. Every weekend Mr Greer reprimanded them or told them they were on a yellow card. Roberto didn't heed the warnings. He continued as he'd done previously. This happened to such an extent that the other boys were too afraid to even tackle him when he was approaching their goal.

Roberto would often nudge Anton in the back or walk behind him just to trip him up. He'd been successful twice, until Anton made sure to either wait for him to go first or to walk alongside Roberto.

He found it odd that either Wagner, who had successfully auditioned to be Roberto's shadow, or Roberto himself, hadn't emerged on the playing field. Mr Greer eventually left the other boys playing amongst themselves while he went inside to check on the boys. Some time had passed before Mr Greer and the two boys came outside. Roberto immediately ran onto the field, barged into another boy who was both younger and smaller, sending him sprawling to the grass.

From there he dribbled the ball towards the goal and blasted a shot at the goal. To his annoyance the goalkeeper saved it. Then he spotted Anton sitting in the shade of the frond and a wicked smile curled the corners of his mouth.

Anton realised there and then that Roberto was laughing at him.

Mr Greer ignored the game and cut straight across the field to where Anton was relaxing. He lifted the tail of his shirt up and removed a sodden paperback book. As he proffered it to Anton the young boy's eyes widened in alarm, recognising his cherished birthday present, ruined.

'I believe this belongs to you, Christiano,' he said, sorrowful, unable to look directly at the boy's face, crumbling right before him.

The paperback dripped water and was bent backwards in his quivering grasp. Christiano (for Christiano was the boy's birth name), tried to open the spoiled book but the sodden cardboard front cover tore in half. Inside the black ink streaked down the glued pages. His crestfallen gaze met his teacher's, seeking an explanation.

Mr Greer steadied himself for what he was about to say. He was aware that Anton (or as he was known then, Christiano) had received the book from his teacher yesterday to celebrate his birthday. He was aware that the boy was eccentric, even unique in comparison to the other boys; that reading was his passion. He silently prayed the boy wouldn't break down and cry in front of him. He wasn't a counsellor or any good when it came to comforting a tormented soul.

'They were in the process of flushing it down the toilet, I'm sorry to say,' he said in a strained voice. 'They will be reported for their transgression.'

Anton knew that all the boys would get was the cane across the palms of their hands. Painful, sure. Nevertheless, Roberto would despise him even more. He'd be blamed for inducing the pain, even though it hadn't been he who'd caught them doing wrong. Five or ten strokes or any other amount wasn't enough as punishment. Roberto wasn't the type of boy who learnt from his misdemeanours. Anton knew this. Mr Greer knew this, too. The other boys knew this better than anyone else. They all lived in fear of Roberto. The goalkeeper who'd saved his shot moments ago would get tripped or smacked upside the head later.

No, Roberto strutted around the brownstone orphanage purely because he could. He believed he intimidated Anton as much as the other boys. The only reason he glowered at Anton was because Anton never showed his fear. This was for a perfectly good reason. Anton didn't fear Roberto one iota. For Anton had faced real fear, pure terror some years earlier and lived to tell the tale.

Roberto's punishment had to be far more severe than the curriculum permitted. His punishment needed to be permanent. Something he'd remember for the rest of his life. Something that would keep him up during the nights reliving the moment his life had been torn apart and a new, less promising one commenced.

Fighting back the urge to cry and scream at the same time, Anton handed the unreadable book back to Mr Greer. 'It's of no use to me or anyone else now, sir,' he said. His Adam's apple bobbed up and down with emotion.

Mr Greer's shoulder slumped and he sighed. Then he nodded in acquiescence. The book indeed was of no use to the boy or anyone else for that matter. However, he refused to dispose of this in the waste basket. What he would do right now is take it to the headmaster's office. When Monday morning rolled around the evidence would be there and the fact that he was an eye-witness to the rotten deed.

'I'm sorry, Christiano,' he said with sincerity.

Anton stared impassively at the shadow of the frond gently swaying to and fro in the mild breeze. He waited diligently until Mr Greer returned inside with the sodden book.

Then he rose, purposely. In that moment all humane emotion dissipated. Neither was his consciousness riddled with rage. He elicited no hatred for Roberto. An eerie, inhuman calm settled upon him now that he was in motion. He strode across the field to where Roberto had just blasted another shot at goal, which resulted in the ball striking the post.

Roberto didn't notice Anton until he was upon him. By then it was too late to react accordingly. His head was yanked back by an unseen force and an arm seized him in a reverse headlock manoeuvre. The young hoodlum was wrenched so that he was parallel to the ground. His whole face ballooned into a mauve hue. His parched lips blanched. Realising all of a sudden he was in a precarious position, he swatted fruitlessly with his flailing arms. Then the agony really began.

Everyone ceased what they were doing and watched in shocked silence. Anton craned his head forward, peering into the purple, oxygen-starved face, seeing undiluted fear in Roberto's protuberant, bloodshot eyes. For in this pivotal moment, no matter how tough Roberto claimed to be, and no matter how much strength he exuded, he was merely a boy. Then his left hand shrouded Roberto's face, fingernails boring into the eye sockets, excavating.

Roberto wheezed, incapable of uttering a single exhalation never mind a word. He wriggled and then groaned as his assailant's kneecap drove itself into the base of his spine. Spittle escaped his gaping mouth. He sounded like an asthmatic emitting a final breath when Anton's hand drew back sharply and crimson lines tore open the child visage.

Mesmerised by this brutal attack, some of the younger boys turned away, gorges rising. The others grimaced but continued to watch. Before Anton had arrived at the orphanage home for boys' they too had been the victim of Roberto's inexorable bullying and harassment habits. Although what they saw was indeed repulsive it had been a long time coming.

But this was only the beginning…

With inexplicable strength, Anton released Roberto. The older boy thumped the ground, spine first. He didn't even have a chance to wipe the blood off his face and touch the scrapes. By the collar of his shirt, he was half-dragged, half-hauled past the goal he'd been shooting at. The frightened, shaven-haired hoodlum thrashed his legs fighting to plant his feet and cease being dragged.

When Anton felt Roberto resisting he heaved him with strength not belonging to a nine-year old boy or most men for that matter. However, he almost lost his balance when Roberto clutched for strands of grass. To hasten what he had in mind Anton stomped ruthlessly on Roberto's head which rebounded off the turf.

By the time Roberto half-recovered from his dazed state, his throat hurt from having his collar pulled taut against his Adam's apple. A hand punched him on the temple and spun him over. Then Roberto blinked and saw the bottom line of barbed wire and understood the pain he'd felt until then was a mere tickle to what was about to befall him.

Anton tore at his scalp and dropped the lower half of Roberto's face onto the barbed wire and applied immense pressure to the back of the bully's skull with his knee. Then he placed his hands around the sides of Roberto's head and onto the barbed wire and pulled the line up and continued to apply more pressure. He roared.

'You laughed at me,' he hissed in a voice that'd terrify a grown man, never mind a bully boy. 'You laughed at me,' he said again. He used all his bodyweight and could feel the barbed wire slicing through the parted lips, ripping the flesh, sawing its way towards the jawbone. 'You think what you did to me was funny? I'll make you laugh for the rest of your fucking life!'

Droplets of blood speckled the blades of yellowing grass around the barbed wire fencing. Then Anton stood erect. He looked over his shoulder at the others who stared in a mixture of awe and trepidation.

'That goes for all of you,' he said in his normal voice, as if nothing horrific had transpired.

In unison the boys nodded.

'He fell onto the barbed wire fence chasing the ball, stopping it from rolling into the woods, yes?'

For the second time the boys nodded automatically.

When Mr Greer returned Anton had returned to his spot beneath the frond tree. The supervisor sprinted to the far end of the field to Roberto's aid. He gently detached the boy who twitched spasmodically and then ran hell-bent to phone for an ambulance.

The boys were indeed quizzed as to what had transpired. They all said the same thing, word-for-word. 'He fell onto the barbed wire fence chasing the ball, stopping it from rolling into the woods, sir.'

Both the headmaster and Mr Greer didn't deduce there was any other explanation. Had it been another boy, perhaps Anton himself, they would have suspected foul play. Nevertheless, Mr Greer and the headmaster did find it odd that not five minutes after Roberto was found trying to flush Anton's birthday present down the toilet he'd had his come-uppance.

Roberto required seventy-two stitches. At no time did he tell anyone who the culprit was. In fact when the headmaster told him the boys said he'd fallen onto the barbed wire fencing chasing the ball, stopping it from rolling into the woods, he sullenly nodded that that was an accurate account.

No one ever so much as breathed a bad word about Anton in the orphanage ever again…

The second he'd removed all his emotions regarding the spoiled book and acted without too much contemplation, Anton had put an end to all his troubles.

That was what he needed to do right now.

Sitting in the Volvo letting his thoughts run away with themselves would induce a mixture of distressing emotions that would hinder his chances of accomplishing his objective.

He needed to act…

41.

HAVING FINISHED the letter, Dean folded the sheet of paper and placed it into the envelope. He wrote the name and full address on the envelope in bold capitals so there could be no mistake as to its destination.

The maître d' arrived promptly, pushing the trolley into the room and expertly extracted the bottle of white wine from the ice bucket and placed it onto the bedside cabinet. He studiously placed a folded kerchief to prevent a damp ring appearing from the bottle's base. Then he removed the dish covering the bowl of ripe strawberries.

Dean smiled crookedly, admiring the diligence and finesse with which the maitre'd performed this somewhat simple task. 'Thank you,' he said. Then without requiring a hint, he slipped a twenty-pound note into the middle-aged gentleman's navy suit pocket.

'And thank you, sir,' the maitre'd said with a slight bow.

I must be a distant relative of the royal family, he thought.

'Here's the letter,' Dean said, proffering it. The white-gloved hand of the maitre'd accepted it. Dean watched him placing it on top of the trolley. 'Please make sure to send it today with this afternoon's mail. It is has more importance than you can imagine.

The middle-aged man nodded, serious. 'I will do exactly as you've requested. You have my word that this very letter shall be sent out with the post today. I hope you enjoy your wine and strawberries, sir.'

'I will, as though it was my last,' Dean said. He opened the door wider so the maitre'd could push the trolley back out into the hallway without scraping the door.

When the maitre'd had taken his leave, Dean closed the door. Then he crossed the room to the bed, propped his back up and stretched out again. He poured himself a generous glass of the white wine and without a hint of haste supped the juice before devouring the succulent strawberries.

A calmness overcame him that quietly surprised him. This mildly perplexed him as the set of circumstances he found himself in ought to have induced panic and terror in abundance. He chose not to analyse the reasoning behind this and closed his eyes. For whatever reason writing the letter to Sandra Hill had been both uplifting and cathartic. It dispersed the cloud of doubt and weakness hanging over him all day long. He'd fight to the death admirably, knowing that whatever befell him good or bad wouldn't change anything. Of course, he'd still prefer to be alive to see how it all turned out. However what would be would be.

Prudently, Dean opted not to drain the entire bottle. He left it for whoever the next guest happened to be or for a member of staff. The strawberries moistened his lips and mouth. Furthermore, the five-minute nap had reinvigorated him somewhat.

His backpack was palpably lighter upon his departure. Before closing the door and locking it shut Dean gazed longingly at the cardboard box of a familiar game someone had left behind on their travels. Then he closed the door.

Tucked under his jacket in the waist of his jeans was the Colt M1911, loaded. As soon as he passed the reception area and out through the lobby, Dean would surreptitiously remove the weapon, survey the parking area and make a dash for his wrecked car.

He took the stairs, as opposed to the lift, holding onto the gold handrail. As he reached the ground floor the overly polite and happy receptionist was emerging from the ladies' room. She did a comical double-take.

'Is everything all right, sir?' she asked, slightly anxious when she saw the key to room 56 in his hand.

'Yes. Everything is great.'

'Are you leaving?'

Dean snorted laughter at that rather obvious observation. 'Yes, Sherlock.'

This time the receptionist laughed aloud and then fell silent. 'Was there a problem with the room or the service?' she said, perplexed.

Shaking his head Dean said, 'No. On the contrary. I enjoyed my brief stay here. But as I told you earlier, miss, I only came here because of some pest haranguing me on my journey. If however I am travelling this way in the foreseeable future I'll be sure to drop by.'

'I'll have to sign you out,' she said. Her voice emitted a touch of remorse.

'Okay,' Dean said. Then much to his surprise the receptionist leant forward and planted a soft kiss on his cheek.

Before he had chance to query the 'what and why', the receptionist hurried forward towards the lobby. Dean understood that discussing it in the reception area would land the attractive young woman in trouble. Instead he closed his eyes for a moment and committed the kiss to his memory.

Thank you.

Every other thought took a backward step while the memory of the kiss lingered like the scent of a woman's perfume as he entered the lobby and approached the broad oak desk.

It was the kiss he thought about when the moment came for it all to end...

42.

WITH THE SHOTGUN in his grasp, Anton crossed the car park to the main entrance to the Holiday Inn Express Hotel. He squinted at the brilliance the cylindrical silencer reflected from the glorious sunshine. The shade of the lobby allowed his eyes to focus without obscurity.

He strode into the hotel like a matador into the bullpen. His whole demeanour exuded confidence. Then he came to a halt and faced the one who'd been his toughest challenge to date. He waited purposefully with inhuman patience. He waited for his intended prey to turn around and face his destiny.

And then he did…

Their eyes met across the spacious lobby. What Anton silently admired was how the prey did not react as he'd done throughout the hunt. Instead he stood motionless with a queer smile on his face and a light shining somewhere deep in his eyes. It was as if they both knew without the other speaking that this was the moment it all came down to. But surely after all the struggle and thwarting him thus far the prey would at least make one last attempt to flee or fight.

Anton saw the attractive young lady behind the reception desk take notice of his big gun. That was all her protruding eyes saw. In the next instant she'd react and another member of staff or guest would intrude. There was no need for that.

Now that the moment of profound realisation had passed the act itself was rudimentary in comparison. Anton marched forward, the empty shell discharging itself from the chamber and, fired at point blank range, obliterating the face of the prey.

If nothing else it erased the look of pity in its eyes and the queer smile.

Even as he turned on his heels and strode back outside, the mere sight of the smile baffled the hunter more than the receptionist being able to identify him if he was ever apprehended. The smile and the pity in those eyes didn't belong to a man who faces death and is seconds away from being erased. He tried to convince himself as he crossed the car park that it was a grimace, not a smile. But not even his consciousness would permit him to lie.

He got into the Volvo and tossed the backpack, which he'd picked up, onto the back seat. He knew Dean had the money on him, as he'd climbed into the Honda Civic and searched for it. All he found was and AK-47 fitted with a suppressor. As he started the car and drove off he could hear the shrieking of the receptionist that threatened to lift the roof off the hotel. But to Anton that was all a background din; not something he wasn't accustomed to. The expression of the face that no longer existed except in his mind persisted, and was all he could think of as he drove out of the car park and joined the M4, heading eastbound.

Why was he smiling and looked at me with pity? he kept asking himself.

43.

IT SEEMED LIKE wherever they went lately there was pandemonium. Yet DI Sark somehow knew that this time there would be a significant change in their ongoing case. Two patrol cars were parked outside the brown and beige bricked façade, side by side. It had been pure coincidence that the two detectives were travelling to Tenby when they got the call on their radio through dispatch that someone had apparently been murdered at this venue.

Now as they took the turning off the roundabout and drove past the Harvester restaurant, DI Jason had to drive up onto the kerb to allow the postman in his van to get through. Customers and staff members emerged from the Harvester and out of the Llandarcy Sports Academy gymnasium. The crowd parted like the red sea as DI Jason drove forward with the flashing blue beacon spilling onto the road in front in neon light.

DI Sark sat in the passenger seat, numb. As they approached the Holiday Inn Express Hotel and spotted a constable vomiting violently on the pavement he closed his window for a moment. He blocked out the sounds of crying, screaming and retching from outside and envisioned his wife, at home, in the kitchen. He saw her in his mind's eye wearing a red plaid apron, standing in front of a hot stove opening the door with gloved hands. The steam that billowed out fogged the kitchen and when it dissipated, DI Sark opened his eyes.

The PCSO who wasn't puking approached them on legs as stable as spaghetti. Sark and Jason flashed their badges. Then DI Jason asked, 'What's the story?'

'Guy got shot at point blank range in the lobby. Some big fucker with a shotgun did it then walked back out again. Security cameras are being checked so they can rewind the footage and make a copy.' He rubbed his ashen face and buried the heels of his hands into his eye sockets. Then added: 'I'd brace yourself if I was you, guys. I'm only not being sick 'cause I've got an empty stomach, I'll tell ya that much.'

DI Sark nodded. 'Good job, officer. Secure the area until further assistance arrives. Who else has been at the crime scene?'

'Uh, all the employees and eighteen customers. All have been evacuated. They're over there.' He pointed to a patch of grass. The employees were of course in uniform and the eighteen customers were dressed in casual clothes. They were all huddled together, some standing, some sitting, all displaying distressed and sullen expressions.

'Anyone witness the murder?' DI Sark asked.

'Just the receptionist. She's been falling in and out of consciousness. We've dispatched an ambulance to treat her for shock. Poor lass was hiding behind the reception desk, shaking like a leaf screaming her head off. She'll never fully recover from this, I can tell ya. Things like this only happen once in a while. I thank the lord Jesus for that, yes'm.'

DI Sark and DI Jason exchanged a brief look that said, 'I wish this kind of thing only happened once in a while; that wouldn't be so bad.'

Patting the uniform on the shoulder, Sark headed to the entrance. He stood in the vestibule. His eyes zoomed in on the dead body sprawled out in a pool of blood, bone and brain matter, like a movie would have to emphasise the effect.

Perhaps if Sark had known beforehand that the cadaver belonged to ex-policeman Dean Ferris, it wouldn't feel as if he'd been punched in the gut. In that moment when his eyes registered the body of a man he knew vaguely everything else fell into place.

It was over.

The hunt had reached its – what many would deem inevitable – conclusion.

And the hunter had caught up to the prey at long last.

This time, however, the ex-drug squad undercover officer had run out of luck. Even a cat only had nine close calls before its time came. Dean had thwarted his adversary for a considerable amount of time. Nevertheless, it had merely been a futile exercise that had ended the only way it was ever realistically going to end.

A pang of hurt and sorrow exploded inwardly. Although Sark had done everything in his power to save Dean from the peril he found himself in, he still felt remorse. He didn't know whether that was because he felt as though he'd failed as a policeman doing his utmost to save an innocent's life or as a man who had to live with the memory thereafter.

As though he moved without any control over his bodily functions, Sark ambled towards the human remains of a brave man that had failed in doing one last good deed. He covered his mouth and nose with the sleeve of his jacket to prevent gagging. The gruesome sight imbedded itself to his memory. Once this day was finally over, sleep would become a distant lover from another lifetime.

And yet all of this came about due to a mob boss's insistence that Dean owed him a favour he couldn't refuse. Yet Dean had done this errand – or at least attempted to do it – without complaint.

DI Sark wholeheartedly wished now more than ever before that Dean had accomplished his task. He didn't know how much money approximately Dean had been hauling. It wasn't important to a certain degree. Nevertheless, what angered the detective more than anything else save all the innocent people who lost their lives, was that this Anton assassin had got away with the bundle and could be anywhere now. Only weariness diffused the anger.

Why though? What was it that made Dean so damn adamant and recalcitrant? Evidently, the man who'd been called 'The black sheep' within the law enforcement had a conscience that was almost Christ-like in modern times.

Failure didn't merely mean embarrassment or disappointment; it came at the ultimate cost. Yet after all the warnings and even pleases, Dean Ferris had taken this mission upon himself like nothing else mattered. Sark admitted silently that was far more courageous and admirable than some of the colleagues he'd worked alongside. And that wasn't an insult or putting their bravery into question either. It was a simple, undeniable fact that the scarcely recognisable cadaver in front of him was the epitome of sacrifice and heroism.

The deed clearly meant the world to him and therefore no matter what mistakes he'd made in the past, they had been overshadowed by the good thing he'd tried to do today.

'I'm sorry,' Sark whispered to the deceased.

The brightly lit lobby reflected his image in the scarlet pool. In it Sark saw his blood-red features. Strangely it appeared he was crying blood.

A hand rested gently upon his shoulder. Sark was startled in spite of himself. When he craned his head back he was relieved to see his partner eyeing the disfigured cadaver. A hollow cavernous niche poured blood, bone fragments and brain matter out onto the drowning linoleum.

DI Jason said aloud what Sark had thought. 'The hunt is over…'

44.

A GLIMMER OF HOPE competed with the horrifying climax to a long, gruelling hunt. DI Sark and DI Jason had spoken with the receptionist briefly, although the paramedics had given the detectives reproachful looks as they assisted her into the back of the awaiting ambulance.

DI Sark didn't want to cling onto a thread of hope, as it had already been cut at the cord at the crime scene. Yet after speaking with the maitre'd he couldn't help but focus on something that had to be more positive than what had transpired in the lobby.

'Just for clarification,' Sark said, making certain they were referring to the correct individual, 'the man in the lobby – the one who died – was the man who enquired whether or not you had stamps, an envelope and a piece of writing paper, yes?'

The maitre'd nodded, not appreciating the tone the detective used, as though addressing a child. 'Yes. I'm not stupid.'

'No one said you were,' DI Jason said, raising his palms in a 'no offence' gesture. 'We just need the facts to be clear in order to prevent a mix-up later on.'

'Man asks for piece of writing paper, envelope and stamps. First class. No first class stamps, but because he's willing to pay five pounds for one first class stamp, a customer who overhears the conversation who has two first class stamps sells them, knowing he'll be gaining. I then took those items to the kind man who gives me a twenty-pound tip. Very generous. He then asks for strawberries and some white wine. I go get them for him. It takes a while. By the time I come back he's written

260

a letter and hands it to me. He says, about the letter, "It has more importance than you will ever know." Or somethin' like that. Anyway, letter is very important and he asks me to make sure the postman takes it with him back to the sorting office with the other mail for collecting.'

The middle-aged man of Italian origins shrugs.

'D'you have any idea who or where the letter was going?' DI Sark asked.

'Sorting office.'

Laughing, DI Jason turned away, shoulders bouncing up and down. DI Sark gazed heavenward.

'Yeah, obviously it's going to the pissing sorting office,' Sark said, doing well not to lose his patience. 'But did you happen to notice where the letter was addressed to by any chance? Or is it quicker and easier to wait for the resurrection of Jesus?'

The maitre'd shook his head in disdain. 'Bad attitude. But no, I do not stick my nose into other people's business. But I did notice its destination was somewhere in a place called Tenby. I only noticed because I'd put it with the other mail at the reception desk.'

DI Sark didn't hear anything the maitre'd had said after he'd said Tenby. DI Jason flicked the laughing off instantly and whirled around. They didn't need to know anything more.

'Maybe it's a letter apologising to her for failing,' DI Jason said, as they made their way across the car park to their vehicle.

Sark shook his head, disagreeing. 'But how could he know that? His death was spontaneous.'

'You told him about how you sussed out what he was doing by intuition. Perhaps his own intuition told him to write a letter to Sandra as a back-up in case he failed.'

'That doesn't make sense, though,' Sark said, visibly irritated. 'There was no package, only a small white envelope with a piece of paper in it. What good's that to Sandra? Ultimately, he's failed and worst of all Anton has got a pay-out for killing Tobias, albeit inadvertently, and many others along the way. Thus his reputation is not only intact but has increased beyond measure throughout the country.'

DI Jason pressed the button for the car to open automatically. They got in and slammed the doors. 'The letter is "of more importance than we'll ever know", according to Dean. Perhaps the letter is a clue.'

'A clue to what?' Sark said, interested in his partner's comment.

DI Jason shrugged again. 'Only one way to find out is to go to Sandra Hill's home and find out.'

'One of us has to stay here to see what the security cameras show.'

'Well, you stay and I'll continue onto Tenby. The letter's not gonna be there until tomorrow, anyway. And most likely, don't pin your hopes on it, 'cause it's probably nothing but a letter of condolence. The letter's not gonna alter the case in any way. What's done is done, as they say. Now those left behind just have to live with it.'

Sark rubbed the nape of his neck where he felt tense. 'Yeah, you're right.' With that said he squeezed his partner's shoulder and got out.

'And another thing,' DI Jason called out as his partner was about to close the door.

'What?'

'Call your wife. Tell her I'll get her a new lamp.'

Sark offered a thin smile. Then he closed the door.

***

Half an hour later, DI Sark was leaning over the security guard watching the monitor in the niche behind the counter. There were three monitors in total behind the desk. One was filming the lobby, the second one was filming the car park area, and the third was rewinding.

Sark had little experience with modern technology. He could work the TV, microwave, Hi-Fi system, computer and his mobile. And even then he'd only acquired basic skills. All the buttons and the black rubber joystick on the desk looked far too complicated for him to decipher if he had to do this on his own.

On the 22-inch screen the receptionist that had paled and been carted off in an ambulance ran backwards towards the exact spot DI Sark was standing. It made what they were seeing all the more surreal.

'Here we go,' the security guard said. He was a big, rotund man who didn't look anything at all what a security guard ought to look like, Sark thought. He wasn't big because he went to the gym everyday and pumped iron, Schwarzenegger-style. God only knew how he'd be able to chase anyone.

Switching off his train of thought, Sark concentrated on the screen and waited patiently for the whole incident to reverse time. *Shame life wasn't that simple,* he thought. If that notion could ever be made a reality someday then he'd find himself out of a job. That didn't seem like such a bad thing at times like this.

'Ready, Detective?' the security guard asked, breaking his reverie.

'Yeah, I am. Are you though? I mean this isn't like watching a movie. This kinda thing sticks with you. I can only suggest that you don't watch it. I can't order that.'

'I'm not scared,' the security guard protested.

'I'm not disputing that,' Sark said, not meaning to offend the guard's manhood. 'But seeing this kinda thing disrupts your sleep. Sometimes ignorance is bliss in comparison to what I come across. I'll let you know when I'm finished.'

The security guard remained motionless, adamant.

'Please,' Sark said in a gentle but firm voice.

Finally the security guard stood up and sidled out of the way.

'Thank you,' Sark muttered, aware that he'd insulted the man. 'Oh, one more thing. Is there any sound?'

The security guard shook his head. 'No. But the stick allows you to turn the camera angle. But that won't work on a recording. But you can hit the red button which gives you a view of the exterior.'

Sark nodded. 'Okay. And stick around. I'm not very good with these things; I might need your assistance.'

At that the security guard perked up. The detective knew it wasn't out of some sick, twisted lust to see the violence unfold. If nothing else it'd give him something exciting to be involved in instead of the banal ennui of his mundane duty.

'How do I get the footage rolling?'

The security guard came back over to the desk and leant over Sark.

Sighing in defeat, Sark said, 'Here, you fly the plane, captain. But when you start getting nightmares don't say I didn't warn you, got it?'

'Jus' wanna help, Detective, that's all.'

Sark gestured that he should get on with it, and then the cordial chat ceased and the screen was all that mattered.

Unlike the old portable TVs that showed what the CCTV picked up, the flat screen picture was clear as good eyesight. The camera was behind them above the wall sconces, more than seven feet high. Sark and the security guard peered closer, absorbing every fine detail. The attractive brunette receptionist with tawny skin and her hair tied in a bun walked past so quickly she'd have been unrecognisable if Sark hadn't seen and spoken to her before. She came back into view, only now her back faced the lens. Then Dean came into view, his body canted to the left, as though he carried extra weight on that side. He leant on the glossy counter, talking amicably to the receptionist. What they were discussing was anyone's guess.

The detective felt like his and the security guard viewing this past event was an intrusion of Dean's privacy. He was alive and burdened with some concealed injury. But that aside, he was well... and smiling. If one were to say content that would be an apt observation too. This, Sark found, was odd.

Then the sunshine was blotted by a moving silhouette. The long instrument with a cylinder at the top end gleamed in the yellow radiance. Then the dim of the lobby enveloped him and the figure was a tall, broad shouldered man with chiselled features, armed with a shotgun.

Although neither the security guard nor DI Sark heard the gun blast, the brilliant, momentary flash of light made them recoil. The spray of clothing blood and something else that was most likely bone fragments and brain matter decorated the lobby. Dean collapsed, a marionette whose puppeteer had dropped his handles unexpectedly.

The next part was worst of all.

Dean lay sprawled out across the shiny linoleum, chest rising and falling far too quickly for it to be anywhere near healthy. His legs, bent at the knees, twitched spasmodically. The towering and menacing figure approached its prey and fired again.

By this time the security guard had turned away and buried his head between his knees. Sark felt pins and needles stab his rosy cheeks. The man they only knew as an assassin called Anton then bent down and carefully turned Dean's nearly headless body over and pulled the backpack off him. Dean's lifeless arms slapped the floor, spraying dark red liquid further across the room. The figure pivoted slowly – gracefully even – and walked back outside.

DI Sark couldn't watch anymore. But he did notice the receptionist rising from beneath the counter and chancing a peek over the top. And although he couldn't hear her screaming or see the face her hands clapped across, the emotions she'd felt resonated somewhere in his thundering heart.

After some time (he couldn't be certain how long exactly), Sark rested his hand on the security man's back. 'You okay?'

The security guard nodded. Then seconds later he straightened up and regarded Sark. 'I shouldn't have watched it after all,' he said, a wiser man after the viewing.

'You'll be all right,' Sark assured him. 'Listen, can you rewind to the moment the perp leaves the building. Only this time show it from an exterior angle?'

The security guard said he could. A couple of clicks and pressing of buttons later and an expansive exterior view showed the whole car park area and The Harvester occupying the next lot.

'Nothing happens here though, does it?' the security guard asked.

Sark shook his head. 'If you mean "death wise" then no. But I wanna see what vehicle our perp is driving.'

Anton emerged, and even from the high angle DI Sark saw the unmistakable frown on his countenance as he stepped off the kerb and headed towards a brown Volvo. Unfortunately, from the recorded angle they were unable to zoom in and be able to see the registration number.

'Does that help?'

Sark faced the security guard who he already thought a lot of. 'It does and it doesn't. We got a brief description of the car he was driving upon leaving the crime scene, but no license plate to narrow it down. But by now my colleagues should've traced the victims he killed to acquire that vehicle to be able to identify it.'

The security guard gave 'thumbs-up' sign. 'Just a matter of time from the sounds of it,' he said, upbeat.

'Naw, not this guy,' Sark said, thinking aloud. 'He's been an enigma for many years for a good reason. He's probably dumped the vehicle by now and changed his identity to look like someone else. He's been doing it for years. That's why they call him "The Chameleon".'

The security guard sat back in the swivel chair, visibly taken aback. 'Sounds like Jack Reacher's worst nightmare.'

'And James Bond and Jason Bourne, too,' Sark added.

Neither man spoke for a minute.

'Is there anything else I can help you with, Detective?'

'Can you cut a copy onto a disk of the incident?'

'Yeah, sure. I can do that right away. Just need to get someone from staffing to give me a blank CD and the necessary paperwork. Won't take too long.'

'Thanks,' Sark said. Then he watched the forensic team begin their assiduous examination of the crime scene, searching for any minor detail or piece of evidence. This time DI Sark thought their presence was fruitless. The CCTV footage spoke a thousand words and all of them with shock right down to the bone marrow.

45.

SANDRA HILL'S drawn, sleep-deprived face reminded DI Jason of Edward Munch's painting of the screaming woman. She wouldn't have been able to have coped with more bad news had he arrived at her home for such a reason. There were dark circles beneath her eyes. Bags appeared to stretch her flesh off her bone. Of course, this was an exaggeration – but only a slight one at that.

DI Jason formally introduced himself, flashing his credentials. Then he said in a clipped voice, 'May I come in, Mrs Hill?'

'What's happened now?' she snapped.

'Nothing bad, I can assure you. But I'd like to explain somewhere a little more private, if you don't mind.'

The grieving mother moved aside but not immediately. She waited for the detective to close the front door behind him and then led the way down the short hall to the living room. 'Tea, Detective?'

'Only if you're making a cuppa.'

'No. I'm having a brandy.'

'Then I'm all right,' he said, deliberately waiting to be invited to sit down.

Sandra poured herself half a shot glass of brandy and motioned for him to sit in the armchair opposite the sofa. 'What's all this about? And don't gimme that crap about how it's nothing bad. The minute you or someone who works for the mob is around there's always bad news. So get to it. You're not welcome here.'

DI Jason cleared his throat, loosening the collar around his neck. 'The man we are certain killed your son has been on the news.'

'Yes, my husband did mention something. But I didn't know if it was true or not. Phoning from the local pub pissed out of your skull isn't exactly convincing.'

'It is true, Mrs Hill,' DI Jason said. 'He's been hunting someone Paul had hired to do a job that involves you.'

Sandra put her untouched brandy on the coaster, alarmed. 'Me?'

'Yes. We believe that this assassin has been hunting a man who used to work undercover for the drug squad. Without going into this man's past and how he and Paul met is by-the-by. What we believe and are almost certain of is that Paul sent this man on an errand to give you a lot of money as a peace offering and to help pay for funeral expenses. You mentioned he's tried to contact you before but after what happened you understandably gave him the cold shoulder. That is correct, ma'am?'

Sandra said it was a fact.

'Since last night the assassin has been murdering Paul's men and anyone who gets in his way. The mob boss who Paul had a falling out over refused to pay this dangerous individual 'cause he killed Tobias when it should've been your nephew, Leo. You know all about that.'

Sandra said she did indeed know that bit of information.

'A couple of hours ago this ex-policeman doing Paul's errand for him was found dead at a hotel on his way here to give you the money. He was killed by the assassin who killed your son.'

'So now you're telling me the same S.O.B. that you've been unable to arrest because you couldn't find your own arsehole with a compass has now come into the possession of how much money?'

'We don't know the exact amount,' DI Jason said, feeling hot. 'But it's a lot. A few grand, at least.'

'You said "Nothing bad, I can assure you". Are you for real?'

DI Jason felt his cheeks flush. 'I meant…'

'You didn't know what you meant,' Sandra said. Her voice never wavered with emotion, but her dishevelled form leant forward. 'You're just a pup still wet behind the ears from the academy. You didn't know what you meant if you had all day to think it over.'

'Mrs Hill, please,' he begged.

She turned away, disgusted. 'What are you doing here? D'you enjoy being the bearer of bad news?'

'If you just let me finish.'

Sandra theatrically threw her arms up in the air. 'Oh God. You are somethin' else. Not content with giving me the news of my son's death but now you've gotta finish your morose tale for my sake. That's what you're gonna tell me.'

She contorted her haggard face. 'If you didn't say it as if you were reading it outta a goddamn textbook I might not mind so much.'

'Apparently,' DI Jason went on, not waiting for permission. All he wanted right then was to say his piece and take his leave. 'Apparently, before his death, Dean wrote a letter to someone residing in Tenby. We believe that letter is addressed to you.'

'A letter? What's this… Dean fella writing to me for?'

DI Jason shrugged. 'That's what we're trying to find out. My partner and I think it has something to do with our investigation. We'd like to be here tomorrow morning – providing it's in tomorrow's post – when you receive it. It's evidence and we'll need it. I'll be staying at the Atlantic Hotel. Can we exchange phone numbers, please?'

The reproachful demeanour Sandra had emanated towards him dissipated instantly. 'Yes, all right.'

'We don't mean to intrude, but the letter may tell us something that can help solve the case. Don't hold me to that though,' he added.

They dutifully swapped numbers. DI Jason gave Sandra his mobile number and he took her home phone number. Then he took his leave and ambled back through the picturesque seaside town welcoming the sunshine and sharp breeze off the shore.

No wonder she's devastated, he thought. *Tobias and his family had a perfect small town life out here. No murders happened here, except on TV and in popular crime novels. Tenby was the epitome of sun, sea and most of all relaxation.*

***

DI Jason got back to his room and opened the doors to the veranda. The wind whipped his hair back off his forehead. It was far too windy and cold to be outside even if there was still some sunlight. He returned inside and perched himself on the edge of the mattress and called his partner.

'What's happening?'

'He left in the Mishar's Volvo. Currently in the process of tracking it down. How 'bout you? You there yet?'

'Just spoken to Mrs Hill.' He went on to explain how she'd rebuked him for daring to call her. 'When I told her the reason she relaxed. And another thing: one of us should inform Paul that Dean is dead.'

Static interrupted their conversation momentarily.

'... hear me now?'

'Yeah,' DI Jason said.

'I already told Paul over the phone. I haven't got time to go back and forth to peoples' houses all day. Paul wasn't related to Dean... and he knew the risk involved.'

'What he say?'

'He asked how it happened, went quiet and then hung up.'

'I'm sure he's not that upset. Probably pissed off with Dean for allowing Anton to get the money.'

'Ah, that's what I thought. But in fairness he never mentioned the money. And it's not something he'd forget. After all, that was the purpose of the errand.'

'Perhaps he's going soft in his old age.'

'The chief wants me to hang around in case we find Anton or the Volvo. There's not much point both of us being with Sandra, anyway.'

'No, I guess not. Okay, I'm gonna get some grub in me before I starve to death. Call me if you hear anything?'

'No worries. Ditto.'

DI Jason hung up. His empty stomach growled.

***

The sun hadn't slipped beneath the horizon for long before the sky turned black. DI Jason shovelled mouthfuls of greasy chips and jumbo sausage down. He'd bought them from a local chip shop in the cobbled streets concealed by the ancient stone walls and returned to the hotel with the lapels of his winter coat turned up. Now he sat in front of the TV watching the national news with the volume turned up.

A recent photograph of Cathy Groves was displayed on the screen, followed by a shot on the suburban street she and her widow resided. A female news reporter who couldn't have been any older than twenty-five stood directly in front of the camera. She wore a red scarf and gloves to match and a duffel coat. Her nose and cheeks were almost the same colour. Behind her the familiar sight of patrol cars and yellow crime scene tape fluttering in the breeze was depressing. Had DI Jason not been without food since earlier that morning the melancholy settling into the pit of his stomach would have abated his hunger.

'Detectives believe that the same man who murdered Tony Nivean, Danny Sampson and Cathy Groves then pursued fellow resident and ex-police officer, Dean Ferris from this crime scene to the Holiday Inn Hotel off Junction 43 on the M4 and shot him twice. Police were also earlier today when the suspect's vehicle was found stranded on the hard shoulder containing the bodies of Jill and Chris Mishar. Their young daughter survives them. Another incident which cost the life of a filling station attendant in a Texaco garage in Cardiff is also said to be related. The deceased's family is yet to be notified...'

DI Jason changed the channel to number four and watched an old *Simpsons* episode. Homer was rushing like a bat out of hell to Springfield gorge to stop Bart from doing a death-defying stunt when his mobile buzzed.

He checked the ID on the tiny illuminated screen, then answered. 'Yeah.'

'We've found the Mishar's Volvo,' DI Sark said.

'Where?'

'A turning just off the A465.'

'Where's that?'

'On the dual carriageway heading towards Neath town centre.'

'Where in Neath is it? Where's Anton?' DI Jason said, putting the bag of chips and half-eaten sausage to one side.

'The car's been left on some back road in Neath Abbey. No sign of Anton. The place is practically deserted, save some small businesses. It's a perfect place to pull over and discreetly disappear. I'm telling you, it's like this guy has planned this whole thing out right down to every last minute detail. There's a canal and a rubbish disposal. A monastery. All on a quiet back road. The only places worth mentioning that could ID him are McDonald's and a car dealership called Trade Centre

Wales. We're asking around now if anyone saw someone of his description. But it's gone six already. He's been gone a good coupla hours.'

'He'll turn up.'

'Will he though? The car was empty. No fingerprints. No loose strands of hair. Nothing. Zip. I gotta bad feelin' 'bout this.'

'No one can remain that elusive after everything's happened,' DI Jason said, believing that and yet doubting himself at the same time.

'He's done pretty well till now. Cascarini was wrong – he's not a chameleon, he's a fuckin' ghost.'

'I very much doubt a man carrying a .38 and a big-as-fuck shotgun walking around any town isn't gonna stay unnoticed for too long.'

A pause. Then: 'We'll see…'

46.

A **TALL,** broad-shouldered man with blond hair curling beneath his ears crossed the main road opposite a primary school. He wore a dark green raincoat and thick black lensed reading glasses. Something long and heavy looking was cradled to his side beneath the coat. Fortunately, this man had used a hacksaw from the boot of a borrowed car to cut the butt off to be able to carry it in a concealed manner.

His old ally, darkness, accompanied him as he ambled, seemingly aimlessly up the main road. A sloping gradient took him past an old church and cemetery. The cemetery was placed bizarrely alongside the playing field of a junior school. Using the zebra crossing, the man walked to the other side. He slipped into the phone box and rummaged in his coat pocket. On the metallic phone it informed him of the amount and how to operate the device. His pockets were full of pound coins and loose change. The number he dialled was a mobile and would guzzle his loose change. But that was a minor concern to the more imperative issue at hand. He fed the coins into the slot and dialled the long number from acute memory. A few cars passed on the main road behind him intermittently. Apart from the droning of passing cars all was quiet.

An elderly man's voice answered after the fourth ring in Spanish idiom.

'Hello?'

'It's me, Marco. I need your help right away. Can you help me?' The man's voice sounded as if it were full of sand or grit.

His mouth appeared to fill the lower half of his chiselled face beneath his prominent cheekbones.

'Ah, the prodigal son remembers me, after all this time.'

'Time is not my friend,' the man who spoke fluent Spanish said.

'When is it?'

'Now more than ever, time is against me.'

'Is your job for your new employer not as good as you first thought?' The old man's tone had an underlying mocking to it.

'No. They refused to pay me and now I'm a wanted man. It's on the news.'

'This is a serious matter I gather, yes?' the old man said, no longer humorous.

'Very,' the man with artificial blond hair said.

'Okay. Where are you now?'

He pivoted and peered through steamy glass to a sign that read Neath Abbey. He told this to the elderly man on the other end and gave him a brief description of his surroundings. Then he waited for an answer.

'Okay,' the old man said, after much deliberation. 'Go to this St John The Baptist Church and keep out of sight. It is dark. No one will see you. You wait there. I'll send an old friend of mine to pick you up and take you to his home in Aberystwyth. You'll have to keep your head down before you can return. When enough time has passed we'll forge a passport and give you a new identity. But no more killing anyone or getting into fights or disputes. That's the best I can do.'

'Thank you,' the man in the phone box said.

'Don't thank me yet. Thank me when it's over and you're safe.'

The man in the phone box terminated the call and replaced the receiver. His thoughts were on the ageing arms' dealer whom he'd helped a couple of years previously before leaving for London, dreaming of making enough money to return to his native land and pay back those who had been good to him.

Now, it seemed, he couldn't even help himself.

***

The sky was as black as coal dust. The air shrunk and felt like a thick duvet with humidity. The blond-haired man's gait that had earlier today been one of purpose and intent was now lethargic, defeated. The burden of his troubled thoughts dragged his head into his chest. The oppressive air swallowing the oxygen did not affect him. Physically he was as fit and lithe as an Olympic athlete. But mentally his impenetrable defence had been shattered by what had transpired after the events in the hotel lobby. His confidence and self-belief and determination had been castrated.

He passed the high, wire-mesh fencing surrounding the front schoolyard without so much as a glance. Instead he kept replaying the scene in the Volvo over and over again on a never-ending loop as though by doing so he'd be able to make sense of it.

After executing his prey and departing the hotel with the backpack, Anton or Christiano or Marco had rejoined the road and skipped going further west on the M4 and opted to take the next left onto the A465. At the second left turning he'd found a convenient place to pull over and not be in full view.

In the hotel car park the assassin had wandered past the bullet-ridden Honda Civic and quite clearly saw the vinyl briefcase lying open in the footwell beneath the passenger seat. Predictably the prey had opted not to leave the money in the car and took it with him so it would be out of sight. He was as certain of this as anything else, because that's what he would have done.

The actual killing of his prey in the end had been child's play in comparison to the previous day's events. He'd crossed the cement parking bay to his car, realising that his prey had welcomed the end. The man with many names understood this. The man he'd been hunting all day had succumbed at long last. He'd succumbed not only to his relentless pursuer but to the task itself. And that was fair, the assassin thought. For the prey had won his respect. He'd out-thought, outmanoeuvred him on many occasions and still the assassin filled his rear view. After all, it wasn't even the prey's money. He was merely the gofer; an expendable gofer for a mob boss on his way down. And, even in hindsight, the one called 'The Chameleon' and 'The Shape' had every right to believe that this was the case.

That was until he opened the backpack.

The backpack contained these items: iodine; gauze pads, a roll of bandages; pepper spray, and a Colt M1911 pistol.

No money was to be found in any of the other compartments. It was this fact and this alone that frazzled Anton's brain. A roiling panic coiled from within like a rumbling thunder growing closer. His eyes stretched the optical nerves, elastic band style. His pulse felt like electricity at the toes and fingertips. What was worse was that old, unwelcome emotion, fear which had arrived beyond the shadows of his former self unexpectedly. His heart mimicked the sound of high-tempo tap-dancing.

In the midst of this unsustainable emotion Anton ripped the backpack open and upended it and shook it furiously. But even while doing this he knew it was fruitless... absurd. The money wasn't in the backpack. That amount of money had not been in the possession of his prey either. He'd felt the Kevlar bullet proof vest beneath his clothing in the lobby and had sighed inwardly in relief that his first shot had been to the head. It seemed instinctual that the amount of money the prey had been hauling from London to the hotel was inside the backpack. He hadn't made a mistake by allowing his haste to betray him.

It was the not knowing that created confusion. The purple blister of lightening behind his retinas highlighted the moment he'd discovered the revelation and knew what it meant.

He'd been defeated...

The indestructible, inexorable killing machine had been outwitted quite remarkably. Even now walking with his chin touching the top part of his muscular chest it amazed him how this had happened. For he still couldn't see how it had been achieved. The prey hadn't known he was going to die when he did. He couldn't possibly have known that Anton was going to take it upon himself to come into the hotel looking for him. He'd barely made it into the hotel alive in the first place.

The prey had been wounded in the back of the upper arm and in the rear shoulder. Anton had seen the geyser of blood spraying out of his target's mouth in shock and pain. That would have been enough for any man to endure, especially under the circumstances. And yet his adversary had remained two steps ahead at all times, no matter what the situation seemed to be on the surface.

What plagued his ever-churning mind was one simple yet unanswerable question: Where was the money?

47.

THE FOLLOWING MORNING DI Jason got a call from his partner who told him they had found an empty vinyl briefcase in Dean's Honda Civic and an empty backpack in the Mishar's Volvo estate.

'Well, we kinda knew that anyway, didn't we? DI Jason said.

'Yeah, I suppose. Listen, I'm gonna make my way to you shortly. I'm just gonna give my wife a quick call. That's if she still remembers me. Probably gonna file for a divorce and get the keys changed. Bloody neighbour next door has been to my house more than me.'

DI Jason didn't know what to say to that sombre comment. It was true that a lot of detective inspectors ended up getting divorced due to their hectic working schedule. It wasn't as if they could clock in at 9am and then clock out at 5pm like most people. Yesterday had been one of the hardest, most gruelling days for everyone. They'd have more luck chasing shadows than catching their perpetrator, and what made it worse was how they'd have a mountain of paperwork and get grilled by their superiors on how they managed to not apprehend him. Instead six people had lost their lives since the day before yesterday.

Once he'd hung up, DI Jason had a full English breakfast. He washed it down with a pint of orange juice, feeling rejuvenated because of the nine-hour deep sleep he'd got. Then he took a hot shower, got dressed and ventured outside.

The sunshine was misleading, for the bitter cold whipping off the shore felt like a blanket of ice on his face. Last night he dreamed of a man with no face, armed with a shotgun and a cylindrical suppressor attached marching into the lobby, shooting dead the receptionist and taking the stairs. The man in his dream kicked open the doors of every room and moved on solely intent on finding him and nothing else. In his dream Jason had heard the din and knew intuitively who it was. He tried to flee the room but when he opened the door ajar and turned his head the faceless killer emerged from another room and headed towards him. He locked the door (not that that would hold him for long) and dove under his bed. This, of course, had been a big mistake. He was giving the impression that the room was vacated and yet he'd locked it from the inside. Evidently, he'd be found out. He rolled out of bed and threw himself to the door and took the chain off, and was about to ease the door open when the faceless killer stood on the other side of the threshold. He didn't even have a chance to be afraid. The door flew inwards smashing him in the face and sent him tumbling backwards. The faceless killer stood over him pointing his shotgun at his head…

…and then he woke up.

Falling asleep again the rest of his deep slumber was a dreamless nothing.

***

Less than an hour later DI Sark entered the lobby and would have walked right past DI Jason had he not called out and got his attention. DI Sark's eyes were a little bloodshot. Dark circles had formed beneath his eyes. His hair although combed appeared unkempt, and the coat he wore was creased.

'Where'd you sleep last night?'

'Fitfully in Skewen Police Station. I must've rolled over at one point, fallen off the couch and bashed my right shoulder.

Big fuckin' bruise there when I looked this morning. You look like you've been holidaying.'

They both chuckled at that comment. It was meant as a joke but in comparison to how they both appeared it wasn't exactly far off being true, either.

'Shall we make our way over to Sandra's?' DI Jason said, serious again.

'Yeah. Where's the car? A police constable dropped me off outside.'

'Let's walk instead. It'll do us good. It's not far from here either before you start moaning.'

As they stepped outside, Sark gazed out across the clear blue ocean and the few people on the beach walking their dogs. It looked so relaxing it made the case seem to be a million miles away. The buildings were all different shapes and hues. Sky-blue, pink, sunshine yellow, purple. *Houses built by adults and painted by children,* Sark thought.

'If we don't find him this is gonna be in the back of my mind for a long time, maybe for ever,' Sark said, thinking aloud.

'I refuse to believe that. The longer he stays in this country the more likely he'll reveal himself at some point. No man like him can restrain his killer instincts for long. No matter how many times he changes his disguise. And as I keep reiterating, as long as we do all we can then that's all we should be concerned about. You only think of the negative aspects. You seem to forget how many crimes we've solved in our short time working together. And I also believe in what-goes-around-comes-around sooner or later. This Anton, or whatever his real name is, will get his come-uppance.'

They walked out of the town and down a long street with a sea view called Marsh Road. On the other side of the long road was a street sign, Newell Hill. The detectives crossed the road and approached house number 15 and steadied themselves. In their hearts they hoped for the best but expected the worst. They'd had their hopes dashed so many times in their jobs that although that mantra seemed pessimistic it did prepare them for the worst.

DI Jason rang the doorbell and shuffled his feet. DI Sark rubbed his haggard face with his palms, hoping he looked at least half presentable.

The door opened and Sandra regarded both men. Then she said in a croak:

'I've got the letter…'

***

Five minutes later they were sitting in the living room. Sandra explained how she'd decided not to open the letter until they arrived. She had no idea what to expect. The probability that the letter was anything worthwhile now that the money had been stolen was for certain. It could however have been hate mail from Dean who knew his minutes and hours of yesterday leading up to his death and wanted to express his feelings. After all, when DI Sark told him that Paul had more than hinted that he was coming to Tenby Dean had understandably been irate.

'There's no point dwelling on the worst, Sandra,' DI Jason said. 'If you'd like us to open it we can and if it's something distasteful then we'll keep it to ourselves.'

Sandra shook her head. 'No. He wrote to me specifically, and went to great extremes from what you said to make sure it arrived. Like my Tobias that poor man lost his life doing something quite remarkable on my behalf. The least I can do is have the guts to read his letter. If it's deemed evidence and you are obligated to keep it as such thereafter then so be it. But it's addressed to me for a reason. He's speaking to me.'

With that said she leant forward, picked up the envelope from where it lay on the oak table and tore it open. The two detectives watched intently as she opened the single sheet of paper and read the dead man's handwriting.

To Sandra Hill,

If you are reading this in the company of the police, then it's safe to say that I am no longer part of this world. My life has been taken by the same man who took your son's. Many years ago I made a mistake that haunted me later in life. My colleagues gave up on me as did the people I thought of as my friends. What was worse was I lost the girl I fell in love with and my family disowned me. But there was one man who helped me in my time of need - your brother. I'm sure that the police have already given you this information. What they might not know is that I had two choices the day before yesterday. One: refuse to return the favour Paul Demato did for me and lose my life there and then or some time later as though I were just another gangster. Or number two: risk my life by doing a good, moral deed that would help a grieving mother in her time of suffering. At first I hated Paul for putting me in this position. He'd only save me so he could use me as a pawn when it suited him. I even tried to hate you for turning your back on Paul, the way my family turned their back on me. But I couldn't. Just like I couldn't hate my family for disowning me (God knows I tried).

During this errand, I saw a lot of other good people lose their lives as well. People who have something to live for, unlike me. My family is religious and I guess to a point so am I. I thought if I could do this one last thing for the greater good, God might see me trying to redeem myself and forgive me when no one else would.

And now I realise that I've been mortally wounded and am struggling to breathe I will never get to meet you and see your face when you get the money to help with the costs of your son's funeral on Saturday. The man hunting me is outside waiting to kill me. At some point I will have to leave this hotel and accept my fate. But I still want to achieve what I set out to do.

But fate or God or both if you like must've seen this too and decided to help me in my quest. At the bottom of the single white bed in room 56 of the Holiday Inn Express in Llandarcy off junction 43 you will find a popular board game, Monopoly. When I saw it and realised what I must do it made me laugh till tears poured out of my eyes.

In school once my teacher asked why I was crying when my caterpillar evolved into a butterfly and we had to go outside and take the lids off so they could fly away. I told her because he was my butterfly and that now he was gone he was as good as dead. During my journey to where I will die I cried for the first time in years. I cried because through all the hate directed towards me by the ones closest to me there were people like you, the detective and the nice lady at the Texaco garage who still cared. Then I remembered what my teacher said, 'Dean the butterfly was – and still is – your caterpillar. But like people who wear out their bodies the caterpillar must change to ascend. You didn't do wrong at all. You did something great – you set your butterfly free.'

I've realised that I'm just a caterpillar who has worn out his body and is ready to become like a butterfly, so I too can be set free.

If you go to room 56 in the hotel I stayed at you will find I did do that one last moral deed for the greater good. Take it, and know that your son Tobias, like me, has been set free.

Dean Ferris

Tears streamed down Sandra's quivering cheeks. The two CID detectives exchanged a glance, not knowing if the grieving woman's tears were a good thing or not

'What's it say, Mrs Hill?' DI Jason wanted to know.

The woman couldn't answer, so she handed him the letter. He read it and then passed it over to his partner. DI Sark read it and when he got to the part which mentioned him he felt tears welling in his eyes. He didn't risk speaking right then. Instead he put the letter down on the table and composed himself.

'Guess we need to get you to the Holiday Inn Express right away,' DI Sark said.

'I'll call the chief; tell him what we know. The hotel is closed for the day after yesterday's events, so getting into the room won't be a problem, and no one has been in that room since Dean that we know of.'

There may yet be a silver lining to this monstrous cloud, Sark thought.

*****

An hour or so later, all three of them found themselves walking down the carpeted hall to room 56. DI Sark had the key and unlocked the door. The forensics hadn't thought of investigating the room Dean used. There wasn't any need, as the murder took place downstairs in the lobby. No one could have foretold these turn of events.

Both detectives gestured for Sandra to enter first, gentleman like. She stepped into the room and crossed to the slightly creased but otherwise immaculate white bed. She glanced over her shoulder, waiting for the detectives to give her permission. They did. Then she lowered herself to her knees and lifted up the quilt and peered into the gloom.

When she slid back out so she was visible again, a Monopoly board game was in her grasp. Hesitatingly, she lifted the lid off the box, and although she'd been prepared she still gasped at the sight before her.

'Fuck me,' DI Jason muttered under his breath.

There in all its magnificent glory was the money for which Dean had sacrificed his life just so she could obtain it and not the ruthless killer. Also, it was ironic that a board game centred round money and property should actually be used to stash bundles of cash, all of it as real as life itself.

'Will this be taken as evidence? Or is it mine now?' Sandra asked.

'No,' Sark said with a glad heart. 'That money is yours. It always was. Our investigation never had anything to do with a large amount of money being distributed via an ex-policeman acting as a courier. It was solely about catching the man who murdered your son and many other innocent people. Take it. Put it in your handbag and do as Dean Ferris suggested.'

The money was no compensation for not apprehending the man with many names. Yet it was a consolation to ease Mrs Hill's suffering. It left a bitter and sweet taste in Sark. No amount of money could ever replace the love of one's own son and the pain that came with the sudden loss. But what he saw sparkling in the grieving woman's eyes that day as they left room 56 and stepped outside and drove back to Tenby was a glimmer of hope. Hope that in the midst of a world-shattering storm there would be a rainbow when it passed.

'God bless that Dean Ferris chap,' Sandra said in a faraway voice in the car on the way back to her home. 'He'll suffer no more pain or anguish. And neither will my sweet Tobias 'cause they're both free...'

48.

ON THE DAY of Tobias Hill's funeral the rain that fell the night before ceased. Now the blades of grass in the rolling pastures glistened like emeralds. The service was concluded by a rendition of Amazing Grace. The burial ground beyond the church had a path cleared of overgrown shrubbery. The pallbearers wheeled the finest mahogany coffin out of the church and down the sloping path. Grieving relatives followed in an orderly fashion, Sandra Hill leading the way.

DI Sark was in attendance. His partner was back at CID headquarters writing up their report. He'd be busy going through all the statements and forensic evidence, trying to see if there was anything they'd missed that would lead them to the perpetrator.

Paul Demato was also in attendance. Initially, Sandra Hill had refused to allow him to come. Yet, providing he did not engage in conversation with her, he'd been permitted. As the coffin was lowered gently next to the hole in the ground, the pastor opened the good book and waited patiently for all the attendees to gather round.

He read loud and clear from the verse he'd chosen, made the holy sign of the cross, and then closed the tome. The burial had come to its inevitable conclusion. Paul who stood directly across the hole from Sandra nodded. Sandra reciprocated the gesture. She was aware of the troubles ahead, regarding court cases, fines and police records Paul was undergoing. His transition to Majorca, Spain, wouldn't be at all easy. He'd be watched diligently, authorities daring him to step out of line again so they could get him behind bars. Sandra had no sympathy. This, after all, was his come-uppance for all the wrongdoing and ultimately being at fault for the reason why her son had died so young in such horrifying circumstances.

DI Sark had observed this nod of distant acceptance. To him though, this felt like a hollow victory, at best. If this had been one of those crime/thriller novels his wife enjoyed reading there would be a nice ending where justice prevailed and the perpetrator was apprehended or died. Instead the force of reality hit him like an artic lorry.

As the congregation dispersed Sark didn't feel the urge to part ways with the coffin. He kept thinking what the point in one's life was. On a good day he believed that good, honest, hard-working folks were angels in training for the afterlife. On days like today he believed that the human race, although evolved, still possessed feral instincts and were no better than any other creature. All full of gluttony and selfishness.

'Thank you for coming,' a female voice said, breaking his reverie.

Sark whirled around, startled. 'Pardon?'

Sandra Hill bravely offered a thin smile and repeated what she'd said.

'Don't mention it,' he said.

'Where's your partner?'

'He's working. This case is not over till it's over,' Sark said, wanting to sound reassuring.

'I won't lie to you, Detective. I won't rest easily till you do get the S.O.B. that tore my world apart and contaminated my soul. But I also know just by looking at you that you'll not rest easily till you do. You're not just doing your job, you're doing what Dean did – giving himself up for the greater good. And you're a good man for that and that alone is enough. God bless you.'

Sandra embraced him and kissed him on the cheek.

DI Sark knew in that moment – apart from the ongoing investigation itself – the most important aspect of his life right then was to get home to be with his endearing wife.

'The letter was the most beautiful thing I've ever read or experienced,' Sandra whispered. 'Don't give up on people, Detective. You inspired him to do something beyond magnanimous. That's something to be thankful for, don't you think?'

'It's because of people like you Sandra I could never give up. I am truly sorry for your loss. But I want to believe that Dean was right; that your son has been set free to someplace where there is no pain or anguish.'

With that said the detective broke free from Sandra's warm hug and walked despondently down the sloping path.

'Goodbye,' Sandra said, loud enough so he could hear.

DI Sark stopped, pivoted and said, eyes smiling, 'Not goodbye, Mrs Hill. Never goodbye to people like yourself. Good journey.'

EPILOGUE

MRS SARK was in the kitchen, standing at the worktop, buttering two croissants. She'd awoken at half past six. The time according to the oven digital clock was 8:44. She'd been reading her Chris Mooney book for an hour. The night before she'd gone to bed earlier than usual. Her husband had come home in the evening, still dressed in his funeral attire.

They'd talked for three hours about everything other than the murder case he was currently working on. Mrs Sark knew her husband well enough to know when he was deeply troubled. Sometimes it was wise not to discuss the ins and outs of her husband's mind, regarding his job. Instead she'd cooked them a chicken casserole. During the night though, she had woken, disorientated by the low groans and moans and the endless stirring from Jonathan lying next to her.

The stillness of the street outside was a rarity. Often on a cold, winter night when her husband was working, the silence seemed foreboding. Now Mrs Sark embraced it. Life on earth on this Sunday morning would commence any minute now and the silence would be an ever-distant memory.

She heard the footfalls of Jonathan descend the stairs preceding his entrance. For a man who slept fitfully and appeared to have had bad dreams he looked quite handsome in his pyjama bottoms and Ghostbusters T-shirt. He brushed the back of his hair down and lowered himself around the dinette table.

'You're up early,' he said, stifling a yawn.

'Ah, but unlike someone I know I slept peacefully.'

Jonathan Sark rolled his eyes. He never could hide anything from his wife, who reminded him of a 1950's commercial or old black and white films where the wife stayed at home doing all the housework and had dinner on the table when her husband returned home. Their life was like that. They didn't send each other text messages throughout the day. Neither of them had joined Facebook and uploaded their pictures and likes and dislikes for the world to see. They had an old-fashioned dial phone and a pink and white classical radio. They watched old films starring the affable James Stewart and Grace Kelly. All in all they kept themselves to themselves, and enjoyed the simplicities of life.

Mrs Sark poured a glass of fresh cold water from the tap and placed the glass and china plate with two croissants on the coaster in front of Jonathan. 'There you go, sweetheart,' she said. Then she pulled the chair out from under the table and sat opposite.

Jonathan thanked her and took a thirsty gulp of water. He knew what was pending but didn't resist.

'Now,' Mrs Sark said in a polite but firm tone, 'are you going to tell me what troubles you so or shall I up and leave you with not even a backward glance?'

Sark smiled, blushing. 'You wouldn't do that, Miss,' he said.

'Oh. And why is that? You seem awfully sure of yourself, young man.'

'Your conscience would fret over what would become of me.'

This time it was Mrs Sark's turn to smile. 'How very true. But seriously. What's going on in that overheated mind of yours that'll be the death of you if you don't start closing that front door every day after work on your work and enjoy life?'

'Well, last night I had two conflicting dreams. Both vivid.'

Mrs Sark didn't interrupt. She let him ease into his narrative and watched him intently.

'The first one was of me and the killer we've been hunting. In this dream I was running – sprinting, even – down this narrow corridor with my service pistol extended, ready to fire. I was chasing the man. I kept thinking of what Don Mario Cascarini told me if I was going to pursue this fellow – that I must be willing to die and lose you. And this was it, I was running full pelt. I came to a corner and put on the brakes. Then I stopped, stood motionless, thinking of your face, memorising every feature, every detail. I thought how much I'd miss seeing you first thing in the morning and kissing you on the lips last thing at night. Then I turned the corner and the man I was after had gone. Presumably, while I'd been considering going ahead and stopping like a coward, the murderer had wasted no time escaping. And I realised I'd failed at my job – but more importantly, I loved you more than anything or anyone else, most of all me. And I thought that was a good thing.'

Mrs Sark's throat worked convulsively. She composed herself before saying, 'And the other dream?'

'In the other dream, I was a young boy. I don't know why but for some reason I was sitting on the bank of a river, fishing. This I found strange because I don't even like fishing. Anyway, I was so busy watching the flowing river I didn't see the man we were hunting materialise from the copse of firs over yonder.' He pointed to his right, as if he were still sitting on the bank at that moment. 'He walked towards me, and for all the splendid sunshine his face remained obscured. A mystery. We didn't speak, but we both knew our roles and needed no further direction.

'I rose and began to follow him into the thicket when in my peripheral sight, I saw you on the opposite bank. You were wearing all white. A white frilly dress with matching sunhat

293

and two daisy bracelets on each arm. You'd never looked so beautiful. My heart ached as I longed to be with you on that side of the bank. Then your eyes smiled and shone like the finest emeralds. It was then as I walked towards my destiny into the valley of the shadow of death that I knew everything was going to be all right, as long as I loved you...

'Then I woke up...'

Printed in Great Britain
by Amazon